DARK SINS

PLATINUM SECURITY
BOOK THREE

KELLY MYERS

1

AVERY

I tuck a strand of blonde hair behind my ear, peer through the camera lens and focus on the happy couple. Snap! I freeze-frame on the perfect shot. *You can literally see the love for each other shining in their eyes*, I think.

I'm happy for my clients, a newly engaged couple, but I can't deny that a part of me is a little jealous. No one has ever looked at me with such adoration. I let out a small breath and take a few more final shots. *Not everyone gets a happy ending with her soulmate, Ave. Deal with it.*

"I think we're done," I say and give them a bright smile.

The couple exchanges another kiss, probably the hundredth since we started the photo shoot, and I place my camera back in its case. "Thanks, Avery," the bride-to-be gushes. "I'm so excited to see the pictures."

"I should have them ready in about a week," I tell her.

"Oh, good! We can't wait to share them with all of our friends and family."

I force another smile and hand my card to the groom-to-be. "I'm glad I could be a part of your special time. If you ever need anything else…"

But, I don't think they even hear me because they're sucking face again.

"Okay, then. I'll be in touch," I say and give an awkward wave. I love taking pictures and photography of all kinds, but, God, sometimes it's hard for me to do the newly-engaged couples and weddings. But, hey, they're my bread and butter so I just suck it up and get the best shots that show off their undying love.

I figure at least half will be divorced within five years, anyway. That's the statistic, right? It's actually probably higher, I think, and head over to my car, beyond ready to leave the park with its Disney-like setting of singing birds, blue skies and smooching couples.

I'm not usually so bitter when it comes to happy couples, but lately, it's been harder for me. I slip into my Jeep Wrangler, set my camera case on the passenger seat and flip down the visor. I open the mirror and study my reflection.

On the outside, I'm 32 with long blonde, wavy hair, blue eyes and a slim build despite my love affair with sugar. I guess I can thank good genes and the fact that I'm nearly 5'8" so I guess my weight just gets evenly distributed over my tall frame.

On the inside, things are a bit more complicated.

I sigh, shove the visor back up and slip on my sunglasses. Being Avery Archer hasn't been easy, I think. But, I try hard not to wallow in self-pity. Everything fell apart for me two years earlier, but I dig deep, push past all of the hurt and live my life the best way I know how.

Because that's what Luke would have done.

As I drive away from the park and back to my apartment, I feel my mind wandering back once again. Trying to make sense and understand how everything went so horribly wrong. I live in sunny Los Angeles now, but grew up in Lima, Ohio, a small town where everyone knows everyone and right now, in November, it was probably 40 degrees out, if they were lucky.

I look up, grateful to see palm trees and not bare, half-frozen skeletal branches.

My older brother Luke and I were super close, only two years apart. I looked up to him and wanted to do whatever he did. My parents adored Luke and thought he could do no wrong. Me, on the other hand? In their eyes, I couldn't do anything right. Nothing was ever good enough and they were always so focused on Luke that I felt the need to prove myself.

It's the whole reason I joined the CIA.

Biggest mistake of my life, I think, as I turn into my parking garage.

I turn my car off and sit there for a minute as the memories come flooding back. Luke joined the Navy after graduating high school and was determined to be a SEAL-- he had found his calling, the thing he was meant to do, and went after it with unrelenting passion and zeal. For Luke, there was no Plan B.

Luke went to Boot Camp and then on to Coronado, California, for phase one of BUD/S, Basic Underwater Demolition/SEAL training. It's a grueling 6-month, trial by fire, selection process where the majority of SEAL wannabe's either quit or get injured. My parents and I couldn't have been prouder. Luke was the best of the best and he was out there proving it.

Navy SEAL training is notoriously intense and few candidates actually make it through. My brother said it was around an 80 percent dropout rate. But, Luke made it through all of the training, became a full member and received his Trident pin. While he continually proved he was one of the elite, I floundered around in my first year away at college, not sure what I wanted to do.

One day, I was walking through the Student Union checking out the various booths set up for a job fair. The moment I saw the Central Intelligence Agency representative, I knew what I wanted to do. I was going to join the freaking CIA. I was super smart, good at puzzles and had a knack for languages. I'd make a great analyst, help my country and make my parents proud.

It seemed like a no-brainer.

So, I majored in Political Science, got my Bachelor's degree and I applied to the CIA. After several rounds of tests and interviews, I was accepted. Then, I had to complete basic training at the Sherman Kent School in Reston, Virginia, just outside of Washington DC.

By this time, Luke had made DEVGRU (Naval Special Warfare

DEVelopment GRoUp), commonly known as SEAL Team Six, which is literally the crème de la crème of warriors. He was based in Virginia Beach and only about a three and half hour drive away which was great.

I felt like Luke, who had gone through so much training, as I went through the Career Analyst Program, or CAP, which gave me a thorough understanding of how to think, write and brief according to CIA standards.

In my eyes, Luke was out there saving the world. I may only have had a desk job, but I was gathering intelligence that would help SEALs like him take down the bad guys. It felt really good.

Then, I fucked up. I fucked up so badly that I ended up killing my brother and his team, losing what relationship I had with my parents and quitting my analyst job.

That was two years ago and now here I am, unable to forgive myself. It's like I'm stuck in limbo. I can't move forward and I certainly don't want to go backward. So, I hover in the middle, drowning in guilt, not knowing what to do.

Just...lost and floundering...

With a sigh, I grab my camera and purse, slip out of the Jeep and walk up to my apartment. It's small but cozy, tucked away in a residential North Hollywood neighborhood in the Valley. It might get obscenely hot here in the summer, but the rent is decent and nobody bothers me.

Nobody bothers me to the point where I kind of have no friends.

Except Liberty. I open the door and my German Shepherd lopes over. I give her a big kiss and leash her up. "Hang on, Libs," I say and head into my bedroom. I change into a t-shirt, leggings and tennis shoes and sweep my hair back into a ponytail. Then, I grab Liberty's leash and we head out for our daily jog.

Liberty loves the exercise and running helps me clear my head. Because no matter how much time passes, I can't let go of the events that happened which caused people who I love to die.

I pick up speed, push myself harder. The cliché claims that time heals all wounds, and maybe it eventually does, but that hasn't been my experience. My scars burn and bleed every damn day.

Working as an analyst was challenging and I enjoyed receiving classified information from a variety of sources, then examining and evaluating it. My old job was to gather information from around the globe from individuals, foreign media and satellite surveillance. Because this information varied in how reliable and complete it was, it was up to me to draw coherent and useful intelligence from it all.

For me, it was like being sent the broken pieces of a vase from all over the world and having to glue them together in the right order to see what the vase looked like.

I was good at what I did until I wasn't. Until I shared information that turned out to be wrong. Deadly wrong. I shake the memories off and Liberty and I finish our run. I feel a little better afterward and give her some fresh water while I eat a couple pieces of chocolate. Then, I hop in the shower.

Afterward, I throw on pajama bottoms and an old t-shirt with the Navy SEAL emblem-- an eagle with an anchor, pistol and trident in its talons-- that used to belong to Luke. I plop down on the couch and Liberty jumps up and lays down beside me. As I stroke her soft black and tan fur, I open my laptop and check my email.

I scan down the messages, mostly from clients, and then pause when I spot one that jumps out at me. I don't recognize the email address, but something makes my spine tingle. I open it up and read the short message: *Avery, I have information regarding Operation Armageddon that will interest you. It will also clear your name of any wrongdoing. G.*

For a moment, I can't move. Can't breathe. I just sit there, frozen with shock, re-reading the message.

Information that will clear my name?

Is that possible? I blink, trying to wrap my head around the idea that maybe the shitshow known as Operation Armageddon isn't my fault. That just maybe I'm not the one solely responsible for sending my brave brother and his team to certain death.

Because they all died except one.

One very tall, very handsome, very muscled man named Ryker Flynn.

I let out a shaky sigh, remembering the first time we met. My brother and Ryker were on leave and dropped in to visit my parents for a few days. They had met at Boot Camp in Great Lakes, Illinois, hit it off and trained together until they reached the top. That weekend, I came home, too, so I could see Luke.

I just wasn't expecting my heart to skip a beat when I laid eyes on Ryker.

With short dark hair and eyes the color of expensive whisky, he made the butterflies in my stomach flutter to life. I'll never forget looking up into his tan, rugged face and being at a complete loss for words when he said hello the very first time.

Damn. My heart still pounds when I think about him.

The attraction caught me off-guard and I thought I saw a spark of interest on his end, but then Luke swept in and they went off and did whatever craziness military guys do when they're on a break. I have no doubt that it involved copious amounts of alcohol and loose women.

Hell, they were U.S. Navy SEALs. The shit they went through to become a part of that elite team...they deserved to let loose.

Later that weekend, my Mom made dinner for all of us and I got to sit across from Ryker and discreetly drool over him the entire meal. While my brother was loud and always talking, Ryker was quieter. Yet, he possessed such a commanding presence. He listened closely to everything I said and even asked me quite a few questions about working as an analyst. When I talked a little about what I did, he looked impressed.

Obviously, neither of us could divulge too much information because everything we did was classified. But, we found a common ground and I enjoyed talking to him so much. Because Ryker listened to me like no one else ever had before. He showed interest, enthusiasm and respect.

Luke and Ryker left the next morning and I usually saw him once or twice a year after that. I lived for those brief visits when he came back with my brother and I always made sure I was home. A couple of times, I even drove to Virginia Beach to see them.

I'll always remember when Ryker came and spent the holidays with us. His parents had died in a car accident earlier that year. He was an only child who didn't have any other close family so, of course, Luke insisted that he spend Christmas and New Year's with us.

It was Christmas Eve and my flight got delayed. My parents complained about picking me up because they wanted to attend Christmas Eve Mass. So, Ryker offered to pick me up from the airport while Luke and my parents went to church.

I didn't expect to see Ryker and instantly regretted wearing minimal makeup, throwing my hair up in a messy bun and being in my comfy old sweatpants. I must've looked a mess after waiting around all day and then flying for hours, but Ryker didn't seem to notice. He greeted me with a big bear hug, grabbed my luggage and guided me to my parents' SUV.

It was the best greeting I ever got and I remember he smelled like pine, all Christmas-like and woodsy. On the drive back, our conversation was easy and light. Snow flurries fell and when we got back to my parents' house, we made hot cocoa. Ryker built a fire and we sat on the couch and talked for nearly two hours. I think it was the best night of my life.

And then I sent Ryker into a bloody ambush. It's a miracle he survived. He barely made it to the extraction point alive and they got him out just in time. His physical injuries were extensive so I can only imagine the mental trauma he sustained.

The guilt I've endured since that night nearly broke me a few different times. But, it's something I've learned to live with and handle. Some days are worse than others, especially birthdays, holidays and anniversaries.

I always had a huge crush on Ryker Flynn and a little part of me wonders if the feeling was mutual. But, everything changed after Operation Armageddon. Any affection Ryker may have had for me disappeared and was replaced by a bitter hate.

Because I was the one who fucked up. I led Luke, Ryker and the rest of their team into a slaughter and I took the blame, the guilt, the fall.

But, now someone is telling me it wasn't my fault? That they have information that can clear my name? It seems too good to be true, but I have to find out the truth. If I can ease my conscience from the crushing burden I've felt these last couple of years, I will in a heartbeat.

But, even more than that, I'll be able to face Ryker, my parents and everyone else who blames me for Luke's and the others' deaths.

And, maybe, I'll finally be able to forgive myself.

I'm determined to find out the truth, but I don't know if I can trust this "G." I'm going to need help. Someone I trust.

I trust Ryker.

Problem is he doesn't even want to look at me anymore. The last time we spoke, he made his feelings for me quite clear: he hated me and would never forgive me for leading his brothers into that massacre to die.

I try to push back the terrible things he said and focus on the hope that this mysterious "G." may have information to help me finally be able to move forward.

I pet Liberty and decide that I'm going to track Ryker down and ask for his help.

Even though he will probably tell me to go to hell.

2

RYKER

"And, I also want to welcome Harlow to the team," Jax Wilder says, holding up his champagne glass. "I'm sorry you're going to have to deal with a bunch of macho Alpha males, but try to cut us a little slack. We're still learning."

My gaze moves over to the dark-haired beauty and Harlow Vaughn tilts her glass with a smile.

We're all in Jax's office, the former LAPD cop who started this firm, Platinum Security, and we use our government training and killer instincts to work as bodyguards, locators, investigators and any other shady job clients pay us to do. We're a ragtag group that consists of former military, CIA and, now, a hacker thanks to the newest addition of Harlow.

Some might call us the bottom of the barrel, but our skills are deadly and we do whatever it takes to get the job done.

"Finally, to Lexi. You've got your hands full with this one," Jax says and nods his dark head toward Griffin Lawson, the ex-CIA operative and pretty boy of our dysfunctional group.

"Thanks a lot," Griff mumbles, arm around the pretty redhead's shoulders.

Griff, my best friend, just returned from New York after helping Lexi find her kidnapped brother and a priceless treasure worth millions. Now he's in love with the little, feisty redhead beside him. They haven't stopped giving each other googly-eyes since I walked in. I have to admit, it's getting to be a little bit much. Griff has always been such a player so seeing him so ga-ga over a woman is strange.

I can't believe my two closest friends are in love. And, it seems that these women have helped them put their demons to rest. I honestly never thought I'd see the day. In fact, Jax is marrying Easton Ross next week.

"But, consider yourself lucky because he's one of the best men I know," Jax adds. "So, cheers," he says and lifts his glass.

"Cheers!" Everyone says in unison and clinks their glasses.

The mood is light, almost festive, and then my cell phone rings. I excuse myself and wander over to the corner, looking down at the caller i.d., and don't recognize the number. Could be a potential client, so I answer. "Ryker Flynn," I say.

There's a pause on the other end of the line. Then, "Ryker? It's Avery."

My stomach drops when I hear the one voice I never wanted to hear again. The angelic voice that haunts my dreams, tortures me on numerous lonely nights and that I've never been able to forget.

No matter how hard I've tried.

Avery Archer, the blonde-haired, blue-eyed she-devil who I love to hate. The woman responsible for the death of my best friend Luke and the rest of my SEAL team.

I'm so surprised that I don't say anything. Couldn't even if I wanted to because my throat squeezes and I don't think I can get a word out.

"Please, don't hang up," she says.

"Fuck," I swear loudly. Everyone looks over and I don't give a shit. I head for the exit, a scowl settling over my face, and I know I must have smoke coming out of my ears.

"Everything okay?" Griff asks.

"No," I growl, storming out of the office. I shove the front door open and stalk outside because I need some air. I take a deep breath then snarl into the phone, "What do you want?"

I hear her swallow. Can feel her taut nerves through the phone line. "I-I need your help."

"Are you fucking kidding me?"

"Ryker, please. I found out some information about...that night. About Operation Armageddon and...well, I don't think things are what they seem."

What the fuck is she talking about? I wonder. She murdered my entire team. How can it not be what it seems? "Go on," I grit out between clenched teeth.

"I don't want to talk about this over the phone. Can we meet somewhere?"

I squeeze my eyes shut. The idea of seeing Avery again is like both a knife piercing my heart and pure exhilaration. God, I had the biggest crush on her until-

"I'll come to you," she says. "I live in the L.A. area."

"So do I," I say.

"Oh! Okay, well, I'm in North Hollywood."

"I'll text you my address," I say and glance down at my large, rugged military watch. "Can you get there by 5?"

"Sure."

"Fine," I say and end the call.

Goddammit. I take a few deep inhales and get my breathing under control again. Then, I text her my address, pull my keys out of a pocket and get in my Expedition. I only live a few blocks over in East Hollywood. I had no idea Avery lived so close. I figured she was still near Washington D.C. somewhere or maybe back in Ohio with her parents.

Avery fucking Archer.

She was Luke's little sister and therefore completely off-limits. But, that didn't mean I couldn't imagine what it would be like with her. Imagine running my fingers through her golden hair and kissing those full, pink lips until they were swollen.

Pink. Every time I see the stupid color, I still think of her. Avery is feminine, delicate and innocent. And, don't even get me started on the way she smells. Sweet like sugar.

I'll never forget the first time I saw her. Luke and I finally got some leave time and went to visit his family in Ohio for the weekend. He talked about his sister, of course, but, holy shit, she was stunning. He had never mentioned that.

I remember my first look and my mouth literally dropped. Avery looked like a model-- tall, slim, bedhead blonde hair and cornflower eyes rimmed in midnight blue. She had curves in all the right places and my head filled with lusty thoughts. I had to remind myself she was Luke's younger sister and I tried to shove all of the inappropriate thoughts away, but it was hard. *So hard.*

That weekend at dinner, we were finally able to talk and I found out she was an analyst for the CIA. Luke had only mentioned that she worked for the government. He hadn't prepared me at all for meeting his sister.

I don't know what I expected. I guess not much and she took me completely by surprise. She was not only incredibly beautiful, but also super intelligent. A force to reckon with, I realized. In any other situation, I would've asked her out and been planning to get her into my bed afterwards, but I couldn't do that with Avery.

So, I just suffered below the belt whenever I was in her presence and then went out and found someone else to fuck. Because I vowed never to cross that line with Avery. She was sweet and innocent, and I was no good for her. Besides, I was constantly traveling the world on classified, dangerous missions, taking down bad guys. I didn't have time for a relationship and I didn't want one. All I wanted to do was take down bad guys, protect my country and make my former military Dad proud.

I park the Expedition in the garage below my condo and then remember what a shithole my place is right now. With an annoyed groan, I get out and hurry up the stairs to my place. I unlock the door and stand there staring at a royal fucking mess. I glance down at my watch and realize she'll be here in less than ten minutes.

Shit. I hit the lights, grab a garbage bag and just start dumping crap in it. Empty beer bottles, fast food containers and various trash. There's a layer of dust on everything and I can only imagine what she's going to think. It looks like a pit. I had a rough couple of weeks recently and then started a new case so I haven't had the time or desire to clean up.

A couple of rough weeks? Yeah, right. In reality, it's been a couple of rough years. I massage my temples and then my hands move over my ears where the tiny hearing aids are hidden. The nice thing is they're custom-made to fit in my ear canals and are pretty much invisible. The bad thing is I'm 34 years old and have hearing loss in both ears because I was too close to an explosive device that detonated.

The same explosion that destroyed my hearing also killed my fellow SEAL team brother so I consider myself lucky.

I hate thinking about that fucking mission, Operation Armageddon, and I try not to. But, it's like when someone tells you not to look into the sun during an eclipse. What's the first thing you do? You look up into the sun. I wish I could erase that night from my mind and that my SEAL brothers were still alive, especially Luke, but that's not possible.

During my training, especially in the first phase of BUD/S, the instructors teach you how to be mentally strong. How to bulletproof your mind and cultivate mental resilience so you can stick it out while everyone else around you gives up. Yes, it's all extremely physically demanding, but there's no way in hell you'll survive unless you learn mental toughness.

Only 1 in 7 trainees makes it through and Hell Week is a special kind of torture. But, what SEAL training really tests is your mental mettle. It's designed to push you mentally to the brink, over and over again, until you are hardened and able to take on any task with confidence, regardless of the odds-- or, until you break.

Ironically, I broke after my career being a SEAL ended. I was supposed to be the toughest in the world and, for years I was, but then I lost that ability. That mental toughness that had made me so successful in my Navy career.

Winston Churchill said, "If you're going through hell, keep going."

I've lived by that advice, but in the last two years, it hasn't been easy. The PTSD, the recurring nightmares, the scars...

I'm incredibly grateful for Griff and Jax or I probably would've blown my brains out by now. God knows, I have enough weapons lying around here to get the job done.

We is greater than me. Along with mental toughness, SEALs also learn to work as a team. It's always about your teammates. No exceptions.

Griffin Lawson and Jaxon Wilder are my team now.

Jax gave me a job, something to do and a way to feel useful when no one else would hire me. And, Griff does what any best friend does-- he listens to my bullshit and steers me away from the bad habits that I can't seem to kick. The self-pity, the guilt, the drinking.

I've punished myself for still being alive while Luke and the others are dead. Sometimes, I wish I would've died with them. It's the dark thoughts like these that always start me on a downward spiral. *Shit.*

I shake my head hard and remember my training: one small step at a time; emotional control; visualize success; small victories.

I breathe in for four seconds, then breathe out for four seconds. I repeat this four times and I'm feeling better. In control again.

My watch reads five minutes to five. I look down at the garbage bag in my hand and realize I don't have enough time to take it down to the dumpster. *Fuck it.* I toss it in my room and shut the door. God knows, Avery won't be going into my bedroom. Even though, deep down, a part of me would love it.

I jog into the bathroom and look at my reflection. I haven't seen Avery in two years and I know I'm not at my best. Far from it. I have shadows under my brown eyes, I've lost weight and my diet consists of beer and pizza.

And, hey, I'm an emotional basket case. Wanna come in?

I run a hand through my short dark hair and wonder if I have time to shave. Two minutes to five. *No.* I ignore the stubble and instead reach for my toothbrush. I may not look great, but at least I'll have a minty fresh breath. I guess that's something.

When I hear a knock at the door, my stomach clenches. Seeing Avery means facing the brokenness inside me and I don't know if I'm ready to do that.

Or, if I ever will be.

1700 hours.

3

AVERY

eventeen-hundred hours. I take a deep breath, lift my hand and knock.

Oh, God, I'm nervous, I think, and wring my hands. Other than this morning, I haven't talked to Ryker since our blowout at the hospital two years ago. I thought going to visit him would be good for both of us and instead it turned out to be the worst thing I could've done.

I hear the door click and, as it swings inward, I almost turn and run away. Instead, I suck in a deep breath, unable to swallow past the sudden dryness in my mouth and throat, and look up into the whisky-colored eyes that I've missed so very much.

For a moment, we just look at each other. It's like the first time we met all over again. I literally can't find the words and he's just as handsome as I remember. Even more so with a light growth of dark stubble and his cropped hair longer than the military-short cut he sported before. He looks older, his cheekbones higher with hollows beneath, and I can't miss the fact that he's lost weight even though he's still muscular as hell.

"Hi."

"Hi."

We both talk at the same time and I can't help but give him a small, shy smile. I hope this goes well. I need his help, but, more than that, I've missed him so much. *So, so much.*

I didn't realize how much until now. Until I'm looking into his shadowed eyes.

"C'mon in," he says and motions for me to come inside.

His voice is just as deep and steady as I remember. But, the warmth and kindness are gone.

I follow him into the condo and look up, studying the back of his dark head and broad shoulders. My stomach somersaults and I'm still in awe by how very tall and strong he looks. When he nods to the couch, I sit down and lay my purse on my lap, clutching the straps so hard that my knuckles are white. *Shit, calm down, Ave. Just tell him what you found out.*

He sits in the chair next to the couch and waits. "Thank you for meeting me," I say and he nods again. "I know it's been awhile…"

When a shadow darkens his brown eyes, I bite my lip. "Um, I got an email and I wanted you to see it." I pull my phone out of my purse, fumbling as I try to pull my email up. I glance up and he just watches me with that cool, detached gaze. Like he wants me to just hurry up and get the hell out of here.

Finally, I get the message open and I turn the screen around so he can see. He reaches over to take the phone and when his huge hand touches mine, I feel the electricity spark between us. A muscle flexes in his jaw and he yanks his hand away fast. When he reads the message, his eyes narrow.

"Who the fuck is G?" he asks.

"I don't know. But, I was hoping you could help me find out."

For a moment, he doesn't say anything, but I can see the gears turning. And, I already know what his internal debate is about. He wants to know more about the doomed operation, but he doesn't want to help me.

The coldness emanating off him is palpable. *Shit.* Coming here was probably a huge mistake.

"Ryker-"

His eyes snap up and pin me with an icy stare. A stare full of blame.

He's definitely not going to make this easy on me, I realize. "I know you've heard it before, but I'm sorry. I'm so sor-"

Before I'm done speaking, he jumps up and I can see his expression turn hard as granite. "Don't," he snaps. "I don't want to hear it."

I close my mouth and watch him stalk across the room and then back again.

"Why are you here, Avery?" He leans down, his face hovering in front of mine, and repeats the question with more force. "Why *the fuck* are you here?"

Most girls might burst into tears and be intimidated by a former Navy SEAL who's 6'4", nearly 200 pounds of solid muscle and up in their face swearing.

But, I'm not most girls. I push a hand against his hard chest, shove him back a step and stand up. "What is wrong with you?" I ask, feeling a surge of anger.

Ryker just blinks, not expecting me to stand up to him. To push back. Well, I'm not some wilting flower and I've grown up quite a lot over the last couple of years. I came here with the hope that he had done some growing up, too, but I can see that isn't the case.

"I told you why I'm here. Whatever information this person has might clear my name. It might help us better understand what went wrong."

"That won't bring my team back," he states in a flat, emotionless voice.

"I know that, but-"

"So, it sounds like it's all about you."

"What?"

"You just said you might be able to clear your name."

"Right," I say carefully. He shoots me a glare and I don't understand why I'm in the wrong here. "Ryker, ever since that night, I've had to live with the fact that I led Luke and five other SEALs straight into a slaughter."

"And, I've had to live with the guilt of not being able to save them so I guess we're even."

My temper flares. "This has nothing to do with being even. This is about trying to figure out the truth. I thought you of all people would want to know what really happened."

Our voices are getting louder and louder. *Shit, this is not going the way I hoped it would.*

"You wanna know what happened, Avery?" he asks, voice turning nasty. "I'll tell you. Your shitty intel said there were no more than 10-15 tangos at that meeting. *Ten to fifteen.* We ran up against at least 80. His whole fucking army was there and they knew we were coming."

His nostrils flare and his chest rises and falls with rapid breaths. Again, he lowers his face right into mine, his brown eyes blazing. "You're the reason my brothers died out in that goddamned Columbian jungle. The reason I almost died. So, if you think I'm interested in clearing your name, think again, little girl. You can fucking rot for all I care."

His venomous words make the last of my self-restraint snap. I pull back a hand and slap his face. The crack of my palm against his cheek is loud and echoes through the room. For a moment, we both just stand there in shock.

"Get out," he hisses between gritted teeth. I look down and see his fists are clenched.

Oh, shit. I turn, grab my purse and swing back around to face him. I can see him struggling to keep his control in check. Suddenly, I feel all of the anger drain out of me. Like someone just pulled the plug. And, instead, all I feel is an aching emptiness.

"I miss Luke every day," I say in a quiet voice.

"We all do."

I let out a breath, push my hair back off my face and walk to the front door. *He's not going to help me.* The realization hits me hard, but what did I expect? That he'd welcome me with open arms?

I pull the door open and, as I'm walking out, I hear his voice behind me. "Congratulations, Avery. Navy SEAL training couldn't break me, but you sure did."

His words cut through me like a knife and when I turn back around, he slams the door in my face. Tears burn the back of my eyes, but I refuse to let them fall.

Completely rejected, I head down the path, climb into my Jeep and hit the steering wheel with a fist. *Well, that went well.*

The last thing I wanted to do was hurt him further. As frustrating as he can be, I know it's because he's in pain. He's like a big lion with a thorn stuck in his paw. He roars and carries on and puts on a big show, but deep down he's hurting.

I want to pull that thorn out, but he just won't let me. I probably should've been more patient, but he really knows how to push my buttons. And, I suppose I shouldn't have slapped him, but he really pissed me off. Doesn't he realize that this whole situation has been just as hard on me?

We *both* lost Luke. They might have been best friends and called each other brother, but Luke really was my blood, my family.

Ugh. Ryker Flynn drives me insane.

When I saw him at the hospital after the doomed mission, he reacted in much the same way. He lashed out, said cruel things and placed all the blame on me. He said things that I'll never forget, that burned into my memory and cut me to the quick.

I remember walking into his hospital room after he was back in the States. For being such a big guy, he seemed smaller, vulnerable, in that bed surrounded by all kinds of equipment and an IV stand. I found out his injuries beforehand and it's a miracle he survived.

Five gunshot wounds that luckily didn't hit any major organs and a knife wound in his shoulder. Not to mention a broken arm and numerous contusions and abrasions. His handsome face was a mess-- stitches on his chin, bruises, cuts and one eye was swollen shut.

But, somehow, he still managed to glare at me.

I walked over to his bed and laid a hand over his, covering the bruised, scabbed knuckles. He had fought with incredible strength to escape that jungle and make it to the extraction point. *Like a ferocious lion.*

"I'm so glad you're okay," I said.

"Why would you think that?" he asked.

He had never spoken to me with such coldness in his tone and I remember I flinched. "I just meant- I'm so glad you made it out of there."

Again, that death stare. *God, he's really perfected it over the last two years*, I think now.

"Well, I didn't," he snapped and pulled his hand away.

For a long moment, I didn't know what to say. "What do you mean?"

"A part of me died out there with them. Shit, I wish I had."

"Don't say that."

"Fuck you, Avery. All of this is your fucking fault and nothing you ever say or do will change that."

I remember it felt like he had yanked the rug out from underneath me. I grasped onto the side of the bed and swayed. His words cut deep and I've never been able to erase that awful conversation. His words still haunt me.

The man I had crushed on for the past few years looked at me with hate in his eyes. I had always believed with my whole heart that Ryker Flynn was the most handsome, kind, considerate man. That he would always have my back and stick up for me. Because even though our interactions had been few and far between, the ones we had were sweet and precious to me. I had cherished each one and tucked them away in a special place in my heart.

"I'm sorry," I whispered.

But, he did not forgive me. Instead, he blew up and I just stood there, at a complete loss for words, as he laid into me like I was a punching bag.

"I'm sorry isn't good enough. It won't bring my team back," he snarled.

I had never seen him look so ugly and hateful. After more yelling, a nurse finally came in and told me to leave because I was upsetting the patient.

God, it was awful.

I don't know why I thought today would go any differently. It's clear that Ryker solely blames me for the shitshow that killed his team and I have shouldered that blame for two years.

And, I've had to deal with the guilt and heartache by myself. You don't talk about classified missions. Especially missions that end in failure and chaos. I have barely any shred of a relationship left with my parents. The moment they heard rumors that I was the one responsible for Luke's death, they never looked at me the same.

All I ever tried to do was please my parents, but I finally came to the heartbreaking conclusion that no matter what I do, nothing would ever be good enough. I learned that after Luke died. That's when I left the CIA and picked up a camera. I always enjoyed taking pictures and during the long, lonely months after losing Ryker's team, I immersed myself in photography.

There's something about capturing a special moment in time and then being able to go back and relive it all over again that gives me joy. I don't have to worry about catching bad guys anymore. Now my job is to capture other people's happy moments and I love it. In a way, it brings me a sliver of peace.

But, if there's a chance that I wasn't the one who fucked everything up that night, I need to know.

For my own sanity and to ease my soul.

4

RYKER

uck me.

I slam the door shut, lift my hands and see they're trembling. I squeeze them into fists, turn and punch the wall.

Like an idiot, I stand there and stare at the hole now in my wall.

Seeing Avery again shook me to my core. I scrub a hand over my lower face and remember the last time we spoke. I was lying in a hospital bed after returning from Columbia. I may have been high on painkillers, but I know I said all sorts of hurtful things just like I did now.

Ryker, ever since that night, I've had to live with the fact that I led Luke and five other SEALs straight into a slaughter.

I guess I never really took the time to see it from her point of view. I saw my side and my brothers' side, but never hers. It's so hard, though, because every time I look at her, I see my slaughtered team. Lost in that jungle, surrounded by 80 armed hostels, unable to escape as bullets and explosives screamed through the darkness.

Watching my team get trapped and killed is something I won't ever just be able to get over or accept. It'll haunt me for the rest of my life.

But, shit, now I feel bad. I tore into Avery when all she wanted was my help. And, no matter what happened, she's still Luke's little sister.

Fuck. I grab the door knob, stalk out and spot her sitting in a Jeep that's parked at the curb. I jog over, walk around and tap on the window.

A wave of surprise flits through her eyes and she rolls the window down. I rest an elbow on the roof and lean down. "I'm sorry," I say.

She glances at the handprint on my cheek. "Me, too."

"I probably deserved that," I admit and turn to take a look in her driver's side mirror. Then, I look back into her blue eyes. "Can we talk?"

Avery nods and I open the door. She slides out and my gaze drops, noticing the way her t-shirt pulls against her full breasts. I turn away, trying to ignore the quickening of my pulse. God, she's more beautiful than I remember. So slim and curvy all at the same time. And, with those stunning blue eyes and bedhead hair, she looks like an angel and temptress all rolled into one.

My groin tightens. *Fuck.* I can't even go there. Not now, not ever. I do my four deep breaths and guide her across the street to a park. We sit down on a bench and I pull my focus back to the matter at hand.

"So, tell me more about this email."

Avery crosses her long legs toward me. "I haven't responded back yet. I was hoping to get your advice."

"I think we should set up a meeting."

"We?" she asks.

I nod. "I'll help you do whatever it takes to find out more about what the hell went wrong that night." I drag in a ragged breath. "I shouldn't have lashed out at you back there. I'm sorry, Ave. You didn't deserve that."

"I think we've both been pretty damaged by all of this," she says. "If I could go back..." her voice trails off.

"I think we both would've done a helluva lot of things differently."

"Yeah, I think so."

As I'm looking into her eyes, my heart speeds up and something in those blue depths won't let go. I can't deny I'm still attracted to her.

Shit, what man in his right mind wouldn't be? Avery Archer is the most beautiful woman I've ever seen. And, looks aside, she's strong and smart.

Christ, she even smells the same as she always did. Sweet like cotton candy.

I always had a thing for her. I'd never admit it and Luke would've chopped my balls off before letting me date his little sister, but it's true. Avery is the one who got away. The one I've always compared every other girl to and none measured up.

"So, what's next?" she asks, breaking eye contact.

"Email your source back."

Avery nods, pulls her phone out and starts typing. I watch her slim fingers tap out a message and then hit send. "It said I'm interested in hearing more and want to set up a meeting."

I nod, meet her blue eyes again. We look at each other for another long moment and it feels like there's so much more that we want to say. So many unspoken things between us that need to be said. "So, how did you end up living here?" I ask, treading carefully. "Last I heard, you were near D.C."

"I quit my job and left the CIA not long after, um, visiting you in the hospital."

I had no idea. "Why?"

"Isn't it obvious?"

I shrug. "You had a good job that you worked hard to get. People fuck up every day at work."

Avery looks off into the distance and clasps her hands. "Ryker...I'm not sure you understand how much failing you, Luke and your team affected me."

I don't say anything. Just wait for her to continue.

"It was horrible knowing I messed up, but after seeing you..." She runs a hand through those golden waves and I want to reach out and touch it, too. Feel the thick strands between my fingers. "I was responsible for your injuries, for every moment of pain you suffered, every bullet that pierced your skin. The knife wound, the bruises, the cuts. I felt terrible because-"

I look up when she abruptly stops. "Because why?" I press.

Her eyes say one thing, but her voice says something else. "Because..." She swallows hard.

Say it, Ave. Tell me you cared.

"Because you were Luke's best friend."

I feel my jaw tighten and give a short nod. I remember the precious conversations we shared, all the moments I wanted to reach out, lift her chin and kiss her. Did she ever feel the same? But, I knew I couldn't succumb to my desires. I had too much discipline to ever follow through with any of my lusty thoughts.

But, now...

Now, when I look into her cornflower eyes and smell that sugary confection perfume she wears, I feel my control slip a notch. What good did it ever do me, anyway? I've spent my life sacrificing for others. For my country and my team, for the people I loved, but lost...

Maybe it's time to do something for yourself, a small voice whispers. I've always wanted Avery, but did the right thing, the honorable thing, and kept my distance as much as possible. It was hard then, but it's a million times harder right now.

Luke is gone. Our careers are gone. My parents are gone. Avery's parents may as well be gone.

I look at her and realize we have no one left.

No one but each other.

But, then I remember what a fucking mess I am. She's way too good for a broken man like me who can't shake the ghosts and who's far more mentally damaged than I ever was physically.

Still, though, if we can at least work together and find out the truth about Operation Armageddon then maybe it will help us both heal. At least a little bit.

I lift a hand, on the verge of laying it over her clasped hands, but then pull back at the last second. *Shit.* It's so ingrained in me to keep my distance from her that I'm scared to do anything. I don't want to frighten her or make her feel like she will owe me for helping her.

Avery looks down at my hand, the blood drying on my knuckles, and frowns. "What happened?" she asks.

I swipe a hand over my knuckles, covering them. "I punched the wall."

Her eyes widen. "Good thing I left when I did," she says, trying to make light of the situation.

But, the fact that she infers I might have hit her rocks me to my core. "Avery, I would never hit you. You know that, right?"

She nods. "I'm sorry. I know you wouldn't. I shouldn't have said that."

"If we're going to work together, we have to trust each other."

"I've always trusted you," she says in a soft voice. "Why do you think I came to you?"

My heart swells and I throw caution to the wind and lay my hand over hers. Her skin is so soft and warm. I feel a shock of awareness jolt up my arm and through my entire body. *Jesus.* "I'm glad you did," I say. My voice comes out hoarse, raw-sounding. I swallow hard and when I pull my hand back, she grabs it in both of hers and squeezes.

"Me, too," she says.

I look down and watch her fingers brush lightly over my hurt knuckles and begin exploring the space between my fingers. Her touch is light, wispy, curious. She turns my hand over and drags her fingers over my palm and my cock stiffens.

"I've always liked your hands," she says.

I suck in a breath.

"They're so...big. And, strong."

I literally can't speak. Just feel all the blood in my body rush south and it becomes crystal clear how goddamn much I want this woman. How much I've always wanted her. Suddenly, I let every thought of her brother, of my loyalties to her family and myself go. Just wash away. I twine my fingers through hers, lean down and kiss her.

And, she tastes as sweet as she smells.

When Avery's mouth opens, I feel a rush of relief and lust pound through me. I slip my tongue past her lips, deepening the kiss that I've been wanting to give her since the moment we met. She slides her silky tongue against mine, exploring my mouth as I explore hers.

Her response blows me away. I never knew for sure if she wanted me like I wanted her.

Now, there's no question about it.

After we devour each other, we pull back and both of us are at a loss. Chests rising and falling hard, we gaze into each other's eyes, communicating on a deeper level than mere words. When she lifts a hand and lays it against my cheek, my eyes slide shut.

Something about this woman feels almost...healing. I press my hand to the back of hers, turn my face into her palm and kiss it. Avery is a light to my darkness. She has a glow about her that's so comforting, unlike anything I've ever experienced before. Being with her like this, I feel emotions I haven't felt in years. Emotions that I thought had died a long time ago.

For the first time in years, I feel hope and that maybe there's a light at the end of this hellhole I've been trapped in.

Suddenly, her email dings and I let go and jerk back. She glances down at her phone. "Check it," I say and shove a hand through my hair. I don't know what exactly just happened between us, but it was intense. I need a minute to regroup and focus on the matter at hand. To get myself under control again.

"It's from him. Or her," she says and opens the new message. She scans it and then looks up at me. "He promises to reveal everything he knows at the meeting. But..."

"But, what?"

"But, he says it will have to be in Columbia."

I feel my entire body tense up. "Columbia?"

"That's where he is."

Never in a million years did I think I'd ever go back to Colombia. Just the thought of stepping foot in that drug-riddled shithole makes my stomach churn.

"If you don't want to go-"

"I'm going," I tell her in a firm voice.

She nods. "Then I guess we should get packed."

We stand up and head back across the street to where her Jeep is parked. "Where in Columbia?" I ask as she opens the door.

I see her swallow and know the destination before she even tells me. "Bogota."

Of course. I lost my team in the jungles of Bogota. I give a sharp nod and resign myself to the idea of going back to the country where my life nearly ended in a hail of bullets. Ghosts haunt those steamy jungles, but I'm determined to go with her and face whatever I need to face so that I can finally move on with my life.

So I can finally be able to forgive Avery. And, most of all, so I can finally forgive myself.

"I'll book the tickets," I tell her.

Avery nods, reaches up and lays that soft hand against my face again. "Thank you, Ryker. I know this isn't going to be easy."

"Nothing worthwhile ever is." I help her into the Jeep and close the door. "I'll be in touch with the trip details."

I take a step back as she starts the car and then drives away.

I have no idea what this trip will hold, but I really hope for two things: that Avery and I can continue where we left off in the park and, above all, I yearn for closure. An end to the all-consuming pain and guilt that I've let wreck my life.

5

AVERY

A s I drive back to my apartment, I pull a candy bar out of my purse and start munching, unable to stop thinking about the mind-blowing kiss we just shared. Well, that certainly cleared up any doubts on my part regarding how Ryker felt about me. *Feels about me?* I have no idea where we stand, to be honest.

All I know is I want to kiss him again. I want more, so much more, but one step at a time. At least we're not yelling at each other anymore. We're on the same page and have a common goal.

I told him I felt terrible because...

Because why? he asked.

I wanted to tell him the truth so badly. Because I care for him so damn much. But, I gave him the easy answer and said because he was Luke's best friend. He has to know now, though, after that hot-ass kiss. And, God, right in the middle of the park. I have never kissed a man in public like that before.

But, Ryker makes me feel things I've never felt before-- desired and utterly wanton.

My hair whips around my face as I pull onto the 101 N freeway and head home. My history with men is practically nonexistent. Every

guy I ever met or went out with never measured up to the lofty standards I had set after meeting Ryker Flynn so I never gave them much
of a chance.

He literally ruined dating for me.

In my eyes, Ryker Flynn was a hero. No man was tall enough,
tough enough or handsome enough. No one possessed that amazing
shade of whisky-tinted eyes that he did. No one even came close to
the hard muscles and military-fit body Ryker had. *And, still has,* I
think, remembering the way his upper arms and chest bulged beneath
his t-shirt.

Oh, Lord, I think. *I want him. Badly.*

I've always wanted him. Despite everything, he's always been
the one.

Everything was always so damn complicated, though. He was my
older brother's best friend and his job was his life. Secret missions
kept him gone for months at a time and I'm sure the last thing he
needed was a clingy girlfriend.

Because for as long as I've known him, Ryker has never mentioned
a girlfriend. Luke once said Ryker wasn't big into relationships and
preferred being single.

But, isn't that what all single people say?

I do, anyway. It's almost a coping mechanism for loneliness that
can strike out of the blue and make you wonder what it would be like
to have a partner. A significant other to share your heart, dreams and
life with.

After trying to date a few different men over the years, I stopped
completely after quitting the CIA. My partner for the last two years
has been guilt and there's been no one else. The only one who's been
in my bed besides me is Liberty. It's been lonely and now I want to
change that.

I want Ryker in my bed.

I want that big, hard, strong male. After that kiss, I feel a surge of
confidence. I know he wants me, too. I could feel the need thrumming
off his hard body.

31

There's something else, though, too. This deep, emotional connection between us that I've never felt with anybody before.

Whatever happens between us, I'm ready.

I'm also scared. There's a darkness in Ryker and, even though I've known him for years, I really know nothing about him. I never realized what a toll the guilt took on him. Maybe because I was too busy wallowing in my own self-pity.

We're both aware now, though, and it's pretty clear we've both spent the last two years in pretty much the same headspace. Enveloped by guilt, regret and sorrow. Maybe it's time to change that.

When I get home, I take Liberty out for a run. But, there's no clearing my jumbled thoughts. My mind is all over the place and flying to Colombia to meet this new source with Ryker is making me anxious. Am I going to finally find out the truth of what happened? Was I a scapegoat and did I take the fall for someone else? I have a million questions.

And, then there's Ryker himself. We'll probably end up staying in some off-the-grid shithole which is fine with me, but will there be one bed that we'll have to share? There's no way I'll be able to sleep next to him and not want more. Not touch him and kiss him.

The thought of being intimate with Ryker makes my toes curl.

I've thought about it before. Quite a few times actually. Wondering what it would be like to feel his huge, calloused hands run all over me. To see his naked, powerful body in front of me and touch him anywhere and everywhere I want. To feel him inside me, hot and hard and moving.

I focus on my running and not the wet feeling between my legs. God, he gets me all riled up.

When we get back, I give Liberty some fresh water and realize I don't have anyone to watch her when I'm gone. *Shit*. I'm not taking her to a kennel. She's a rescue and if she thought I abandoned her, I'd never forgive myself.

This is where having friends would come in handy. Unfortunately, I don't have any anymore since pushing them all away.

I reach for my phone and call Ryker.

"Hey," he says.

I don't expect him to pick up so fast and I'm in the middle of swallowing a big gulp of cold water. "Hi," I manage, still out of breath from my run.

"Are you okay?" he asks.

"Yeah, sorry. I just finished running." He doesn't say anything and I catch my breath. "I have a bit of an issue," I say and look down at Liberty.

"What's that?" he asks in a husky voice.

My stomach drops. God, he sounds sexy. His voice is deep and rich and warmth pools low, gathering between my legs. "Um, well, I have a dog and don't have anyone who can watch her while I'm gone."

"You do? What kind of dog?"

I forgot how much Ryker always loved animals and I smile. I honestly didn't think I could like him any more, but guess what? Now I do. "German Shepherd. She's a rescue so I don't want to board her."

"Hell, no. She'll think you abandoned her. What's her name?"

"Liberty. Do you know anyone who could watch her?"

"I think so. Let me call you back."

We hang up and I throw Liberty a wink. "Sorry, Libs, but Ryker will not be babysitting you. He'll be with Mom." Liberty gives a woof and I itch behind her ear. A minute later, Ryker calls back "Hi," I say.

"Hey. My friend Jax and his fiancée Easton can watch her."

"And you trust them?"

"With my life," he says. "Trust me when I say Liberty will be living the life of Riley while we're away."

"What do you mean?"

"She'll be staying at Easton Ross's Hollywood Hills mansion and will be pampered in every way."

"Easton Ross the actress?" I ask in disbelief.

"Yep. It's quite a place."

"And, she's engaged to your friend?"

"Jax Wilder. He owns Platinum Security where I work. By the way,

I got our tickets. We fly out at 0900 on Delta with a stop in Atlanta. Looks like it'll be about ten hours total."

"That's a long flight."

"Yeah, flying on a commercial sucks."

"Too bad we couldn't hop a ride on a military plane."

"Yeah."

"Okay, well, that means I should drop Libs off tonight."

"I can pick you up and drive you over."

"Are you sure?"

"Can you be ready in half an hour?"

"Sure. Thanks, Ryker."

"See you soon."

My heart skips. *Yeah, see you soon*, I think. "Okay, Liberty, baby. Let's pack your gear and get you ready to spend some time with a movie star at her mansion."

Liberty's tail swishes back and forth.

An hour later, I'm sitting on the floor across from Easton Ross in her Hollywood Hills mansion and it's totally surreal. Easton is even more gorgeous in person with raven curls that just touch her shoulders and bright red lips that pop on her porcelain face. And, Jax Wilder is her complete opposite with a sleeve of tattoos and an intense, almost dangerous look about him.

Of course, Liberty adores her and Jax both.

But, I think Ryker loves her most. He's so damn adorable, stretched out on the floor, rubbing her belly and kissing her furry face. I wish he was doing that to me, I think.

Jax and Easton watch me closely and Easton is full of questions about our trip. When Ryker tells Jax we're going to Colombia, he grabs his phone and calls someone named Griff. "Apparently, Ryker is off to Colombia with some girl," Jax says and glances my way. "Sorry, no offense."

Griff gives a loud exclamation and Ryker rolls his eyes. "Tell him to get over here and I'll let you guys know exactly what's going on."

Jax may look wary about the situation, but Easton looks positively delighted. When Griff arrives, Ryker introduces us. His bright blue eyes assess me closely and I get the feeling he already knows about me. Or, at least heard my name before. I wonder how much Ryker has told him. He shakes my hand and then Easton tells them to go get beers in the kitchen while she and I chat.

I watch the three best-looking men I've ever seen head toward her huge, state-of-the-art kitchen. Jax is dark and mysterious, a total bad boy, while Griff is good-looking in a yummy Brad Pitt kind of way. Both are covered in tattoos and keep exchanging looks. But, to me, Ryker blows them both away. To me, he's perfect.

Ryker looks over his shoulder as they walk away and I give him a small nod.

"So," Easton says and smiles at me. "How long have you and Ryker known each other?"

I can feel the third degree coming on, but I decide I like Easton. She's so classy and put-together. She reminds me of an Old Hollywood starlet. And, she's sincere which makes me feel comfortable.

"He and my brother Luke met at Boot Camp and went through Navy SEAL training together," I say. "Then, we met not long after when he brought Ryker home to visit my family in Ohio. So, going on ten years?"

"Ten years?" Easton's green eyes glow with interest. "And, you two are just friends?"

I feel a blush heat my cheeks and I nod. "We only saw each other once or twice a year."

"And, what do you do?"

"I'm a photographer. I mostly shoot weddings and special events."

She arches a slim, dark brow. "Really? I need to hire a photographer for our wedding."

I look down at the engagement ring on her small hand. A huge square-cut diamond with an emerald on either side. It's blinding. "Your ring's gorgeous, by the way."

"Thank you," she says. "But, not half as gorgeous as the man who gave it to me."

It's clear how much Easton is in love and I wonder what it would be like to be so in love with a man that you want to spend the rest of your life with him.

"Can I have your card?" Easton asks. "If you're not already booked, I'd love to discuss having you shoot our wedding."

"Sure," I say. I pull a card out of my purse and glance toward the kitchen, wondering what that trio of handsome men were discussing in such low, deep voices.

6

RYKER

"That's *Avery Archer*?" Griff asks and runs a hand through his perfectly-mussed brown hair. I nod and he studies me closely. "You okay?"

"Yeah."

"Is she the one who called you earlier at the office?" Jax asks.

"The phone call that made me flip out? Yeah." I admit.

I know Jax doesn't know much about my past and now isn't the time to delve into it, but I want to catch him up. Griff knows me better, but even he doesn't know all the gory details. Nobody does.

"My best friend in SEALs was Luke Archer, Avery's older brother. We met at Boot Camp, went through BUD/S together and basically just hit it off. Eventually, we both made DEVGRU, The Naval Special Warfare Development Group."

"Better known as Seal Team Six," Griff says.

"I know that impresses you for some reason," I say, "but, it's just a job title. DEVGRU SEALs just get to go on 'sportier' missions." Even though I try to make light of it, Griff isn't having it.

"It impresses the hell out of me," Griff says and glances over at Jax. "It's all secretive as shit, but I know you trained for a long time, spent 5 years on a regular SEAL team before you could even apply for

DEVGRU. Then, God knows all the shit you had to go through before being accepted. You were part of a Tier One Special Mission Unit. Not an easy accomplishment, brother. So, yeah, I'm damn proud of you. Deal with it."

"Thanks," I mumble, feeling my face redden under all the unnecessary praise. Yes, I worked my ass off to be a SEAL and to be a part of DEVGRU, but who gives a fuck? It's just a job title like I said. "Anyway, we were sent on a mission to take down a target, a drug lord, who was supplying weapons to terrorists. Operation Armageddon."

I take a deep breath and know it's okay to talk about it. To tell these guys, my closest friends, what happened. "We went down to Columbia on bad intel. The whole situation was jacked up. No joy." I press my palms against the island countertop, stare down at the fresh scabs on the knuckles on my right hand. "I lost my whole team. Barely made it out myself."

They offer me silent support, not pushing, just letting me go at my own pace.

"What's Avery's connection? Other than being Luke's sister?" Jax finally asks.

"Avery was the CIA analyst whose source provided the bad intel."

Griff sucks in a breath. "Fuck."

"I blamed her for everything, hated her for the past two years. Or, so I thought." They wait for me to continue. "Apparently, a source just contacted Avery about having new information that will vindicate her. So, we're going down to meet them in Colombia."

"I don't feel good about you two going to fucking Colombia," Jax says.

"Me, neither," Griff agrees.

"No choice, brothers. We have to see this through. Find out if she was purposely fed bad intel."

"If you're going in, you need all the information you can get. I'm going to have Harlow do a deep search. Give me names, whatever you can, and we'll see what she can find out."

"Thanks, Jax."

He hands me a pad of paper and a pen. I write down names, dates, contacts, anything and everything I can think of about Operation Armageddon. I slide it over and feel a little better. It's good to know these guys have my back.

"You need anything-" Jax says.

"And, we will be down there in a heartbeat," Griff finishes.

I reach out and Griff and I slide our palms, link fingers and bump knuckles. Our signature handshake. Then, I turn to Jax and show him how it's done. I give Griff a half-smile like we just initiated Jax into our secret club.

"So, concerning blondie out there..." Griff says and gives me a questioning look.

"What about her?" I ask, instantly protective, defensive.

"You two were always just...friends?" He quirks a brow.

"Always. She was Luke's little sister. That meant off-limits."

"You're a stronger man than me," Griff says.

Not really, I think. I've always desired Avery and now that Luke is gone...A part of me wonders if he'd actually be happy that we found each other and that we're trying to find the truth in this whole mess. I kind of think he would.

And, even more than that, I can say I don't hate her anymore. My feelings have always been strong for her and now they're swinging in the opposite direction.

"I guess whatever happens, happens," I say in a low voice. "I'm done holding back."

Griff smirks. "There's my boy. When you didn't look twice at Harlow, I got worried."

"I thought sleeping with employees is against the rules," I say.

"It is," Jax reminds us with a good-natured scowl.

"Avery is different. She's...special."

"The one that got away," Jax says.

I don't admit or deny it.

"Well, she's back, buddy," Griff says and slaps me on the back. "Time to figure it out."

Later that night, after my usual 5-mile run, I pack a suitcase and Griff's words reverberate in my head.

Time to figure it out.

Yeah, it was definitely time. Past time.

And, if that didn't give me enough anxiety, I have to face the fact that tomorrow at this time, I'll be back in Colombia. My head feels like it's going to explode. I pull out my SIG Sauer P226 and place it in a foam lockbox with extra ammunition. I'm not taking any chances down there.

I'm not sure how going back to Columbia is going to affect me. Shit, I should've just gone to talk to a shrink like the military suggested two years ago. But, no, I thought I had it handled. Everything under control.

I give a snort. *Yeah, not even close.*

Ever since the Charlie Foxtrot that was Operation Armageddon, I feel like I'm a man on the verge of drowning. I'm paddling so hard, but I keep sinking under, sucking in water. And, considering not drowning was pretty important since the "sea" was one-third of my job description as a SEAL, it's a strange feeling.

My mind wanders back to BUD/S training when we went through drown-proofing. That just means they bound our hands and feet and threw us into a pool. Naturally, you panic at first, but you have to dig deep mentally and very quickly learn how to get up for air.

Now, I'm trying to figure out how to get up for air. My feelings for Avery are all over the place. I've gone from hate to desire in the blink of an eye and I'm having trouble processing it.

I shake my head. I can't deal with this right now. Time to take a shower and go to bed because it's going to be a long day tomorrow.

I wander down to the bathroom, slip out of my t-shirt and kick off my jeans. I grab a fresh towel and freeze when I catch a glimpse of my reflection in the mirror above the sink. My eyes move from the jagged knife scar on my front shoulder below my clavicle and down my side where I count one, two, three scars from bullet wounds. On the opposite side there are two more round scars from being shot.

I don't remember much about the pain when it first happened. I was running on adrenaline, lost in a jungle full of tangos, just trying to get to the extraction point with the rest of my team. But, they surrounded us and, one by one, I watched the others fall.

Until I was the last one left.

DEVGRU is divided into color-coded squadrons and I was a part of "the tribe," or the Red Squadron. Our logo is a Native American Indian and it fit us well. We were fierce warriors and fought to the death. We took out a lot of bad guys, but we didn't stand a chance that night.

Six of us against 80 of them!

When I woke up in the hospital, all bandaged up and loaded up on painkillers, I knew someone had fucked up. I never would've guessed it was Avery. But, word gets around and it didn't take long before a SEAL friend from another squadron visited and filled me in on all the dirty details.

And, then, when I was at the lowest point of my life, raging with hurt and anger, Avery walked into my room. All angelic-looking with pity in her eyes. She was the whole reason my tribe was dead and I was laying in that bed.

I'm so glad you're okay.

At that moment, I was so far from okay. Every sentence out of her mouth just made me angrier and, to be honest, I had to struggle to hear her because my hearing was impaired after a grenade exploded too close to me.

I was frustrated and I wanted to throttle her. Instead, I said the most hurtful things I could think of so she would leave. I hated the pity, didn't want it. I knew I was a broken mess and, even after my wounds healed on the outside, the inside remained raw and fresh.

For the first time in a very long time, I feel a tenuous thread of hope. That maybe finally I'll be able to find peace. Maybe going back to Columbia will be a way to finally put the demons in my head to rest.

God, I hope so.

After a quick shower, I drop into bed. I'm exhausted. Today was emotionally-draining and I never expected to see Avery Archer again much less agree to go to Bogota with her.

I can fall asleep anywhere and within seconds. I also jump awake at the first sound, ready to go. Guess that's what happens when you're military. Tonight, the second my head hits the pillow, I'm out.

When the nightmare starts, I'm with my team again. The six of us, in full tactical gear, move through the jungle as one, total focus on the mission ahead. It's straightforward and well-planned out. Intel suggests 10-15 tangos and our main target is Antonio Castillo.

Their little group left the safety of Castillo's compound earlier and they headed deep into the jungle for a meeting. Antonio Castillo is an asshole and a drug lord. If that isn't bad enough, he's also selling weapons to terrorists.

And, that's why we're here. Our mission, Operation Armageddon, is to neutralize Castillo and end the flow of weapons to our pals in the Middle East. Seems simple enough. Unfortunately, the majority of information provided by the fucking CIA is wrong.

From numbers to locations to weapons.

It isn't long before we find ourselves in the middle of Castillo's own personal army. When the shooting begins, all hell breaks loose and our well-thought-out plan goes out the window. Instead, our mission becomes one of survival.

Castillo's men close in on us and, before I realize it, I'm within combative range which means the bad guys are 7 yards or closer. It's not a good feeling. Within this close distance things happen fast, really fast, and a gun is pretty useless.

I pull my concealed knife and face three men. They all charge me at once and I manage to take one down. Then, a second. But, the third one stabs me in the shoulder with his knife. I keep going, though, can't stop because if I stop, I'm dead.

I suck it up, ignore the pain, and slam into the fucker, driving my knife into his gut. As he's falling over, I see Luke go down, two guys slashing at him. I launch myself into them and neutralize both bad guys. But, Luke is not in good shape.

This is where the nightmare takes a turn from what really happened.

I look up and we're surrounded. A sea of enemies, all pointing knives, guns, assault rifles and grenades at us.

There's nowhere to go. No escape.

Suddenly, someone lifts a rocket-propelled grenade against his shoulder and fires. The warhead screams straight toward me and explodes in my face.

I jump awake, sweat dripping down my body and a scream caught in my throat. *Fuck.* That was more intense than usual. I haven't had a dream like that since right after I left the hospital. I pull in a deep breath and blow it out once, twice, three, four times.

Just when I start thinking I'm doing better...bam!

I fall back and throw an arm over my eyes, knowing that I'm done sleeping for tonight. Maybe tomorrow night will be better.

I hope so, anyway.

7

AVERY

The following morning, I meet Ryker at the airport. We check our luggage and Ryker has a small black box which I'm guessing holds his SIG Sauer, a SEAL favorite. After he fills out a card declaring the weapon, he opens the box to reveal the gun and then locks it.

Yep, I'm right. Guess when your big brother was a SEAL you just start catching on to certain things.

We go through security, head down to the gate and before long, we board the plane. Ten hours is a long time to travel. But, we're both used to flying and I know Ryker is especially accustomed to long flights since he used to go all over the world.

We take off and I look out the window, watching as we head out over the Pacific Ocean, moving higher up into the cloudless sky. The plane makes a wide circle and comes back around over land, and we head toward Atlanta, Georgia.

Fifteen minutes after takeoff from LAX, I lean back in my seat and cast a sidelong glance at Ryker. His ridiculously long legs extend out, touching the opposite wall, and his ankles are crossed. I'm glad he chose the emergency exit seats because there's plenty of extra room to stretch out.

He's fiddling with his earbuds which are all tangled up and he's concentrating so hard that I can't help but smile. "Need some help?" I ask.

He looks over and shakes his head. "I used to have to tie and untie knots underwater. I think I can get some stupid earbuds undone-"

The cord snaps in his big hands and I bite my lip to keep from laughing.

"Goddammit."

I cover my mouth, but I can't stop my shoulders from shaking.

It doesn't take him long to notice. "Ha ha," he says, not in the least bit amused.

"Sorry. It's just- the look on your face…" I burst into a fit of laughter.

It takes a moment, but a reluctant smile finally curves his mouth. "It's really not that funny."

"I know," I say, "but, you know when you just can't stop laughing?" I press my lips together, trying to hold it in. "You just looked so serious and I knew they were going to break."

Suddenly, I remember the last time he made me laugh this hard. It was three years ago and I had driven to Virginia Beach to meet Luke. We were supposed to spend the day together and had plans to visit a nearby animal sanctuary.

Growing up, we had always loved animals and took care of all the neighborhood strays or any sick animals we stumbled across. We bottle-fed baby squirrels who fell out of a tree in the backyard, mended broken bird wings and one time we even saved some baby opossums that were still clinging to their poor, dead mother on the side of the road.

It also happened to be my 29th birthday and Luke knew I'd love visiting the rescued animals. Our parents made sure to teach us kind-ness and compassion toward all living creatures, and growing up, our house sometimes resembled Dr. Dolittle's.

When I arrived at the base that morning, Luke was a green-faced mess and had caught some kind of stomach bug. He felt terrible and I had no intention of making him spend the day with me out at the sanctuary.

"But, it's your birthday and you drove all the way down here," he had said. "I feel terrible."

And, that's when Ryker offered to go with me.

I have to admit, as much as I loved my brother, I was so excited to be spending some time alone with Ryker. We drove out to the animal sanctuary and I remember how easy the conversation flowed, how comfortable I felt around him.

The six-acre property had large horse and cow pastures, a red and white barnyard for the smaller animals, an organic vegetable garden and lots of trees and shade for the nearly 200 rescued animals.

We hugged cows, cuddled turkeys and gave pigs tummy rubs. Looking into the eyes of those animals who had been abused or abandoned tugged at my heart. It also made me realize how much Ryker loved animals, too.

And, that made me fall even harder for my brother's best friend.

I remember we were hanging out in the barnyard area with all kinds of different critters including chickens, sheep, goats and turkeys. I was crouched down in the dirt feeding a baby lamb and Ryker bent over to fix the laces on his boot which had come untied.

And, out of the blue, an ornery goat charged him and headbutted his backside. The look on his face was priceless and I dissolved into peals of laughter. I mean, I cracked up so hard, I was shaking. Nothing could stop me and I doubled-over and laughed so hard, I had tears in my eyes. At some point, Ryker joined in and we both fell back in the middle of the barnyard, unable to stop howling.

With dust covering us, we eventually got up and brushed ourselves off. We smiled at each other and I'll never forget when he reached out a hand and wiped a smudge of dirt off my cheek. There was a heat in his eyes that I'd never seen before and my stomach somersaulted.

On our way back to the base, we stopped for ice cream cones. Both Ryker and Luke teased me endlessly about my sweet tooth. They both agreed I should weigh about 50 more pounds. But, it was my birthday and Ryker insisted on getting me a sugary treat.

It's funny how some details I'll never forget. Like how I got a scoop of mint chocolate chip ice cream and Ryker got peanut butter chocolate, but then we each wished we had gotten the other flavor. After a few licks, we swapped cones.

I'll also always remember the way he looked at me while we finished those cones. Almost like he wanted to lick me, too.

But, nothing ended up happening. We had a great day and he drove me back to base like a complete gentleman. Even though I was kind of hoping for a birthday kiss. I said goodbye to Luke and Ryker offered to walk me out to my car.

I tossed my purse on the passenger seat and turned around to thank him for a wonderful day. And, he was standing right behind me, so close, so that when I turned around, I was practically in his arms. I smelled his pine-scented soap and stood there, frozen.

"Happy Birthday, Ave," he said. Then, he leaned in and brushed his lips against the very edge of my mouth. I'm not sure if he meant to get as close to my lips as he did, but something inside of me melted. My heart pounded as I watched him walk away.

And, when he glanced over his shoulder, I couldn't miss the simmering look in his eyes.

A few years later, that heated look turned to ice.

We have a brief layover in Atlanta and then we are up and flying toward Columbia. The longer we travel, the more I can feel Ryker begin to tense up. Anxiety rolls off him in waves and I was really hoping that going back might help him heal. Not give him a damn nervous breakdown.

Forty minutes outside of Bogota's El Dorado International Airport, Ryker looks positively green. Suddenly, he gets up and walks up the aisle toward the bathroom. When he returns a few minutes later, his rugged face is pale and he's chewing a piece of gum.

I think he probably just puked his nerves out.

I look down at his big hands, clutching the armrest hard, and I slide my hand over his. I don't say anything and a few seconds later, he turns his hand over to hold mine.

We don't let go until the plane lands.

Then, it's a whirlwind as we get our luggage and head outside. It's cooler than I expected and not very sunny. We grab a taxi and head through the city toward the hotel. Graffiti and murals decorate walls and buildings giving it an urban edginess.

"I booked us at the Wyndham," Ryker says. "Ten minutes from the airport and 0.3 miles from the American Embassy."

"Sounds good," I say and reach for my phone. I pull up my email and let this mysterious "G." know that I'm here and ask about meeting up tomorrow.

It doesn't take long before we check in and head up to our room. It's nothing glamorous, but I do immediately notice the two double beds beside each other. I pull my suitcase over to the bed next to the floor-to-ceiling window and plop down. It's been a long day and my stomach growls.

"Hungry?" Ryker asks with a small smile.

I nod. "Hungry and tired."

"Room service okay?" He grabs the menu on the desk and I nod. Then, he walks over and sits down beside me on the bed. The mattress sags and when his big, powerful thigh presses against mine, I inhale a deep breath, trying to focus on the menu choices.

But, his warm leg is thoroughly distracting.

"What sounds good?" he asks, his voice low and all gravelly-sounding. And, far too close.

My stomach drops and I remember our kiss in the park. He is a really good kisser and the way his mouth moved over mine...God, he makes me want more.

That kiss was worth the almost ten-year wait.

"Um, I'll get the burger and fries. And, how about a cerveza? And, something sweet for dessert."

"You're reading my mind, Ave." He gives me a smile. Then, he's up, taking that yummy thigh away, and placing the order.

My gaze drifts across his broad shoulders and large muscles that flex with every move he makes. He's so freaking built. My eyes drop and slide down his back, stopping to admire his tight, round ass. My mouth waters and I'm so busy staring at his delectable backside that he turns and catches me.

I instantly look away and feel my cheeks redden. Ryker doesn't say anything, but I can see him pull in a deep breath. "Chow should be here in 30. You wanna shower first?" he asks.

I swallow down the humiliation of my perusing eyes and nod. I grab my pajamas and cosmetic case and head into the bathroom. After I close the door, I drop my stuff on the counter and my eyes slide shut. *Oh, God. He knows.* I want him so badly and it's written all over my face.

I look down at the pajamas I brought-- a short, pink nightshirt-- and imagine Ryker pulling it up over my head. *How am I going to sleep next to him tonight?* Even though we have separate beds, I could easily reach across the gap and touch him.

Shit. It's been a long time. A very long time since I've been intimate with a man. If anything happens between us, I worry that I'll screw it up. What if I'm not good enough? Not experienced enough to please him? Or, God forbid, he's not attracted to me?

But, he kissed you earlier. Kissed you thoroughly.

I step into the shower and can't turn my mind off. If I disappoint him in any way sexually, I would absolutely die. Like be on the first flight out of here. *Calm down, Avery. You're being ridiculous.*

You're also jumping the gun. No one said you're having sex tonight. Jesus, get a grip.

Even so, I lather up with my pink sugar shower gel then smother myself in the matching body cream and fragrance. I slip the little nightshirt over my head, spritz my wet hair with a conditioner and then slide my feet into a pair of powder-pink slippers with little fuzzy balls on top.

When I walk back out, Ryker is at the door, accepting two covered plates, a tray of cookies and a couple of ice cold Pilsens. He tips the hotel employee who casts an appreciative look in my direction before leaving. Ryker turns, hands full, and freezes as I walk over.

"Here, let me help," I say and take the plates from him. I saunter over to the small table, feeling him watching me, and set them down.

He follows me over, slowly, and then pops the Pilsen open. As he drinks, I notice his gaze dip down and check out my bare legs.

When I sit, I pull the short nightshirt down as much as I can and cross my legs. And, Ryker is still staring. "Nice slippers," he finally says.

I look down at them and make a face. "What's wrong with them?" I ask.

"They're very girly."

"If you haven't noticed, I am a girl."

"Oh, I've noticed," he says in a low voice.

My stomach does a little flip as I lift the cover off my plate. He finally sits down and we both start eating.

"You take forever in the bathroom," he says between bites.

"Oh, I'm sorry," I say.

"What do you do in there, anyway?"

He truly looks baffled and I suppress a smile.

"Um, well, lots of things." He pops a french fry into his mouth and raises a curious brow. "I have to take off my makeup, wash my face, brush my teeth, shower, shave, put on my lotions and creams." The look on his face is hysterical. Like he has no clue what I'm talking about. "Let me guess. You'll be in and out in under ten minutes."

"Five minutes," he corrects.

Military men, I think with a smile.

It doesn't take Ryker long to eat either and soon he's up and rummaging through his suitcase. "Any word yet from your contact?" he asks.

I pull up my email and shake my head. "Not yet."

He grabs a few things and then heads for the bathroom. "Keep checking," he says over a shoulder.

Oh, you bet I will, I think and check out his ass again. He closes the door and I picture him getting undressed. That big naked body under the shower spray. I reach for the Pilsen and swallow the rest of it down in one long gulp.

The moment Ryker walks back out, I can sense the change in him. He wears a t-shirt and long shorts. He's clean-shaven and I get a whiff of whatever woodsy, pine-smelling soap he uses. It makes me tingly. But, he seems more distant, caught up in his thoughts. Dark thoughts.

I know being back here is hard for him and when he walks over to the mini bar and pulls out a small bottle of vodka, I feel awkward. I want to comfort him, walk over and wrap my arms around him. But, what if that makes him even more uncomfortable? Which I'm pretty sure it will.

Instead, I pretend to check my email.

But, beneath my lashes, I watch him walk over to the window and down the bottle as he looks out over the city. And, so it goes for the next 45 minutes as he tries to drown his sorrows. Three tiny alcohol bottles later, he drops down on the edge of his bed, cracks open a fourth bottle, and runs his fingers through his damp hair.

Enough. I get up from the chair, walk over and stand between his long legs. I take the bottle out of his hand. He looks up, half-drunk, as I take a sip and shiver. A little liquid courage could never hurt anything.

"You want to talk?" I ask and hand him the bottle back.

He takes a swig. "No."

Of course not. "I wish you'd tell me what's going on in there." I brush a few fingers along his temple, down over his ear.

And, he jerks away like I burned him.

Shit. What did I do?

I'm so confused. I've seen the lingering looks, felt the heat between us, and the second I touch him, he pulls away. *Why?*

"Ryker?"

A muscle flexes in his jaw. Finally, he looks up at me. And, those whisky-colored eyes are swimming in pain. I step closer between his open legs, my knees hitting the mattress. Pulse pounding, I lay my hands on his hard chest and feel him tense beneath the t-shirt. His hands fly up, snake up around my wrists and pull them off him.

He's rejecting me, I realize with a sinking heart.

"What's wrong?" I ask.

But, he just shakes his head and releases my wrists, throwing me off-balance.

I take an unsteady step back and feel a rush of sympathy. This is all my damn fault. For the first time, I understand what the last two years have done to him. *My poor warrior.* "You may not want me, but, please, let me help you."

Finally, he meets my gaze. "You think I don't want you?" he asks in a harsh whisper. "Fuck, Avery, I've wanted you since the first day we met."

My heart stops and I search his eyes for the truth. "But, you just pushed me away," I say, not understanding.

He lets out a ragged breath and grasps my hips. "Because I have nothing to offer you. I'm broken, Avery."

I feel his long fingers dig into my sides and realize how much he's hurting. "Ryker," I whisper. "Let me help." I cover his hands with mine, pull them up and hold them. *So big and powerful.* I place a kiss on first one then the other. "Please."

When he doesn't say anything, I place one of his hands over my heart. "Focus on me. Not the past." My heart thunders beneath his warm hand. We both start breathing more heavily and my nipples grow hard beneath the thin nightshirt.

His gaze drops, broad chest heaving, and I know he notices.

I drag his hand down to cover my breast. "Touch me, Ryker." His palm curves around my breast, then lifts and squeezes. My eyes flutter shut and I let out a sigh. "Do I feel good?"

"So fucking good," he rasps.

"Then touch me. Let yourself feel good."

At the invitation, he lifts his other hand and covers my right breast. I place my hands over his, encouraging him. Cupping, molding, kneading.

"It's just us. You and me," I say. My head falls back and Ryker slips his hands out from beneath mine, grasps my hips and yanks me forward. My eyes snap open and I gasp.

Caught between his legs, I look down and notice the very large, hard ridge pressing up against his shorts. When his hands skim up the outside of my thighs and move up under my nightshirt, I reach around his neck, leaning into him, knowing that he's about to find out my panties are soaked.

But, he doesn't venture there just yet. Instead, he caresses my bare back, hands moving restlessly up and down. His gaze drops to my lips. It's almost like there's an internal debate going on inside his head.

And, I'm glad passion wins.

Ryker leans in and captures my mouth in a kiss that sets my soul on fire. Our mouths meld, tongues stroking, hands groping. It's intense and on a deeper level than I've ever experienced before. That I ever knew existed.

When we finally break apart, panting, it's like I've just come up from underwater. I gasp for air, claw my hands through his cropped hair and press into his hard body.

And, he pulls back. *Shit.*

Through hazy eyes, I watch him set me away from him, lower my nightshirt and touch a strand of my hair. He toys with it for a moment and when he finally looks up, his whisky eyes are full of regret. "I'm sorry, Ave."

"Ryker-"

But, he shakes his head. "This can't happen."

Disappointment surges within me. "Why not?" I ask in a breathy voice.

"Because I'm not good enough for you, Avery."

"Ryker, don't be a martyr."

All of a sudden, it's like a shield snaps down over his eyes, his face, and he gives me that perfectly blank look that I despise. "Trust me. You'll thank me later."

With a frustrated groan, I turn away and drop down on my bed. *No, I won't thank you later,* I think. Dammit, why does he have to be such a saint around me? I know he's had sex with other women. *Lots of other women,* I think darkly.

Yet, when it comes to me, he consistently pulls away. I would think it's because he's not attracted to me, but I know that's not true. I can literally feel the heat pouring off him and the sparks shooting off me.

The moment we touch, it's like some kind of chemical reaction on the verge of blowing.

I pull the blanket up around me and bury my face in the pillow. At this point, I don't know if I'm ever going to be able to convince him to let his guard down. His walls are too high and sturdy.

A fucking fortress that he uses to keep me out.

He has this way of turning off his emotions like a light switch. The last time I saw him look so blank and unemotional was at Luke's funeral, not long after our blowout at the hospital.

Everyone who came to the funeral was utterly devastated. So many people loved my brother and the church was packed with family and friends from school, the neighborhood and the Navy. I've never seen anything like it. Standing room only.

I remember searching for Ryker through the crowd and eventually saw him standing off to the side by himself in his Navy uniform. He stood ramrod straight under a stained-glass window, looking so stoic and clean-cut. And, that blank look on his face gave me a chill.

There were three parts to Luke's funeral and it was the longest day of my life. The funeral mass at the church lasted around an hour and when the priest took some time to talk about Luke and what a wonderful, patriotic life he'd led, I felt sick to my stomach. If it weren't for his patriotism, he'd still be alive. And, then when he said Luke was happy now, safe, and with the Lord, I bit my lip so hard it bled.

Happy? How could Luke be happy knowing he had been brutally killed in a foreign country and his life was over at the age of 32? He never found love or got married or had a family. My parents sobbed beside me and I just remember getting more and more angry.

I know they say life isn't fair, but this was beyond unfair. This was tragic and heartbreaking on a level that ripped a hole in my soul. My older brother had been my hero and, in my eyes, completely invincible. And, now he was cold and in a box, his body riddled with bullet holes. I'd never see his charming smile or hear his contagious laughter again. There'd be no more teasing banter back and forth, no more holidays spent together, no more birthdays or phone calls or hugs where he told me how proud he was of me.

Because he always did. My parents lavished him with praise and attention and he deserved it. But, he also knew that meant I didn't get much. And, that was fine, I could live with my older brother being the superstar and center of attention. But, Luke always made sure to turn some of that praise and attention my way.

Luke Archer was a good man. One of the best. And, the fact that he was gone now filled me with a bitterness. But, the reality of the situation was I had provided his team with the bad intel that resulted in their demise.

He was dead because of me.

I hadn't really let that thought sink in completely yet. And, when I finally did that day, my world began to crumble. The guilt felt like acid and it was eating away at me.

After the church service, we drove over to the military cemetery. Ryker was one of the men who helped carry my brother's casket, right up in front with my Dad.

The burial ceremony at the grave site was even harder than the church service. The funeral honors bestowed on Luke by his Naval brothers brought me to tears and because he had been active duty and a posthumous Medal of Honor recipient, there were body bearers, a seven person firing detail, an Officer-in-Charge (OIC) and a bugler.

The flag remained draped over his casket during the service and near the end, the clergyman stepped back from the head of the grave. The OIC signaled the firing detail to attention and all military personnel in uniform, and there were a lot, rendered the hand salute.

The firing detail fired three volleys on the command of the Petty Officer-in-Charge and then a bugler played TAPS.

It was fucking heart-wrenching and I looked over at Ryker, his hand is a frozen salute. Finally, his gaze flickered over in my direction. And, it was like his brown eyes were empty, completely devoid of any emotion.

After TAPS, the military personnel terminated their salutes and the clergyman offered a final benediction. Finally, Ryker and another soldier removed the flag off the casket and started to fold it.

I watched his large hands move with such respect and precision as they folded it so perfectly. I don't know what it was-- maybe the way he took such care-- but, something about it completely overwhelmed me and more hot tears slid down my face.

When they finished, Ryker gave the flag to the Officer-in-Charge who walked over to me and my parents. It was in the shape of a triangle with the blue field visible. He handed it to my Mom and said, "On behalf of a grateful nation and a proud Navy, I present this flag to you in recognition of your son's years of honorable and faithful service to his country."

Then, he stepped back and saluted.

We all broke down and he offered his condolences. After returning to the head of the grave, the honorary pallbearers which included Ryker, walked over and rendered their condolences.

Ryker was last. He shook my Dad's hand, hugged my Mom and then turned to me.

And, it was like time stood still.

I looked up into his stoic face, not knowing what to do or say. A muscle ticked at his jaw and something finally flashed in his brown eyes.

Hate.

It was cold and controlled and my heart broke.

He mumbled a condolence then turned on his heel and walked back over to my brother's casket.

It felt like he had just punched me in the gut.

As the mourners filed away, my parents and I slid into the back of a black sedan. We still had one more part of this torturous day to get through and that was a gathering at the local veteran's hall where a catered lunch awaited everyone. I was dreading it. All I wanted to do was go home and sink into my bed for the next month. I wanted to forget this nightmare.

I wanted my brother back.

As our car drove away, the OIC saluted us. I remember I glanced out the window, gaze searching for Ryker. He's so tall, towered over everyone, so it was easy to find him. He was at the grave. Everyone else had moved away, but he stood next to Luke, and a big hand laid on the casket.

And, then his head dropped between his shoulders.

At that moment, I saw all of his stoicism disappear and Ryker Flynn broke.

There's nothing so heartbreaking as to see something that you thought was unbreakable shatter into a million pieces.

Later, as I picked at my plate of food at the hall, I realized that Ryker never showed up to the luncheon.

8

RYKER

Pushing Avery away is the hardest thing I have ever done in my life. Harder than any training or battle. Harder than Luke's funeral. I flip over, turning away from her and pull in an uneven breath.

Even though she's in the other bed, I'm so aware of her. She smells like some delicious sugary confection and all I want to do is devour her. It's been almost half an hour since we turned out the light and I stopped things before they went too far. And, I'm still hard as hell. *Fuck.* How am I supposed to sleep when my cock is ready to have sex? Demanding to have sex.

I am the biggest idiot, I think. It's been too long and the woman I want more than anything just let me know she wants me, too. And, what do I do? Play the hero, the noble warrior who doesn't need to have sex with the beautiful woman.

Yeah, right. I am so tempted to go crawl into her bed right now. Sink into her warm curves and luscious body. I need to take the edge off from being here in Columbia and I thought drinking would help. But, there's only one thing that will help me right now.

Fucking Avery.

I flip back over onto my back and throw an arm over my eyes.

When her hand brushed down my face and over my ear earlier, I jerked away. She doesn't know about my hearing loss or the tiny aids I wear. She also doesn't know about the nightmares and how I wake up screaming sometimes. Or, how I try to cope with alcohol. There are too many things I want to protect her from knowing.

She's too good. *An angel.* And, I don't want to taint her with my darkness, my unforgivable sins.

Maybe I am a martyr because I'd prefer to suffer alone. I refuse to drag her down with me. She doesn't need to see the blackness that tortures me.

The problem is that I am still wildly attracted to her. So, while my mind says one thing, my heart and cock are on a completely different page. Lucky for me, I'm a SEAL and mental toughness overrides everything else.

Well, kind of. I look down at the tented sheet and groan. *Fuck, I need to do something about this.* I glance over at Avery who faces away from me and watch the even rise and fall of her back and shoulder as she breathes. Good, she's asleep. I throw the covers back, pad into the bathroom and release the throbbing ache from my shorts.

I've been busy at work lately and before that, I slid into one of my depressions so there's been no hook-ups in awhile. So, of course, my cock has to remind me now, of all times. I wrap my hand around the thick length and start pumping. Leaning forward, hand on the counter, I work it hard and fast, thoughts of Avery filling my head.

And, then I hear her behind me, pushing the door all the way open. I freeze, on the verge of coming, and look up to see her in the mirror. Her gaze drops, blue eyes widening with what looks like... appreciation.

"I could've helped you out with that earlier," she says. She takes a tentative step closer. "I still can," she adds in a husky voice.

Oh, God, I don't have the willpower to turn her away and I am ready to explode when she moves up beside me and reaches down, wrapping her delicate fingers around me. My vision blurs the moment her soft hands touch me. It's like heaven. Her touch is so light, like a whisper, and I wrap my hand over hers, guiding it up and down. Faster, harder, until my whole body trembles.

When the orgasm hits, it's like a freight train slamming into me. The hot liquid inside me shoots out between our fingers and across the counter, and I utter a guttural groan as my body releases all the pent-up energy that's been making me so damn crazy.

I tug my shorts back up, grab a towel and gently wipe her hands and then the counter. I feel like I was a pressure cooker and all of the steam inside me was just released. It's a relief and my head feels clearer. I take Avery's hand, lift it to my lips and place an open-mouth kiss in her palm.

Our gazes hold for a moment that seems to go on forever and we don't communicate with words. More like with our hearts or souls or something. It's strange. Whatever is happening between us...I don't have the strength to keep pushing her away. I feel some of my walls begin to collapse and decide that if we're going to explore this thing between us, I don't want to rush it.

I guide her back to my bed, pull her down with me and wrap my arms around her, loving the way her body curls into mine. When I place a kiss along her hairline, she snuggles down into my embrace and sighs.

We both instantly fall asleep and I don't know about her, but it's the best sleep I've had in years.

Morning comes too soon and waking up with Avery is the most pleasant experience I could ever imagine. Her soft blonde hair tickles my nose and that sugary scent she wears makes me think of better times. When I was younger and carefree and my parents were still alive.

I grew up in a small town in Ohio, ironically not too far away from Luke and Avery. Life as a boy was everything I'd ever wish for a child. I didn't have any siblings, but I had friends, school and played endless sports. My parents were kind and loving. My Dad was my hero and since he was former military, I wanted to follow in his footsteps. More than anything, I wanted to make him proud.

It's the reason I pushed myself so hard. I joined the Navy and set my sights on becoming a Frogman because it was the highest I could achieve. All through my training, he encouraged me and was my biggest cheerleader. When I finally received my Trident pin, my Dad was in the front row and whooped the loudest "Hooyah!" of all.

Five years ago, while I was on a mission in Afghanistan, my parents died in a car accident. I have no other family so losing them made a huge hole in my heart. Luke was there for me and welcomed me further into his family, inviting me over for holidays and vacations.

I always felt bad because it was clear that Luke was the favorite and Avery always seemed to rank second in their parents' eyes. I never understood why because she's so damn amazing. Gorgeous, smart, determined.

Now, I look down at her, burrowed in my arms, and place a kiss in her golden-blonde waves. We've both lost so much and somehow found each other again despite the pain and anger that originally separated us.

I'm not going to lose you again, I promise her.

It's early, probably around 5:30am, but that's when I normally wake up. I can't help it. Back in the Navy, we got up at 4 or 5 am, so technically, this is sleeping in for me. I slip out of bed and disappear into the bathroom. Memories from last night instantly heat my blood. I'll never forget looking up and seeing her reflection in the mirror. The expression on her face. Instead of disgust or revulsion, she was turned on. Which turned me on.

I throw on a t-shirt, black cargo pants and boots then head down to the cafe to grab us a couple of coffees. When I get back up to the room, Avery is sitting on the couch, thankfully dressed and not in that too-short nightgown, typing an email.

She pauses and gives me a shy smile. "He wants to meet in a couple hours. Just outside of town." I nod, walk over and hand her the coffee. "Thank you."

"No name yet?"

"Just G. still. But, he said to look for the American with dark hair."

I sit down beside her. "I don't know what this guy's going to tell us, but I hope it's worth coming all the way down here for."

"It's worth it," she says. "Even if he tells us nothing."

I look over and her blue eyes shine. "Ave…"

"I know we had a rough start the other day and I'm sorry."

My mouth edges up. "For slapping me?"

But, she's completely serious. "For everything, Ryker. I never meant to hurt you. Ever."

"I know," I say softly. And, it's true. I know in my heart that Avery never purposefully did anything to hurt me or my team. But, the anger took me over and I wanted to lash out at somebody. Needed to hate and blame someone. Unfortunately, she's the one who bore the brunt of it.

"I'm sorry, too," I say. "Losing Luke and the others was the hardest thing I ever experienced and I needed someone to blame."

"It *was* my fault," she says. "I mean, I thought it was, anyway. If we find out differently, I can't tell you what a relief it'll be."

"I know, baby," I say. "C'mere." I pull her into my arms and stroke her hair, her back. I feel her body relax into mine. "I guess we both have some healing to do."

I hold her as long as I dare then draw back and brush a blonde lock out of her eye. "Wherever we're headed for this meeting, I want to get there early. Do some recon."

Avery nods. "Good idea. I'll finish getting ready and we can go."

I watch Avery get up and eye the sway of her hips as she walks away. My groin tightens and I remember the sight of her hand pumping me. *Shit.* I stand up and give my head a shake. *Time to focus on the mission at hand, Flynn.*

While Avery is in the bathroom, I check my SIG Sauer then slip it in the waistband at my back. I also brought my pigsticker, a straight blade, which I tuck into my boot. I'm ready to get some answers from this contact, but I'm not stupid. As hopeful as Avery is to clear her name, a part of me wonders if this is some kind of setup.

Why would this person contact her out of the blue about a mission gone to shit two years earlier? Some part of the puzzle is missing and

I scratch the back of my neck. Whenever something doesn't feel right, I get this itch there and no amount of scratching will make it go away.

That's why I'm going in prepared and wary. I'm not sure what's going to happen, but I know one thing for sure: no one is going to hurt Avery and I will protect her with my life.

We leave the hotel soon after and take a taxi to the address "G." gave in the email. It's off the beaten path and a hole-in-the-wall bar. I have the driver pass it and drop us off up the road a bit. "Doesn't look like the safest place," I say as we hike back up and around the back of the building.

I want to check it out and know every entrance and exit point before we go inside. I count doors and windows, making mental notes of everything I see. "He thinks you're coming alone, right?" I ask.

"Yes. I didn't tell him about you."

"Good girl," I say absently and check my watch.

Avery tilts her head back and reads the crooked sign above the door. "La Serpiente?"

"The Snake," I translate.

"Yo sé. Hablo español, el guapo." Before I can comment, she squares her shoulders and reaches for the door handle. "Listo para hacer esto?"

"I have no idea what you're saying, but it's sexy as hell," I say. She tosses me a wink and I want to kiss her senseless. Instead, we head into the dark, seedy-looking bar for locals-only.

9

AVERY

When we walk into La Serpiente, every pair of eyes turns in our direction. Luckily, there are only about a half dozen patrons in here and I'm so grateful to have Ryker with me. He's bigger than all of them put together and when he puts on his serious face, he's downright scary-looking.

If they're smart, no one in this place will mess with us.

Ryker zeroes in on a man sitting at a table in the corner with a cerveza in front of him. He places his large hand at my back and guides me over. When we reach the table, the bearded man with shaggy dark hair nods to the two empty seats across from him. He appears to be around 35 years old and looks from me to Ryker with accessing silver-gray eyes.

"Glad you made it down, Avery," he says in a cool voice. "Who's your friend?"

Even though his look is dirty-hot, his voice is cultivated, educated. *An interesting combination*, I think.

"Ryker Flynn," Ryker answers. "There's no way she was coming down here alone."

Those silver eyes narrow, and I can practically see his thoughts whirling. "Ryker Flynn...you're the one who made it out alive. Well, barely."

"Who are you?" I demand. "And how do you know about Operation Armageddon?"

"Grayson Shaw, but call me Gray. I'm a former CIA op and I've been keeping tabs on Antonio Castillo for years." He leans forward and smiles, but there's nothing friendly about it. "But, that's our little secret, okay?"

I'm not sure how I feel about this man. A mysterious air surrounds him and I don't get the impression that I can trust him. I hope I'm wrong. "Why did you reach out to me?" I ask.

"Because you were set up and left out to dry."

"So what? How does that affect you?" I ask.

As though it's an afterthought, he shrugs and adds, "I have a sister. You remind me of her a little."

I'm not sure I'm buying what he's selling, but at this point, I have to hope he's legit. "So, the bad intel I passed on was knowingly fed to me?"

"That's about it. You and Red Squadron took the fall because someone on the inside was profiting from their relationship with Antonio Castillo."

"You're saying Castillo had a CIA op in his pocket?" Ryker asks, voice laced in disbelief.

"I'm not just saying it, I know it." Gray pulls a file from his jacket and slides it across the table. "That's the communication I found between Castillo and Valkyrie."

I flip the file open and see a page full of decoded chatter.

"Who the hell is Valkyrie?" Ryker asks, looking down at the file.

Gray shrugs. "I don't know. I just know he's CIA because they're the only ones who knew about the Armageddon op other than your guys."

Ryker's brown eyes narrow. "My side wouldn't have sabotaged their own."

The two stare at each other for a moment too long and I can feel the tension build. It's like they're challenging each other.

"Hence, why I said CIA," Gray says smoothly.

"Do you think this agent is still active?" I ask.

Again, that shrug. "Who knows? If I were to guess, I'd say they made a fortune informing Castillo about every movement against him, retired and are now living off their dirty money." Gray studies me then taps the tabletop with a finger. "You could trace the agent's identity back through your original source. Who was that?"

"His name was John Miller."

"Obviously, an alias. What else do you know about him? Anything?"

"Just that he only liked to talk to me. Claimed he trusted me."

Gray makes a face, rolls his eyes. "More like he thought you'd be easy to dupe."

"Thanks a lot," I say, getting irritated.

"Sorry, but look what happened."

I've had enough of this guy, I think. *Pompous prick.* "Let's be clear," I snap, eyes flashing. "I got fucked over because someone was greedy, Shaw. Not because I was weak or bad at my job."

Beneath the table, I feel a hand curve over my knee and squeeze. I glance over at Ryker and see him struggling to hold back a smile

He's proud of me. It makes my heart expand. When I turn my attention back to Gray, I notice something new surface in those silver eyes. Respect, maybe?

"Duly noted, Miss Archer," he says.

"So, why have you been keeping tabs on Castillo?" Ryker asks.

Gray doesn't answer right away and instead just sort of mulls over the question. "He's a bad guy. I don't like bad guys."

"That's a pretty generic answer," Ryker comments, not buying it.

I have a sister.

His earlier words reverberate through my head and suddenly I make the connection. "Castillo hurt your sister, didn't he?"

Gray's eyes widen just a bit in surprise then he gives a sharp nod. "Murdered her, actually. Ever since, I've made it my mission to bring that fucker down."

"I'm sorry," I say and Ryker looks away in disgust, mumbling a curse under his breath.

"Like I said, Castillo is a bad guy." He nods to the folder. "If you can use that information and clear your name, your conscience, then I'm glad. You both seem like good people."

Gray pulls a card out of his pocket and slides it to me. "If you need to get in touch with me, here's my number. While you're here or when you're back home. I don't know anything more about Operation Armageddon besides what's in that folder, but if you need anything else...don't hesitate to call."

I take the card, put it in the folder and we all stand up.

Gray offers a hand to Ryker and they shake. "I'm sorry about your team," Gray says.

Ryker gives a nod. "And, I'm sorry about your sister."

"Thank you for reaching out to me," I say. "This changes everything."

"Good luck," Gray says then turns and slips out a side door. *Gone like a ghost*, I think.

Ryker and I head back out the front door. It's another cool day and not far away I see a small river. We wander over and sit on a log near the bank. "What do you think?" I ask.

"I think he's legit." Ryker looks down at the folder in my hand. "I have to take a closer look, but if what Shaw says is true, then my team was sacrificed because whoever this Valkyrie is was on Castillo's payroll."

"The entire mission was compromised to protect him." I shake my head, push my hair off my face and gaze out over the water. "I need to track down my old source. See if he knows Valkyrie's real identity."

"I'm going to call Griff. He's also a former CIA op and may have some contacts. Harlow, our computer specialist, might be able to dig up some more information, too."

"If none of that pans out, we're back at square one," I say, voice glum.

"Don't forget where we are, though," he says.

For a moment, I don't know what he means. But, then it hits me. "In the belly of the beast."

"Exactly. Castillo's compound is close. If I could find a way in-"

"No. It's too dangerous. Besides, we have other leads to check out first." When he doesn't say anything, I touch his arm. "This isn't a suicide mission, Ryker. Get that kamikaze look out of your eye."

"We're just so close..."

"Hey, look at me." He turns his head and I lay a hand along his stubbled jaw. "I can't lose any more people I care about, okay?"

A light flares in his whisky-colored eyes. "Okay. Sorry."

When we get back to the hotel, I plop down on the couch and Ryker calls Griff on speaker, pacing back and forth like a restless lion. I can hear the camaraderie in their voices and they're closer than I originally realized. I'm glad Ryker has someone close like that in his life. I wish I did, too, but any close friends I had in Ohio, I lost touch with when I moved East to work for the CIA.

And, since moving to Los Angeles in the wake of my brother's death, I haven't felt very social. I know it's my fault that I have no girlfriends, but at least I have Liberty. She makes me smile every day and loves me no matter what. Maybe, after all of this is over, I'll have Ryker. At least as a good friend.

I hope so.

After speaking with Griff, Ryker calls Harlow. I haven't met the new Platinum Security computer specialist, aka hacker, but apparently Griff used to work with her when he was CIA and she's extremely talented. Ryker sits down next to me and introduces us.

Harlow has a breathy, sultry voice and I imagine she also has the looks to go along with it. It must be a requirement to be hot as sin to work at Platinum Security, I think, gaze on Ryker's muscled upper arm and the tattoo that peeks out beneath his shirt sleeve.

"I checked out everything you wrote down for Jax," she says. I can hear her fingers typing over the line. "Antonio Castillo has his own little private army known as the United Forces of Colombia or UFOC. They're comparable to the Medellín Cartel. A very powerful, highly organized Colombian drug cartel and terrorist criminal organization."

"Oh, great," I say. "So, he's like Pablo Escobar's spirit animal."

"You can say that again," Harlow says. "He has a secret, highly-guarded compound in the Columbian jungle somewhere, but I'm still trying to locate its exact position."

I glance at Ryker, but he doesn't comment any further on the compound. "What about the code name Valkyrie?" Ryker asks. "Our contact revealed Valkyrie was the CIA op who was working with Castillo and warned him that we were coming in to take him out."

More typing. "I'll see what I can find out," she says. "If we can find out Valkyrie's real identity or even another name then I can follow the money trail. Castillo would've wired payments, probably to an offshore account, and I can track that all down with my programs and that'll provide a connection between the two. Proof that they were working together."

"Thanks, Harlow. We'll be in touch." After Ryker hangs up, we open the folder we got from Gray and carefully read through the various communications between Valkyrie and Castillo.

"I wonder how Gray got this," I muse.

"He was CIA, Ave. Just like Griff. Those guys are so fucking sneaky. They're in and out of a place and no one's the wiser."

"Um, excuse me, but I was CIA, too," I tell him and cross my arms.

"No, I know, but they were operatives, out in the field."

"Just because I had a desk job doesn't mean I had less important training."

He sighs. "I didn't mean to downplay your work. It's just a different kind of work from someone who is out in the trenches," he clarifies.

"Less dangerous, you mean."

"Exactly."

"I disagree." I can see him grit his jaw, but it's true. Just because I wasn't sneaking in and out of foreign countries doesn't mean my job didn't have its fair share of challenges and dangers. "I may not have had bullets flying around me, but realistically, most operatives don't because their missions go smoothly. Like you said, they're in and out without the target ever knowing."

He eyes me for a moment and must see the spark of annoyance in my eyes. It's a pet peeve of mine that people think less of a woman who works for the CIA as an analyst than say a man out in the field. "Did you see Zero Dark Thirty?" I ask.

"Affirmative," he says, a smile hovering at his lips.

"Then you should remember it's based on the fact that it was a woman who found Osama Bin Laden and because of her dogged persistence, he was finally captured."

He gives a nod. "I also remember the SEALs who rappelled from the helicopter, broke into the compound and finally got him."

Dammit. These Alpha men always have to be right, I think. "You're a smart ass, Flynn. You know that?" I punch his arm.

He lets out a chuckle. "What? And you're not?"

"Can we at least agree that it was a team effort?"

"It's always because of teamwork," he says, voice quiet. "SEAL training teaches you a lot of things, but what's the most impor-tant...We is greater than me."

"Luke used to say that," I say.

10

RYKER

uke. Goddamn, I miss my friend.

A wave of melancholy hits me and it must show on my face because Avery touches my arm. "You gonna punch me again?" I ask.

"Sorry," she says with a sheepish look. "You just really know how to rile me up."

"The feeling is mutual," I acknowledge. My mind drifts off and I remember when Luke and I first met at Boot Camp. We both had the same goal-- to be the best. Funny thing is, though, we never felt like each other's competition. There was an instant camaraderie and respect. We thought it was cool that we were both from small towns in Ohio and wanted to be SEALs. From that point forward, we pushed and challenged each other, but also had each other's backs.

Then, at BUD/S, we were swim buddies which basically meant we were never out of each other's sights for the next seven months. After that, we attended sniper school together and on it went until we became full-fledged SEALs. Luke was my buddy, but also my brother in every sense of the word. I would've died for him.

Turns out, he died for me.

Shit. I suck in a deep breath.

"What is it?" Avery asks in a soft voice.

"Just thinking about Luke," I admit.

"I miss him every day," she says.

"Yeah."

For a moment, we're lost in our thoughts. Then, Avery smiles. "Did you know that if he wasn't a SEAL, he wanted to be a pro-surfer?"

I laugh. "I'll bet he changed his mind after surf torture."

"What's that? Something you did in BUD/S?"

I nod. "It was pretty basic. We laid on our back in about six inches of cold surf, linked arms and waited."

"Waited for what?"

"Until the instructor said we were done." She frowns. "I remember laying there next to Luke and the instructor just kept saying the same thing over and over-- 'We aren't getting out until three people quit, we've got nowhere to be, we can do this all night long. All you need to do is quit. It's easy.' And, Luke looked over at me and said 'Fuck that.'"

"That's my brother," she says with a fond smile. "How cold was the water?"

"Fucking freezing. But, that wasn't even the real challenge. The real test came after we got out of the water and had to face the ocean in a wet t-shirt with a constant 15 knot wind blowing on us. It was brutal."

"Jesus," she whispers. "I don't know how you guys did it. Any of it."

I see admiration flash in her blue eyes and feel proud of Luke and myself. "Because quitting was never an option. We had the desire to accomplish a goal and nothing was going to stop us. Not even hypothermia."

"Mental toughness," she says. "You can't fake it."

"No, you can't. You just commit to a goal and complete it." I think about the last two years and how I broke mentally. Maybe it's time to set a new goal. To forgive Avery, forgive myself and heal, once and for all.

It's then that I realize I'm already halfway there. I do forgive Avery. Every terrible word and thought I've had or said to her, I regret. And, not because the true fault lays with Valkyrie and Castillo, but because Avery is a good person who never had anything but good intentions.

I feel a new calm and peace begin to fill me and look up at her angelic face, gathering my courage. "Avery..." She studies me with intent blue eyes, waiting for me to continue. "I want you to know how sorry I am. For everything. I regret adding to the hurt you already had after your brother died. Can you forgive me?"

Avery nods. "Of course. I get it. We've both said things that we didn't mean."

"It's just hard, you know. Dealing with feelings flipping all over the place." When she nods, I don't think she really gets what I am trying to say. I swallow down my nerves and pin her with a stare. "You have to know..."

"Know what?" she asks in a soft voice.

"Know that I had a crush on you from day one."

Something lights up in her eyes. "Really?"

"You were the most beautiful girl I'd ever seen," I admit and see a flush rise in her cheeks. "I thought you looked like an angel with eyes the color of the ocean and hair like sunshine." I reach out and take a golden lock between my fingers. "I still do."

"Ryker..."

I let go of her hair. "But, you were Luke's little sister so I knew you were off-limits."

Avery looks down, lost in thought, then reaches out and touches my hand. "I'm not off-limits anymore," she says and slips her fingers through mine.

My pulse spikes and I twine my fingers through hers, too. Those few words hit me hard, literally make me hard as hell, and I pull her closer and kiss her. The kiss is soft for a second before I lose all semblance of self-control. I plunge my tongue into her mouth, kissing her hard and deep. My hands wrap around her waist and drag her onto my lap so I can have better access to that delicious body of hers.

"Ryker," she murmurs, and tilts her head back. I drag my mouth down her throat, licking my way to the delicate dip of her collarbone and swirl my tongue inside the hollow.

"You taste so good," I whisper. "So sweet."

When I slip my hand under her shirt and over her flat stomach, I can't believe I'm touching her. Avery was always everything I wanted but thought I could never have. I dip my fingers in the waistband of her pants and tug them down. I want to taste more of her, the very core of her.

I lay her back on the couch and move over her body, determined to find out if her pussy tastes as sweet as the rest of her. I grab the black satin panties she wears and pull them down, while shoving her shirt up and trailing my mouth lower over her stomach...down her hip...along her inside thigh.

So beautiful.

"Ryker-" she pushes up on her elbows and I look up to see her glazed blue eyes watching me intently.

I raise a brow and flick my tongue along her inner thigh, licking up, on a mission.

"Um…" She squirms beneath me, trying to clamp her legs together.

I pause. "What's wrong, baby?"

Her face flames and her chest heaves up and down. "I've never…I mean no one's ever…" Her brow furrows.

Ah, my angel has never been eaten out, I realize. *Christ, her innocence turns me on.* "Just relax," I say. But, I can feel how tense she is so I move back up her body and capture her lips with mine, kissing away her insecurities, soothing her nerves.

When she begins to relax, I slide a hand down between us and cup her. She jerks at the intimate touch and I drag my mouth over to her ear, whispering words to reassure her. "It's just me," I murmur. "Open your legs, baby. Let me make you feel good."

I start stroking between her legs and she lets out a shaky breath, digging her nails into my back.

"Oh, God," she cries and begins to writhe against my hand.

I can't help but smile against her ear. She's so responsive. I suck her earlobe into my mouth and revel in how gloriously wet she is. When I slip a finger inside her, she bucks her hips and begins to pant.

"I'm going to go back down and lick you until you come," I whisper. Her nails stab into my back. "Is that okay?"

"Mm-hm," she breathes.

I kiss her again then start my journey back down. I have two fingers inside her now, moving in and out, and can feel the pressure building up within her. When I reach her dripping center, I close my mouth over her clit and suck.

Avery slams a hand against the couch and her body tightens around my fingers. "Ryker," she gasps, panting and writhing beneath me.

I shove my hands under her ass, lift her up and lick up her folds with a flat tongue. Again and again until she's whimpering and trembling. She's hovering, right at the edge, so I wrap my lips around her clit again and suck deep.

"Shit, God, *oh, shit*," she cries and arches up. Her body shudders hard and I look up watching as the orgasm hits her. Her eyes slide shut, her head falls back and pleasure rolls through her. I don't think I've ever seen anything so beautiful.

I lower her back down against the couch and slide back up her body. Her eyes flutter open and a dazed smile curves her mouth.

"That was amazing," she purrs.

"I'm glad you liked it," I say and nip her chin. "I'm always here for you, Ave. Whatever you need."

"I want to be there for you, too," she says, voice husky.

Oh, God, I think, my cock ready to tear through my pants. I feel like I hit the goddamn lottery. As her hand slides down, my fucking phone rings. I hiss out a breath, pull back and snatch the phone up.

"Ryker Flynn," I say between gritted teeth.

"Hey, it's Jax. And, I've got Griff and Harlow here with me."

I suppress a groan and shift on the couch, trying to get more comfortable, but it's damn near impossible. "What's up?" I ask and then hear the irony of my greeting. Other than the obvious, anyway.

"Harlow found the location of Antonio's compound," Jax tells me.

"And, satellite images show it's barely occupied right now," she says. "Just a few guards."

I raise a brow and look over at Avery.
If I want to breach the compound then now is the time.

11

AVERY

No. I shake my head. I don't care if the place is completely empty. Breaking into Antonio Castillo's compound is a death sentence.

I am not going to let him do it. At least not alone.

"Where do you think Castillo went?" Griff asks.

"Who knows? When my team was tasked with taking him down, he was in the middle of the goddamn jungle. I think it's the only safe place he can hold meetings."

"Do you think there's anything in there that could confirm Valkyrie's identity?" Jax asks.

"Possibly. Harlow, you had mentioned tracing it back through money transfers. If I can get in there and pull his hard drive, then you'd have a place to start looking."

"Definitely," she concurs.

Dammit. It's too dangerous. *But, a good idea,* I think.

"Currently, it looks like his paramilitary group is off fighting a rival so he could be with them," Griff says.

"He could be anywhere," I say. "And, he and his entire army could return tomorrow for all we know."

"I can keep my eye on the satellite images," Harlow says.

"What about security?" Ryker asks. "Can you breach it?"

"I can breach anything," she says nonchalantly.

"Are you sure?" I ask.

"I can take care of cameras and alarms, but you'll have to do the rest."

"Shit," Jax says. "If you do this, we should be there with you."

"We don't have the luxury of time," Ryker says. "I can be in and out by the time you two even board the plane."

"It's too much for one person," Jax worries.

Ryker looks at me. *He wants my help*, I think. "I'm going, too," I say.

"The fuck you are," Ryker growls. "I'll reach out to Grayson Shaw, the contact we met earlier today. He has a personal vendetta against Castillo so he may want to be involved. He also may have some inside information that could help. Harlow, can you get the structural layout of the compound?"

I glare at Ryker. *If he's going then I'm going*, I decide.

"I've searched," she says. "I haven't been able to find it yet."

"Shaw might know. I'll give him a call as soon as we hang up. Anything else?"

"I'll send you the compound coordinates, Ryker," Harlow says.

"Great, thanks."

"Be careful," Jax says.

"Don't take any unnecessary chances," Griff adds.

"Roger that," Ryker says. "I'll be in touch."

After he disconnects the call, he glances up and it's clear I am not happy. "I do not want you doing this. It's not worth the risk."

"Baby, I've done things a lot more dangerous than this."

"Yeah, but I didn't know about those things. I know about this and I'm going to be worried out of my damn mind."

"This is our shot to discover who Valkyrie really is. We need to take it," he says.

I squeeze my hands into fists. *Shit.* I know he's right, but if anything bad happens, I'll never forgive myself. "I'm going with you."

"No, you're not."

"Yes, I am.

Ryker clenches his jaw. "If you go then I'll be worried the whole time. If I know you're here and safe, then I can concentrate better on the mission."

"You're a pain in my ass," I tell him and frown.

Ryker smiles, lifts a hand and rubs at the frown line between my brows. "I promise I'll be careful."

I shake my head. "This conversation isn't over."

"Yes, it is."

"No, it's not." He lets out a frustrated breath, but I don't care. I know I can help him. "What if Gray can't go? There is no way in hell that you are going in there alone."

Ryker grabs the card Gray gave me earlier and makes a show out of punching the number into his phone. I roll my eyes. *He can be so difficult,* I think, and cross my arms. Big, tough former Navy SEAL who thinks he's indestructible. But, he's not. He's only human, made of flesh and blood, and therein lies the problem.

"Gray? It's Ryker Flynn." He hits the speaker button after I motion to him that I want to hear the conversation.

"Ryker, what's going on?" Gray's cool voice asks over the line.

"Any chance you have any information about Castillo's compound that might help me breach it?"

"You're shitting me, right?"

"I just received intel that he and his army are otherwise occupied so the place is practically empty. I'm going in to retrieve his hard drive and could use a little intel. Or, backup, if you're interested."

"I have schematics of the compound."

"How accurate?"

"Pretty damn accurate," he says. "And, yeah, I'm interested in doing anything that'll take that motherfucker down."

Ryker lifts his gaze to meet mine. "Let's go in tomorrow." As he rattles off where we're staying, my heart sinks. I do not want him doing this. Last time he went after Antonio Castillo, things did not end well.

They continue to talk, making plans, and my stomach churns. He's about to get an earful the moment he hangs up. Breaking into Castillo's compound is stupid and reckless. It's the type of thing that could get him killed.

And, I don't need his death in my conscience.

Shit. I stand up and begin pacing. My gut feels all wrong about this, but Ryker is a seasoned warrior and I know there's no way I'll be able to talk him out of it. He's trained and confident, but he's also emotionally involved.

I stalk over to the floor-to-ceiling window and gaze out over the city. The sky is getting dark and thunder clouds hang low and threatening. It looks like there's going to be quite a storm tonight. There's going to be one inside, too, I think, when I go off on Ryker.

So many things could go wrong and the more backup he has, the better. *I'm going,* I decide. Even if it's just to be a lookout, I know I can help. Ryker keeps forgetting that I am a CIA-trained agent. I did some fight-training and I am not scared to face Antonio's goons.

I don't want to fight with him, but he needs to understand that I can take care of myself. I've been doing it for a long time.

With a sigh, I continue to stare out the window and listen to the rest of their conversation. So, apparently, those two are competent enough to go break into the compound, but I'm not. I clamp my jaw together and run through various arguments in my head.

But, he's more stubborn than a mule. No matter what I say, he's going to disagree.

And, then it hits me.

Why don't I just follow them? By the time I reveal myself or they realize, it'll be too late.

Ugh, what a pain, though. I'll have to go separately and be sneaky when I could just tag along with them in the first place. Thunder rumbles and I see a bolt of lightning brighten the sky off in the distance.

I also don't have a weapon. Ryker has his SIG Sauer and knife, but even that's not enough. He's going to need more tactical gear. Their conversation turns to weapons the moment I think about it. Gray says he can supply anything they will need. For the most past, anyway. I hear him mention a Garmin Foretrex GPS, AR-15 with flash suppressor and SIG Sauer P226.

A chill runs down my spine and raindrops begin to splatter against the window. Ryker hangs up with Gray, but I don't turn around. Just keep looking out the window, my thoughts spinning and ominous.

I feel Ryker come up behind me and wrap his arms around my waist. But, if he thinks it's going to be that easy, he has another thing coming. I pull away and spin around, my temper spiking. "I can help," I insist. "And, I don't appreciate you writing me off."

He lets out a long sigh and doesn't say anything. Instead, he breathes in and out a few times. Probably trying to keep his temper in check. Well, mine is about to spiral out of control.

"You listen to me, Frog," I say and poke my finger against his chest. "I am a former CIA officer with field training just like your buddies. You're going to need as much backup as possible tomorrow and I intend to help provide it."

Ryker looks down where my finger just stabbed him a few times and raises a brow. "I hear what you're saying, Ave. But, the answer is no."

My eyes narrow and I'm pissed.

Who does he think he is? I wonder, seething.

"For your information, I am good for more than just a handjob, Ryker Flynn."

12

RYKER

God Almighty, she will not take no for an answer.

I pinch the bridge of my nose, struggling to keep my temper under control, and my next comment as politically correct as possible. "Gimme some fucking credit, Ave. I know you're good for more than that. But, your training is nothing like what Gray and I have been through."

Avery rolls her eyes. "I may not have been through BUD/S, but I know how to shoot a gun and take down an opponent. You're going to need backup. Gray isn't enough. Especially if there are more guards than Harlow says."

"Avery!" I roar.

"What?" she yells.

Fuck. Why can't she get it through that pretty little head of hers that she is not going to Antonio Castillo's compound with us? *No fucking way.*

My voice drops and, instead of loud and bossy, it's low and lethal. "You are staying here. End of conversation." When she opens her mouth to respond, I cover it with my hand. "End. Of. Conversation."

Avery bites my finger and I yank my hand back with a curse. She gives me a defiant look then seems to rethink her approach. I can see the gears turning in her head a mile away. "Fine," she suddenly says. Then, she turns on her heel and walks away.

Feisty little shit. She's going to give me an aneurysm.

She's also lying, I think.

I stalk after her and she's beside her bed, rifling through her suitcase. "Give me your word," I demand.

She looks up, blue eyes flashing. "What?"

"Promise me that you won't follow us tomorrow."

Avery gives me an angelic smile. "I promise."

"Dammit, Avery, I'm not fucking around. It's too dangerous and you need to do as you're told."

"Do as I'm told?" She snorts.

Shit. Poor choice of words. "I know you think you're tough and strong," I say, trying a new tactic. "And, you are. But, this is about more than that. This is about being able to overpower a specially-trained soldier who is going to come at you with deadly force. It's about being able to handle an assault rifle. It's also-"

"If you're just sneaking in and out, why should any of that even matter?" she asks.

My mouth drops open. Closes. Why is she being so dense? So obstinate? "Holy fuck. I feel like I'm banging my head against the wall. What are you not understanding?"

She marches over, so fearless and determined to convince me to take her that my heart softens just a fraction. "I'm not understanding why it's okay for you to potentially sacrifice yourself, but not me!"

Thunder rolls and lightning brightens the sky outside.

Sacrifice herself? Absolutely fucking not.

"That is not even an option," I say. "So, get it out of your head."

"You are so annoying!" she yells. She stomps up and again shoves that finger into my chest again. "Just so you know, I can take care of myself."

Quicker than a bullet being shot from a gun, I grab her hand, twist it up behind her back and push her up against the wall. My mouth lowers to her ear. "So, do it. I've got you. I'm the enemy. Now get away from me."

She bucks against me, trapped between the wall and 200 pounds.

"You're not going anywhere, little girl."

"You're a bastard," she says, cheek pressing into the wall. "You didn't even give me a chance-"

"Neither will they," I hiss in her ear, pushing my hips into her, pressing her harder into the wall, trying to prove my point.

No matter how hard she tries, she's pinned, unable to break away from my steel grip. *Good.* I'm pissed and tired of arguing about something so ridiculous.

"Let me go," she orders.

"Is that what you'll tell the bad guys?" I taunt.

With a grunt, Avery swings her hips to the left and brings her right hand down against my groin in an open-palm slap. A *hard* slap.

"Goddammit!" I roar. I let her go and she spins around, fists up in a fighting stance. I lean over, hands on my hips, and draw in a sharp breath. *Great, now my fucking balls hurt.*

"I didn't want to do that, but you gave me no choice."

I straighten up and she doesn't look sorry at all. "I'm done with this conversation. I'm also done playing games with you. I have recon to do."

When I turn and walk away, I hear her let out a huff and outside thunder crashes. I'm not feeding into her tantrum any further. I have way too much research to do on Castillo, his whereabouts, his army and his compound.

I drop down on the couch with a grunt. *Damn.* She hit me harder than I thought. *Hellion.* I should've known she'd pull something like that. How she can look like such an angel and have the devil's temper is beyond me.

Rain pounds against the glass and the next boom of thunder makes the whole room vibrate. *It's one hell of a storm raging out there,* I think. I just hope the storm in here is over.

Gray sent me an email with the layout of Castillo's compound and I study it. The damn place is huge. A fortress. I forward the images to

Harlow and then continue to look through the pictures, trying to determine the best way to breach it.

Hmm. Between the satellite images Harlow sent and the drawings from Gray, I can determine that there's a concrete wall that surrounds the entire property. Probably at least ten feet high with a main gate in the front. Guard towers on each corner of the wall soar up another ten feet or so.

Using the jungle as cover, our best bet would be to scale the wall on the right-hand side which faces the rear of the house, and then sneak in through the back. I check out the various rooms on the ground floor and try to determine where his office could be. Since I don't have any interior images, it's really anyone's guess. Gray and I will have to do a quick, thorough sweep to find it.

Once we reach the office, I'm going to rip that hard drive right out and stuff it into my bag. I'm not doing the ghost op CIA crap where I sneak in and out without anyone the wiser. I want that asshole to know someone took his files. I want him to worry, to panic, to stay up at night trying to figure out who stole his shit and wonder what they're going to do with the information.

I scratch my fingers through my cropped hair and realize it's awfully quiet. Avery is just out of my line of vision, around the corner, and I can't help but wonder what she's up to. A second later, she storms past, ignoring me completely, and into the bathroom. Bam! She slams the door behind her and I roll my eyes.

She can be mad. I don't care because I know that making her stay here and keeping her out of harm's way is the best thing I can do for her. And, right now, protecting her is my number one priority. My responsibility.

When I hear the shower turn on, an image of her naked body pops into my head. Naked and wet. *Oh, Christ.* She really knows how to piss me off and then turn me on all in the space of minutes.

Outside, the storm takes a turn for the worse. As I scroll through the compound schematics again, the power flickers. *Uh, oh.* If we lose power, we're going to be stuck in the dark together and it's too early to go to sleep.

My groin tightens. Not much you can do in the dark, but there are a few things we could try.

Avery just needs to get over herself.

Although, I have to give her credit. That little maneuver she pulled earlier was impressive. Though, my privates might not agree.

God, she's a handful. But, who better to handle her than me?

Thinking back to what she said earlier, I have a feeling she hasn't been handled by too many men. If I understood her right, I'm the first man to go down on her. How is that possible? The better question is how can a woman taste so damn good?

I swallow hard, listening to the shower, and feel my cock come alive. I want to taste her again. I want to sink into her and give her the best orgasm she's ever had in her life. And, this time I don't want any damn phone calls interrupting us.

The lights flicker again and I look up at the rain-spattered window. There aren't any candles in the room so I get up and head to my suitcase where I have a pack of six-inch chemlights tucked in a side pocket. One snap and a quick shake, and a green light will illuminate the nearby surroundings. The ones I have will last up to eight hours.

While Avery is still in the bathroom, I slip out of my clothes and into my long shorts. The room is warm so I don't bother with a shirt. Last time I wore these shorts, Avery took me in her hands and jacked me hard. I can't get the erotic image out of my head and groan.

Not sure if that'll ever happen again. But, I'm hoping the shower helped cool her temper off a bit. As I head back over to the couch, the bathroom door opens and Avery walks out in a cloud of steam.

We both freeze. She's in that short little nightshirt again and I can't help but check out her long, bare legs. Right down to those little slippers with the poof on top. *God, she's so sexy.* At the same time, I notice her blue gaze dip and move over my chest. I make sure to stay fit so I know I'm ripped and I like seeing the appreciation in her eyes. It definitely makes all the hours I spend working out worth it.

But, then I remember the scars. The knife and bullet wounds and my heart drops. I don't want her seeing the ugly reminders of that terrible night so I turn and move away, back to the couch. I drop the box of chemlights on the coffee table and realize she's still looking at me.

"What's that?" she asks and nods to the box.

Before I can respond, the lights flicker. Once, twice and then go out completely, plunging us into blackness.

13

AVERY

I hear a snap and an eerie green glow fills the space between me and Ryker.

"Chemlight," he answers.

"You certainly come prepared," I comment. Now that it's darker and harder for him to see where I'm looking, I check out his chest and abs more thoroughly. *My God, he's built,* I think and my stomach somersaults. Like a freaking stallion. *So strong, so many muscles.* I think I feel my ovaries snap to attention and salute.

Six pack? *Um, no.* Ryker Flynn has a damn eight pack.

It is borderline ridiculous.

But, so very, very nice. I feel the urge to run my hand over his abs, follow each indentation, but then I remember that I'm still mad at him. Or, at least trying to be. *Jerk.*

"Avery…"

My stomach drops at the huskiness in his voice. *Oh, no.* He's going to turn all sexy and hot now and I'm going to crumble.

Is that so bad? I ask myself.

"Your body is ridiculous," I blurt out.

I think he's smirking, but it's hard to tell in the dark.

"What does that mean?" he asks.

"It means you should eat some sweets. Maybe a cookie or a donut?"

"I ate something sweet earlier," he says in a low, suggestive voice.

A lump rises in my throat.

"And, I'd love to have some more."

"Stop it," I say. My voice comes out far too husky and he starts toward me. Like a lion stalking its prey.

"Can I ask you something?" He stops in front of me and the green light glows between us.

Oh, God, I have no idea what he's going to ask me, but I have a feeling it's going to be extremely personal. And, probably very inappropriate. I let out a breath. "It depends on the question."

"How many men have you been with?"

"I don't think that's any of your business," I tell him. But, there's no force in my voice and he moves closer. I look at the large tattoo on his upper right arm. It's a frog skeleton holding a trident. "Nice ink," I say, trying to change the subject.

His arm flexes. "Is it a secret?"

I huff out a breath. "Why do you even care?"

He picks up a lock of my damp hair and rubs it between his thumb and forefinger. "I find it fascinating that no one's tasted you but me."

My stomach starts to do little flips and wetness pools between my legs. *Damn him.* He's so distracting with that tattoo and those yummy abs and dirty talk. "It's hardly fascinating," I say.

"It is to me."

"Ryker-"

"Tell me," he whispers.

I bite my lip. "Well, technically...one."

Heat flares in his eyes which now glow green from the chemstick. "How can you be so beautiful and so innocent?" he asks.

"You don't know me very well," I say, trying to keep my voice light.

He lays his hands on my hips and we're a breath apart from each other. I feel the heat radiating off his big body and my earlier anger dissolves away. Replaced by a hot spike of desire.

"I want to, though," he whispers, leans in and begins kissing my neck. "I want to know you better than you know yourself."

"That's not even possible," I say, trying to keep my distance. But, it's getting harder and harder with him whispering in my ear and dragging his warm mouth along my throat. I release a shaky, little sigh, trying not to touch him.

His soft lips move up, kissing along my jawline, and his warm breath tickles at my ear. "Sure it is."

I pull back and lay a hand on his chest. "I'm still mad at you," I tell him. But, suddenly, all I can feel is his hard, warm skin and it's like an electrical current passes between us. Like a bolt of lightning.

"Then let me make it up to you."

Before I can respond, he sweeps me up into his arms like I weigh no more than a child and carries me over to his bed. He lowers me down, his big hands roaming all over my body, and I feel tingles wherever he touches.

He grabs the edge of my nightshirt and works it up. Up past my now soaking panties, up over my stomach, over the curve of my breasts. He pulls it all the way off and tosses it. Then, he moves in between my thighs, capturing my leg between his, rubbing against me.

My eyes flutter shut when I feel the hardness in his shorts and I remember how perfect he is down there-- long and thick and smooth. I reach down and grasp the waistband, sliding his shorts down his narrow hips. His cock springs free and I wrap my fingers around him.

"You're so hot," I whisper and begin stroking the pulsing flesh. His breathing increases, becoming more raspy, and I squeeze very lightly. "I'm sorry I hit you here."

"Fuck, Ave." His hips jolt and I slide out from beneath him, moving down his body, dropping kisses along his ridiculously ripped chest and abs. I lick along a groove, making my way down to his cock which juts up proudly.

God, he's big, I think. When I take him into my mouth, he tangles his fingers through my hair and his hips lift right up off the bed. I suck, pulling him deep, right to the back of my throat. Ryker groans and pulls me back up, rolling me over.

Suddenly he's back on top again, kissing me hard. His dark head drops to my breasts and he swirls a tongue around one nipple then the other. His tongue knows exactly how to torture me and I run my fingers through his short hair, trailing my nails down his rock-hard upper arms.

When he reaches between my thighs, I arch up against his hand. My hips begin to grind like they have a mind of their own and I can't handle the pulsing waves that start rolling through my lower body. "Ryker, oh, God!" I cry.

"Come for me, Ave." He strokes my slick folds, sliding a finger up inside me and my inner walls contract. I cry out, digging my nails into his arms. The pleasure is too much and I let out a moan and sink back into the pillow.

Ryker reaches over me and then I hear the crinkle of a foil packet tearing open. Lost in a haze of pure content, I watch him roll the condom down and move back between my legs. I can't believe this is happening. That Ryker Flynn, the man I've always wanted most, is about to be inside me.

"Do you know how long I've wanted you?" he asks.

God, it's like we're on the same wavelength, I think.

"Not as much as I've wanted you," I whisper.

"Impossible," he says and spreads my legs further apart.

When I feel the tip of him press at my entrance, I lift my hips. I want every last inch of him deep inside me. *I just hope that's possible,* I think. A tremble runs through me and I feel my skin stretch around him. "Oh, God," I say and tense up.

Ryker pauses, reaches down and begins massaging my swollen clit. "You can take me, Ave. Relax."

I do as he says and wrap my legs around his waist, opening all the way. He pulls back then slides in deeper. Pulls back again then glides in further. I stretch until I think I can't stretch any more. "I need all of you. *Now,*" I hiss and dig my nails into his upper arms.

He plunges the rest of the way inside, smothering my cry with a deep kiss. I arch up and begin moving with his measured strokes.

When I meet his gaze, those whisky-colored eyes that I love so much penetrate my very soul.

Gazes locked, he drives deep, thrusting harder and I drop my face into his shoulder, as he pounds into me over and over. I can feel his control slip, his tempo going off beat, and I think the whole damn bed is slamming against the wall at this point. I want to scream, but instead I bite his shoulder as ripples of pleasure overtake me again, pulsing through me until I come harder than ever before.

Above me, Ryker's whole body tenses then shudders. "Ave," he groans and explodes in an orgasm that rocks through his entire body. He drops down next to me, burying his face in my hair. "Holy fucking shit," he rasps.

"Ditto," I say.

It takes us both a long moment to get our bearings, to recover.

When his heavy breathing begins to return to normal, he pulls back and looks at me with what almost looks like wonder. "What?" I ask and trace a finger down his rough jaw.

"You just wrecked other women for me," he says then captures my mouth in a long, hot kiss.

Oh! I think, and slide my tongue against his. Several long moments later, I pull back and give him a wicked, little smile. "Good," I whisper.

"Hellion," he says then slips out of bed to dispose of the condom. He returns a moment later and wraps his arms around me, pulling me close. I lay my head against his chest, caught in the warmth of his embrace, and relish the feel of his big, warm body pressed against mine.

We lay like that for a long time, just listening to each other breathe.

"Tell me something about Luke," I whisper. "Something that will make me smile."

Ryker threads his fingers through mine and thinks for a moment. "Luke was my best friend. The best man I knew. Also, the biggest smart ass. He could come up with a sarcastic remark for everything."

I chuckle and watch our fingers glide in and out of each other.

"No one ever made me laugh so hard. We used to stay up half the night and just joke about everything. And, he was always dirty. I used to tell him to get his ass in the shower, but when we'd be out on patrol for days on end, up to our necks in swamp water, he'd always say I will tomorrow. When other guys would razz him about it, I'd just say let him stink."

Ryker takes a strand of my hair between his fingers and plays with it. "We were swim buddies, you know. One time we were on a two-mile training swim and he got a cramp in his leg. He was in agony and I seriously thought he was going to drown. When I tried to help him, he told me to leave him alone and mind my business. That he'd work it out or drown. Well, he used some stronger words than that, but you get the idea. He was stubborn as hell. Just like you."

A soft smile curves my mouth.

"He was the finest man I ever met, a natural leader. If something went wrong, he'd take the blame. He never threw anyone under the bus and was loyal to a tee," Ryker says. "I miss him, Ave. I miss him so much."

"I know," I whisper and lift his hand up and place a kiss between his large knuckles.

14

RYKER

I'm glad Avery and I talked about Luke. It's important to remember him. The happy, funny and loving person he was, the good memories we have.

Unfortunately, I also have bad memories and sometimes they return no matter how hard I try to escape them. And, tonight is no exception.

I fall asleep, Avery snuggled up in my arms, and it's perfect until the nightmare comes again. My team and I are back in the Columbian jungle, surrounded by Castillo's forces, fighting for our lives.

After I get stabbed in the shoulder, I kick out, connect with my opponent's leg and he goes down. I waste no time using my knife on him. Meanwhile, I hear Luke call for help. He's not far away fighting off three attackers. *Shit.* I take off to help him, but several more bad guys jump me on the way over.

At 6'4", I'm a pretty big guy, but three against one is never fun. We battle it out and it's the brutal kind of close quarter combat fighting that leaves people mortally wounded or dead. And, I don't want to die. Not tonight.

And, then Avery rises up in my mind. Beautiful, innocent-looking Avery with her cornflower blue eyes and golden blonde hair. She is a reason to fight, I tell myself. She's also a reason to live. Because before I leave this world, I make myself a promise.

I'm going to kiss Avery Archer. I'm going to know what those luscious lips feel like brushing against mine. I'm going to find out once and for all if she tastes as sweet as she smells. The closest I ever got was after we visited the animal sanctuary. I wished her a happy birthday, leaned in and, as much as I wanted to take her in my arms and kiss her senseless, I merely brushed a chaste kiss at the corner of her mouth.

And, I regret not going in hard and doing what we both wanted. It's the only time I can honestly say I didn't give my normal 110 percent when I should have. I should have captured her mouth in a kiss that left her breathless and trembling in my arms. A birthday kiss that she'd remember for the rest of her life.

Out here, lost in the jungle, fighting this vicious paramilitary group, Avery keeps me alive. She makes me carry on when my shoulder bleeds relentlessly and then I get shot. Once, twice, three times.

Motherfucker.

I go down hard, but don't give up. No way. The adrenaline keeps me moving, crawling forward, reaching for my SIG Sauer, turning and firing up at a soldier who is about to pull his trigger again, but this time his barrel is aimed at my heart. He drops dead on the jungle floor.

One of my team members, Josh, grabs me and pulls me over to a tree. "You're okay," he says, propping me up against the cool bark. My head falls back and I look up at the thick canopy above and see Avery's blue eyes. He packs some mud into my shoulder to stop the bleeding.

"Where'd all these assholes come from?" I ask, struggling to stay present.

He shakes his head. "I don't know, but comms are down. We need to get to the extraction point."

"I don't even know where the hell we are anymore," I say.

And, like every dream, things begin to alter from the real way they happened. Josh disappears and I hear Luke's voice again. "Ryker! Help me!"

I spin around, looking for my friend, but I don't see him anywhere. All I see is goddamn green jungle everywhere I look. Now I better understand what Vietnam must've been like. And, it fucking sucks.

"Luke!" I yell, turning in a circle, unable to find him.

"Ryker!"

All of a sudden, more bullets whizz past and I dive to the ground.

And, I come face to face with Luke's blood-smeared face. He's riddled with bullets, but still alive. And, strangely enough, I realize he has nearly the same color of eyes as Avery, just a little darker.

"Luke," I rasp and take a quick inventory of his wounds. *Fuck*. Too many to count and his breathing sounds all wrong. Wheezy like he has a collapsed lung.

"I'm okay, right?" he asks.

"Yeah, buddy, you're fine," I say, even though I know I'm lying. "C'mon, we're getting out of here now."

"I...can't," he says, eyes rolling back in his head.

"Suck it up," I say. Then, I pull myself up, ignoring my wounds, and reach down for my best friend. He looks on the verge of passing out, but I drag him up and throw him over my shoulder. He's heavy, but I don't care. No way am I leaving him in this godforsaken place. Either we both make it out or neither of us do.

I glance down at my GPS and instead of seeing our exact location and distance to the extraction point, the numbers are flipping, constantly changing. Like I'm lost in fucking Wonderland. I don't know where to go and a wave of panic washes over me. I search for the sat phone, but it's long gone.

So, I just head in the direction that I think is right, but I'm not sure. With each step, Luke gets heavier and heavier. I stumble a few times, but keep pressing on through the jungle. All around me I hear the screams of my other teammates as they fall. My heart bleeds for them, for Luke, and just as I'm on the verge of collapsing, a bad guy comes out of nowhere and tackles us.

I hit the ground hard and suddenly Luke is gone. It's just me and this soldier. We circle each other, knives in hand, and he lashes out at me. I dodge the blade, jumping back and spin, slicing through the air and aiming for his side.

My knife finds its mark and the guy screams in rage. He launches himself at me, slashing back and forth, not even aiming, just trying to stab me anywhere and everywhere. I spin and kick him hard, but he doesn't go down. He's like a fucking, demented ninja, darting all over the place.

A sharp pain makes my vision blur and I look down to see his blade sticking in my side. I pull it out, see my blood dripping down the gleaming silver edge, and drop it on the ground. He launches into me again, tackling me to the ground and suddenly has another knife in his grip, trying to plunge it into my throat.

I grab his wrist, my hands shaking, as I try to hold him back. We're eye to eye, struggling, and the blade drops closer to my neck, now barely an inch away. I muster up all of the strength within me and shove as hard as I can. The guy lifts up and falls back.

Like a striking Cobra, I move fast and land on him, digging my knee into his chest, pinning him in the dirt, and I wrap my hands around his neck. His eyes go wide with surprise as I squeeze. I'm going to wring the life out of him.

"No!" he rasps, flailing beneath me. He punches out, but his failed strikes only make me more angry. I tighten my grip, fingers digging into his neck, leaving red, murderous marks.

"Just fucking die!" I yell and squeeze with every ounce of strength that I have left.

"Ryker!"

My grip loosens. *How does he know my name?*

"Ryker, stop!"

What's going on? I look around. *Who's calling me?*

"Wake up!"

Then, my eyes snap open. And, I realize in sinking horror that my hands are wrapped around Avery's neck. Trying to squeeze the life out of her.

Jesus. I let go and she gasps, reaching up to touch her neck, eyes wide.

Shock fills me and I can't miss the look in her blue eyes. Fear. She's looking at me like she's terrified of me.

Oh, fuck. I feel sick to my stomach and get out of the bed. *What did I do?*

"I'm sorry," I manage to say and grab my shorts. Then, I walk away on legs that feel like noodles, all wobbly. I go into the bathroom, slip my shorts on and splash some water on my face. *What in God's name did I just do?*

When I step out of the bathroom, Avery stands there, a sheet wrapped around her. "Ryker?" She takes a step toward me and I move away.

Jesus, I can't believe I had my hands wrapped around her neck. And, I was squeezing. Hard.

"Are you okay?" she asks, eyes full of concern.

Me? What about you?

"Are *you*?" I ask.

Avery nods. *Thank God,* I think, feeling a bit of relief. But, when she moves closer, I take another step back. Obviously, I need to stay away from her. I would never physically hurt her and the fact that I almost did kills me. Literally, rips me up inside.

"You need to stay away, Ave," I say.

"Don't be ridiculous," she says. "It was a dream. A nightmare. It wasn't your fault."

"What if I didn't wake up in time? What if I would've hurt you?" I slide a hand through my short hair. "I'd never forgive myself."

"You're not going to hurt me." When she reaches out, I stumble back, bumping into the couch.

"You don't know that," I say, my voice raw. "The nightmares are so vivid sometimes. It's like I have no control over myself."

"I trust you."

"You shouldn't."

Avery lets out a sigh. "Please. Come here." She opens her arms to me and as much as I want to go, I can't. My feet are frozen, won't move, because I refuse to put her in any kind of danger and will protect her from everything. Including myself.

"Go back to bed, Avery."

Her blue eyes bore into mine. "You're not coming with me?"

I shake my head. "I'll sleep here."

"But, I want you next to me."

God, she is making this so hard, but I am not going to cave. Her safety is too important. "It's better if I stay away from you. Please, Ave."

She thinks over my words then slowly nods. "Okay," she finally relents. "Take some time. But, I want you in my bed again tomorrow."

Not gonna happen, angel.

I watch her walk back and slip into my bed. It's for the best, I tell myself.

This is exactly why I can't have a normal relationship with a woman. No matter how much time passes, I can't get over these demons. I drop down on the couch, angry at myself. I should've been more careful. I should have woken up sooner, more quickly.

But, God, I was locked down tight in that nightmare's jaws. I couldn't escape.

And to hurt Avery, of all people…

Fuck. I rub my eyes hard and fall back against the cushion. *You're an idiot, Ryker, if you honestly thought you could have a normal relationship with her.* Now you've slept together and it has to end before it ever began.

Because I am ending it, I tell myself. Effective immediately.

I feel awful. I know she cares about me and God knows I care about her, but I can't put her through the nightmares with me. It's not fair to her. She deserves someone who isn't broken. A man who can give her everything she needs and deserves.

And, Avery deserves the world including a happy marriage with a loving, normal husband and children. I can't give her that. It would be selfish of me to keep her in my life and in my bed.

I let out a low curse, lay all the way down on the couch and shove a hand behind my head. Instantly, my mind returns to earlier when I went down on her in this exact spot and tasted how sweet she really is. Thinking about her and the things we did is going to torture me the rest of my life.

A part of me feels like we came so close to happiness. Like we were right on the verge of something amazing and that maybe we could've made it. But, then my goddamn demons had to surface and destroy any hope I foolishly had for a normal future.

I'm pathetic, I think. Always falling prey to the nightmares. Never being able to fully escape their grasp.

I used to think I was so strong and that nothing could defeat me. I was a goddamn Navy SEAL and could kick anyone's ass. I prided myself on my mental toughness.

Ha. Not anymore. I guess no one is indestructible and I'm proof of that. No matter how strong or smart you are, everyone has a weakness and can be taken down eventually.

It just hurts my heart knowing that I'm going to have to break Avery's heart in order to save her. I know my feisty angel isn't going to accept what I have to do. She's a fighter and knows what she wants. So, if she decides she wants me, it's going to be a battle royale.

Or, maybe not. Maybe she'll get sick of my bullshit and figure life is just better and easier without some scarred, broken mess of a man who can't shake his haunted past.

Either way, I know I have to let her go.

And, I know it's going to kill me.

15

AVERY

I'm not going to lie. Waking up to being choked was not a pleasant experience and a little bit terrifying. But, I know Ryker didn't mean it. He would never hurt me. Not in a million years. Of this, I have no doubt.

Unfortunately, he doesn't believe it.

Oh, my poor warrior. He's battled the shadows for too long and all I want to do is help him. I felt the walls starting to crumble, but now they're up again. Higher and stronger than ever. I squeeze my eyes shut and press my face into his pillow, breathing in his scent.

Outside, the rain still comes down, but the thunder and lightning are done. Inside my heart, though, there's a storm raging. I'm going to fight for my man. He has gone through too much heartache and has experienced more loss than anyone should be expected to handle in one lifetime.

One person can only be so strong. Ryker Flynn needs me. He needs help healing and only love will do that. I want to give him that love, reach into the dark shadows and pull him back out into the sunlight.

I open my eyes and look toward the couch where he lays now. It's around the corner, so I can only see his bare feet, crossed at the ankles and propped up on the armrest, hanging over the floor. I want more than anything to go over there and guide him back here, into bed with me. But, he's freaked out and I know he needs some space right now.

I think he's more freaked out than me and I was the one getting choked.

Tomorrow, he and Gray are going to break into Castillo's compound and he needs to be 110 percent focused on the mission. But, now he's going to have this on his mind, too, and that worries me. If anything happens to him, I will not handle it well.

Quite frankly, I will lose my shit.

When you let people in, there's a risk you will lose them. I understand this, but that doesn't make it any easier when it happens.

It's not going to happen, Ave. Ryker is an expert at what he does. No one in the world is more highly-trained than a US Navy SEAL to handle bad guys. It's what they live to do-- they have the talent, patience and fortitude to get the hard jobs done that no one else can or wants to do. Well, except maybe their equal, the Army's elite Delta Force. That's why they work in conjunction so much. Because they're the biggest badasses out there.

For a long time, I can't fall asleep so I just listen to the rain splatter against the windows. Almost two hours later, I sigh and sit up. My gaze moves over to the edge of the couch where Ryker hasn't moved in quite a while so I figure he must be sleeping. Then, I realize he doesn't even have a blanket.

I slip out of bed, pull the sheet off my bed and tiptoe over to the couch. My heart catches in my throat when I look down at him sleeping. He's lying on his side, one hand beneath the edge of a pillow, his other hand tucked under his chin. His breathing is deep and he looks at peace, not caught in the grip of some bad dream, and I'm grateful.

God, he's so handsome. The couch can't be comfortable because he's too big and his long legs are bent, knees hanging over the side. My gaze moves down his rugged face, taking in every detail, from his cropped hair to his closed black lashes to his angular jaw covered in dark stubble.

His neck is long and meets shoulders that meld into arms that could only belong to a warrior. The large muscles might be at rest, but they're no joke. So strong and capable. He can probably bench press 300 pounds which is like two and half of me.

There's fit and then there's military-fit. Ryker falls into the latter category, no doubt about it. I check out what I can of his chest. He's curled toward me with arms in front of him so it's hard to see, but it's quite apparent that he's built like granite. Smooth and hard.

As my gaze slides lower, I spot three scars from bullets and I know there are more. He was shot five times. Five bullets and a knife couldn't take down my man. So, I'll be damned if a nightmare will.

I'm going to help you, I think. I draw the sheet up over his long legs and drape it at his waist. *I promise.*

In the morning, we both get ready and decide to go down and get a coffee. He doesn't mention what happened, but I can feel him pulling away. He's keeping his distance and being extremely quiet. I know his mind is on the mission so I don't want to bother him. But, at the same time, I miss his large hand at my back and the other small touches that I'd been growing accustomed to feeling. I miss catching the lingering, heated looks. I miss the conversations whether we were joking, plotting or fighting.

I hate that he's pushing me away. I suppose there's one way to get him fired up again, though. After the mission, I'm just going to have to seduce him. I told him that I wanted him back in my bed tonight so I'm going to pull out all the stops to make sure it happens.

After all, he's only a flesh and blood man. He'll succumb. Eventually, anyway.

Ryker hands me the coffee and I thank him. The rain stopped earlier and it looks like it's getting sunny out. *I could use some warm sunshine on my face,* I think. "Want to go for a walk?" I ask.

Ryker glances down at the huge watch on his wrist. Gray won't be here for hours and he has gone over the mission plan a thousand times. I give him a small smile and tug on his arm.

"C'mon, big guy," I say. "You're looking pale. You can use some sunshine."

"I guess," he concedes. "But, just a quick walk. I have to get back up there and go over everything again."

He glances down at my fingers, still on his arm, and I let go.

"How much can you bench press?" I ask out of the blue.

"What?" he asks. I can hear the surprise, but also a trace of amusement in his voice. "Why?"

I shrug and throw him a flirty smile. "Just curious. I know it must be a lot so give me a number. Impress me."

"I can bench press you," he says and his mouth edges up.

I'm happy to see the beginning of a smile back on his face. "Yeah. Like two of me."

"Two?" He scoffs. "More like three," he brags.

I raise a brow. "Just so you're aware, I'm not as skinny as you may think. But, thanks," I add and take a sip of my coffee.

"You're light as a feather," he says.

"Again, thank you. But, no. I weigh 120 on a good day."

Ryker does a quick calculation in his head and then gives me a nod. "Three of you is 360. That's what I can bench press. Exactly."

"Three hundred and sixty *pounds*?" I ask in disbelief. "No way."

He shrugs a wide shoulder. "Any guy in good shape should be able to lift 100 pounds more than his body weight. I'm in a little better shape than most guys, I guess," he says.

"I'd say so, He-Man. Geez."

He laughs.

There it is. I smile, glad to see him warming up to me again. It's going to take some work and time, but I'm going to come in like a wrecking ball and knock down those damn walls of his once and for all.

As we walk down the street, I notice what looks like a farmer's market going on down an alley. "Let's go get something to eat," I suggest, eyeing all the fresh fruit, vegetables and other goodies.

We turn and make our way into the alley full of endless stalls and vendors. It's crowded with locals and some tourists. It doesn't take me long to spot some type of yummy-looking cookie. "Ooh, look," I say and drag him over.

"I think you can sniff a sweet out a mile away," he says and smiles.

"You better believe it," I answer, checking out the stall with what the woman tells me are *obleas*. The paper thin wafers are filled with *arequipe*, some kind of caramel, and she adds a little strawberry jam on it.

We both get a couple and Ryker pays her. I waste no time taking a bite and it's sugary heaven. "Oh, wow, delish," I say. We continue through the crowd and I check out a table full of black pottery.

A couple stalls over, I admire some bright-colored shawls and swipe up a sombrero. I put it on and pose. "You should definitely get one," I tell Ryker and hand him the black and white hat. He sets it on his head and the vendor and I laugh.

"El sombrero vueltiado is a macho symbol of Colombia," the vendor says.

"Well, no one is more macho than this guy," I say. A blush rises in Ryker's cheeks and it's too adorable. "Mi hombre es muy guapo, ¿no?"

"Si, señorita. Grande y fuerte."

I buy the hats.

"Your Spanish is impressive," Ryker says, pulling the sombrero off, as we walk away.

"Gracias," I say.

"Ever going to let me know what you're saying?" he asks.

"Posible," I answer with a sly smile. "Oh, look!" I point to a table with emeralds on display. "These can't be real," I say under my breath.

"You can buy emeralds all over Columbia. They may not be great quality, but probably straight out of a local mine." His whisky-colored gaze dips and meets mine. "Want one?" he asks.

I realize he's serious. But, then, I spot a cart with dark Columbian chocolate bars and that's more up my alley. "I'd rather have some of those," I say and head over.

Ryker laughs and trails over behind me. "Only you would choose chocolate over emeralds, Ave," he says.

"Leave me and my sweet tooth alone," I say over my shoulder.

We pick out a few different bars to take home and, while he's paying, I wander past a stall selling frozen fruit juice pulp. It all looks so good. Across the way, I see some coffee and know we have to take some of that home, too.

While I look at the different flavors, I hear someone come up beside me and I turn, assuming it's Ryker. "Look," I say. "They have chocolate-flavored-"

The jolt drops me to my knees. It feels like needles stabbing through my side when the stun gun touches me. Then, I feel myself being tossed over a shoulder and spirited away, down the rest of the alley and around the corner.

I want to call for Ryker, but I can't find my voice. A bag drops over my head and someone secures my hands with a zip tie before tossing me into the back of a vehicle.

Oh, my God.

By the time I get some mobility back in my stunned muscles, it's too late. I'm bouncing around in the back of the van, on my way to only God knows where.

I'm being kidnapped, I realize.

16

RYKER

As I pay for the chocolate bars, I glance over my shoulder and see Avery pause at a booth that sells coffee. Columbian coffee is some of the best in the world, so we will definitely need to get some to take home. I thank the vendor, add the chocolate to the bag of souvenirs that's getting heavier and turn around.

I start walking across the alley, my gaze searching for Avery's blonde head. She sticks out like a sore thumb so when I don't immediately see her, I frown. *Where did she go now?* I wonder and start walking down further.

Probably sniffed out some more sweets, I think and can't help but smile.

But, then I catch sight of her blonde head and my heart sinks in dread. She's hanging over some man's shoulder and he's moving fast. I drop our souvenirs and take off, running after them at full speed. At the end of the alley, I spin around the corner.

Two white vans idle at the curb. No one is around and suddenly one of the vans peels off, tires smoking.

No. Even though I can't see her, I know they have Avery.

The moment I start running after the first van, the other van's back doors swing open and two masked men jump out, blocking my path.

I skid to a halt and they immediately pounce. But, I'm ready. The first man throws himself into me and I stumble backwards, slamming into a dumpster. I drive my knee up into his gut and, as he drops, the second man attacks.

I manage to throw a punch before the fucker on the ground pulls out a taser. I see it a moment too late and he pulls the trigger. When the volts hit me, it's like a thousand knives stabbing into my leg and I drop. He doesn't let up, making sure I stay down, and Christ, it hurts. Every muscle in my body spasms then refuses to move.

I struggle to get up, but my mind and muscles just won't connect. The two masked men each grab one of my arms, yank me up and throw me into the back of the van. As it takes off, the fucker with the taser hits me again and all I can do is roll onto my back and groan.

Helpless, I watch as they zip tie my hands and then pull a bag over my head.

I'm not sure how long we drive. Forty-five minutes, maybe, but I'm guessing we're heading into the jungle because the road gets rougher, no longer paved like in the city, and every so often, I can hear leaves and branches brush against the vehicle.

My mind and muscles start to feel normal again and I wonder where the hell they're taking me. I'm assuming Avery and I are being taken by the same men and to the same place, but as of now, I don't know anything for sure.

Why did they target us? And, who exactly took us? I don't think they were just out to kidnap a couple of random tourists. Something more nefarious is happening.

I need to figure out a way to escape. When I pull myself up into a sitting position, a voice yells, "No te muevas!"

I may not speak Spanish, but I know when someone orders me not to move. I lean back against the van wall and patiently bide my time. Right now I'm at a huge disadvantage because I can't see what the hell is going on around me. Eventually, though, they're going to take the bag off my head and I'll be ready to strike.

Finally, the van stops. I hear some quick exchanges in Spanish and I wish I knew what they were saying. I'm not fluent like Avery, but I do catch a couple of words-- el jefe which means the boss and la mujer which means the woman.

Is Avery the woman they're talking about? God, I hope so.

I can't see what the hell is going on, but the back doors of the van open and someone yanks me out. My captor shoves the barrel of a gun into my temple and, in accented English, says, "Move it, gringo."

Then, he shoves a hand into my back and I stumble forward. I walk, trying to look down and see something, but the bag is pulled tightly closed. The asshole doesn't warn me about the stairs and I trip, slamming my knees into the tiles. "Fucker," I hiss.

The pistol slams against the back of my head for my little comment and stars flash in the blackness all around me. I force myself to stay upright, though, and take one step at a time. Hopefully, closer to Avery.

We walk down a long hallway, take a couple of turns and then he shoves me into a room. It's quiet, except for the sound of birds outside, and a hand pushes me down into a chair. The bag is ripped off my head and I look around. I'm in a library with a desk and built-in bookshelves fill each wall.

My captor is a big guy, a little shorter than me, but heavier around the midsection. He's definitely enjoyed too many *obleas* smothered in strawberry jam. He holds a SIG Sauer P228 and has a mean face with a heavy brow. "You will stay here until El Jefe is ready."

"Who's your boss?" I ask.

"No questions."

I want to know if they have Avery here, but I bite my tongue. The last thing I want to reveal is that I care about her and how much she means to me. I'm not about to give them any ammunition to use against me.

I know how to keep my mouth shut and hold up under duress in a torture-like situation. But, if they threaten Avery, all bets are off.

I close my eyes, pretending my head still hurts from getting hit in the back of the head, but, really, I'm picturing the drawings of Castillo's compound from Gray. Mentally, I compare the images with the walk I just took, counting steps, doorways and turns that we took.

It matches up exactly with how I remember the drawings.

Shit. I had planned to break in here and now here I am. At least I'm pretty sure I'm in Castillo's compound. Very discreetly, I pull at the zip tie, testing the tightness, and think about the knife in my boot.

I can get out of my bindings in a second and escape this place in a heartbeat, but I'm not in that big of a hurry. Besides, if Avery is here, I'm not leaving without her.

More than anything, I'm curious. I want to know why I'm here and I want to talk to El Jefe because that can only be one person.

It has to be Antonio Castillo.

I thought he was out in the jungle somewhere fighting his rival drug lords, but it seems he's back. How in the hell does he know about us? Then, I think back to our meeting with Gray. I don't know him, but I'm pretty positive that Gray isn't the traitor.

It was someone in the bar, El Serpiente, who must've seen us or overheard part of our conversation. I'm sure Castillo has informants all over the place and probably shares a nice reward with them when they give him intel on enemies.

Just like he did with Valkyrie.

I don't want Castillo to know we're looking for information on Operation Armageddon and Valkyrie. If he thinks we're connected to the CIA or SEALs, we're not getting out of here alive.

Because men like Castillo think they're above the law and that they can murder anyone who gets in their way. They thrive on their power and believe they're invincible. Their egos are enormous and they're used to getting them stroked by their score of underlings.

After waiting almost another half an hour, the door finally opens and I get my first up close look at Antonio Castillo, the drug king of Columbia. The man I was tasked to take down two years ago and failed. The man who had my entire team slaughtered.

He looks me over with dark eyes that look black as sin. He's not very tall, has a thick mustache and wears some kind of khaki uniform. I guess from his faux military group.

It takes every ounce of strength within me to keep my expression neutral, but inside I'm seething. This asshole is responsible for the death of thousands of people via his paramilitary force, UFOC, and he supplies terrorists with military-grade weapons.

I want this fucker to go down.

I keep my breathing even, my face expressionless. The problem is this guy's like a snake who disappears in his jungle camouflage at the first sign of trouble. Just like the Taliban who hides in their mountain caves. But, I'm coming in with a daisy cutter and I'm going to flatten his whole fucking operation. Blow it up and clear out this whole section of jungle til there's nothing left but dirt.

"Who are you?" Castillo asks. "And, why are you meeting with a former CIA agent?"

I merely raise a brow.

"I know all about Grayson Shaw and his dead little sister. He's been a thorn in my side for years, but one of these days I'll finish him off. In the meantime, though, I have an empire to run."

"I know all about your empire," I say with a note of disgust.

"And, what do you know?"

I clamp my jaw together.

Castillo takes a step closer, eyes squinting at me. "Who are you, gringo?"

I don't say a word, just meet his gaze.

"I'm trying to be civil. Treat you like a proper guest. But understand, I do have ways to make you talk."

"I'm curious," I say and he narrows his snake-like eyes. "Why'd you come back here and question me yourself?"

"Because Ryker Flynn," he says and holds up the driver's license that was in my wallet, "I want to know why you're down here meeting with a former CIA agent, asking questions about me."

Shit.

"Maybe we should go ask your pretty blonde companion," he says with a nasty smile. "She may be more willing to talk than you."

I maintain my stoic look as best as I can even though I'm freaking out inside. *Oh, God, he better not lay a hand on Avery or I'm going to kill him,* I think.

Castillo pulls out a cigar and clamps it between his teeth. He seems to be weighing his options. "Let's go," he says and motions to his guard.

The goon yanks me up out of the chair and guides me out into the hallway. We walk down to another section of the house and I'm glad it's farther away so I can check out the other rooms, the general layout, taking inventory of all exits points.

When we reach a room at the back of the house, a guard unlocks the door and ushers me inside. I immediately see Avery in a chair, also zip tied. *Thank God.* Happiness flares in her eyes when she sees me, but I give her a discreet look, hoping that she will keep quiet and not reveal anything.

The guard shoves me down into the chair next to Avery. I try not to pay too much attention to her, but I give her a quick once-over and she appears unharmed. Nearby, Castillo lights his cigar up and takes a couple of puffs. He looks from me to Avery and then back again.

"So, Mr. Flynn, is this your *amor?*"

I ignore his question. Just like all the others.

Castillo turns his attention to Avery. "And, what is your name, *hermosa?*"

"Avery Archer," she answers, looking him straight in the eye. Her voice sounds strong and unwavering, and I've never been more proud.

That's my girl, I think.

"What exactly are you and Mr. Flynn doing in Columbia?" Castillo takes another puff of his cigar.

"Oh, you know. Just a little vacation."

Castillo strokes his mustache, then says, "I'm getting that feeling I get when someone is lying to me." His eyes narrow and he stoops down so he and Avery are face to face. "Are you lying to me, Señorita Archer?" Castillo asks.

Oh, shit.

17

AVERY

Oh, shit, I think. But, I hold Antonio Castillo's gaze and don't falter. With bad guys like this, it's important to always look calm and in control. Even when you're not.

No fear, Ave.

"No," I say, keeping my voice even. But, he doesn't look convinced.

"Hmm," he says and wanders over to the other side of the room. "And, I suppose Grayson Shaw is just an old friend who you wanted to catch up with, no?

For the first time, I notice several covered stands on the far wall. Antonio runs his hand along the black cover that hides whatever is beneath and I feel the first tinge of unease.

"Are you familiar with any of the exotic creatures that thrive down here in the Columbian jungles?" he asks.

"Not specifically," I say. Beside me, Ryker shifts in his chair and I know the knife is in his boot. If we can just get Castillo to leave then we'd have a chance to escape.

"Well, then let me introduce you to some of my favorites." Castillo pulls the cover and I see several glass aquariums. In the first one is a coiled snake. "This is the Bothrops asper, also commonly called the

113

equis snake because of the "X" pattern of its scales. It's a member of the pit viper family," he says.

I'm not feeling good about his collection of dangerous animals and I swallow hard.

"It has a deadly reputation and is extremely unpredictable. Would you like a closer look, Señorita Archer?"

"No, thank you," I say.

Castillo chuckles and moves on to another aquarium. This one holds a large brown spider. "The brown recluse," he says. "They can give you a nasty, toxic bite."

I tilt my head and eye the big spider. I remember learning a little about them when my Dad discovered a few hundred living in a wood pile in our backyard in Ohio. Their bite can make you feel pretty sick, but rarely kills. *I'd rather take my chances with the creature I know is less dangerous,* I think.

Castillo moves to the last aquarium where a tiny yellow frog sits. It looks harmless, even kind of cute, but I'm sure it's not as innocent as it looks. "And, finally, the golden dart frog." A cruel smile curves his mouth. "This tiny frog is the world's most poisonous animal. It carries enough poison in its skin to kill up to 20 humans just by touch alone."

I squirm in the chair, pulling at the zip tie around my wrists, but to no avail. The plastic just cuts into my skin, leaving deep red marks that are on the verge of bleeding.

"So, now I'm going to ask you one last time. Why were you meeting Grayson Shaw?"

Neither of us says a word.

I think the perverse side in Castillo is glad because now he gets to call his guard forward and begin the threats.

I'm ready for him, though.

"String him up," he orders.

No. Not Ryker. *String me up instead,* I want to yell.

But, the guard grabs him, pops up on a chair, and hitches his bound wrists high above his head, up on a metal hook attached to the ceiling. Ryker's long body stretches to its limit and he's practically on the balls of his feet.

My heart sinks.

Unable to fight back, much less move, Ryker hangs there. One nod from Castillo and the guard hits him in the gut with a meaty fist.

"No!" I yell. "Leave him alone!"

But, the guard continues to punch him. In the stomach, side and then a strike to the kidney. Ryker grunts with each blow. Then, all of a sudden, Ryker lifts his legs and kicks out with booted feet, catching the guard in the center of his chest with a hard thwack.

The guard drops to the floor like a sack of potatoes.

A wave of triumph washes through me.

"Get out," Castillo hisses and kicks the guard as he struggles up. As he stumbles out of the room, Castillo circles Ryker, but stays just out of his immediate reach. Even with his hands bound and pulled up tightly above his head, Ryker is a force. All brute strength and dangerous looks.

When Castillo pulls a switchblade out of his jacket, my gaze snaps up and meets Ryker's. Castillo flicks the blade open and he trails it along Ryker's middle. He digs the point into Ryker's abs and a spot of bright red appears on his t-shirt.

"Stop!" I yell. Ryker shakes his head, willing me to be silent, but I can't take it. I can't sit here and watch this asshole inflict pain on the man I love.

The man I love.

The realization hits me hard and fast. I guess on some level I've always known. Since day one, Ryker Flynn has been the only man for me. The one I've compared every other man to that I've met. No one ever even came close to the lofty standards he set that first day my brother introduced us.

Honorable, handsome, strong. The list goes on, but he also has some not-so-great traits that have the power to rile me up fast. Like his stubbornness, overprotectiveness and occasional arrogance.

Even so, it doesn't matter. Because this beautiful warrior is all mine and I love him for all the good and all the bad. I love him for exactly the way he is and I wouldn't change a thing.

"Don't hurt him," I say. "Please."

Castillo looks from me to Ryker and he must see how I feel. *Dammit.* Now he's going to use my feelings against me.

Instead, though, he closes the knife and wanders over to the last aquarium. Castillo slides a pair of gloves on and my heart begins to thump harder. He opens the lid, reaches in and lifts the creature out.

The tiny frog sits in his palm and I feel a fury like no other rise up in me. If he puts that thing anywhere near Ryker, I'm going to launch up out of this chair and slam myself into him.

But, he walks past Ryker and stops directly in front of me. "A dart frog's poison permanently prevents nerves from transmitting impulses which leads to heart failure. Death occurs in less than 10 minutes and there is no cure."

Lovely, I think, my eyes on the little bugger.

"Now," Castillo says and kneels down in front of me. "Why don't you tell me what you're really doing down here. Or, you can hold my golden dart frog. Would you like that, Señorita Archer?"

"I happen to like frogs," I say and give Ryker a sideways glance. "But, I'd prefer to borrow your gloves for this one."

Castillo laughs. "I don't think so."

I try not to flinch and keep completely still when Castillo sets the tiny frog on my thigh. *Shit.* If it somehow touches my skin, I'm as good as dead.

My gaze lifts and meets Ryker's.

"Leave her alone," Ryker growls.

"Jefe!"

Castillo looks up and one of his men motions for him. "There's something you should come see," he says. "Right away."

With a frown of annoyance, Castillo scoops the frog up and places it back in its aquarium. "When I return, I want answers or you're going to have an up close and personal encounter with the pit viper."

The minute he leaves, Ryker straightens up. "Avery, get my knife."

I stand up, hurry over to Ryker and shove my fingers into his boot. I manage to grasp the knife between two fingers and pluck it out. With a little maneuvering, I turn it around and slice through my zip tie. The plastic falls away and I jump up on the chair and stretch up to free Ryker.

When his hands drop, I feel a bit of relief. But, I know we're not out of here yet. I hand him his knife back.

"Stay back," Ryker says. Then, he moves over to the first aquarium, pulls the lid off and tips it over.

"What're you doing?" I ask.

"Giving Castillo an up close and personal encounter with a pit viper." The coiled snake begins to unwind and, as it slithers out of the glass enclosure, Ryker grabs my hand. "Stay behind me. There's probably a guard."

I give Ryker room as he pulls the door inward. He moves like a ninja-- silent, swift and deadly. By the time the guard realizes he is there, Ryker drives the blade upward and the guard drops dead. He swipes the blade across the man's uniform, cleaning the blood away and stowing it back in his boot. Then, he retrieves the dead guard's gun.

Without a backward glance, Ryker takes my hand again and we move forward. It's kind of scary to see firsthand how good he is at this. But, I know in order to be a competent SEAL, to stay alive in a hostile environment, that he and Luke both had to kill.

Kill or be killed.

Back against the wall, we make our way down the hall, quickly and with purpose. Ryker must've memorized the compound's layout because he seems to know exactly where we're going. I'm incredibly grateful he spent so much time preparing because this place is huge.

"This way," he whispers and leads me into a room. There's a large glass door on the back wall and we hurry over to it. On the way, we pass a glass case that displays an emerald that's the size of my fist and I do a double take.

Ryker slides the door open and we step outside. "We need to get over the wall," he says.

I glance up at the huge concrete wall that soars above us and I get ready to climb.

"I'm going to boost you up," he says. The moment he leans down, a shot fires out of nowhere. Ryker shoves me down to the ground, covering me with his large body, and squeezes off a shot. Not far away, a man falls.

"Get back inside," Ryker orders, pulling me up. I race back into the house for cover as he turns and fires on another guard. *Shit, I wish I had a weapon.* I glance around the room and the first thing my gaze lands on is the huge emerald in the glass case. It's stunning, but hardly helpful. Then, I notice a carved stone statue on a pedestal. It's heavy as hell and I heave it up, ready to knock someone unconscious.

I peek out the door and see Ryker tangling with two guards. He holds his knife, legs akimbo and in a fighting stance. They circle each other for a moment before one of the guards launches into him. They go down, tussling on the ground, and I waste no time sneaking up behind the second guy and I lob him over the head with the statue. He drops to the ground, out cold, and I grab the knife out of his hand. Meanwhile, Ryker finishes off the other guard with an upward slash to his gut. He shoves the dead guard off him and stands up.

"C'mon," he says. In one quick motion, he drops and laces his fingers. "Up you go."

I step on his locked hands and he boosts me up, hard and fast. I fly up, grab the top of the wall and swing my legs over so I'm facing down, ready to offer a hand to Ryker. He takes a few steps back, races forward and jumps. He lands in the middle of the wall like a damn spider and uses each nook and cranny to dig his fingers and boots into and propel himself upward.

"I got it, go!" he says.

Of course, he does. My man is beyond impressive. I start to turn and lower myself. The moment I let go of the wall, I see another guard storm out of the house, an assault rifle aimed at Ryker. "Look out!" I cry and hit the ground in a roll.

The sound of machine gun fire echoes through the night and I hear the other side of the wall shatter in an explosion of breaking concrete.

Oh, my God. No, no, no.

18

RYKER

Just before Avery drops, I see her eyes widen in horror so I let go of the wall and land in a crouch. A moment later, a guard sprays the wall with an AK-47. I duck behind a thick tree for cover and lift the gun I took off one of the dead guards.

I align the rear sights and pull the trigger. The headshot takes him down and I stash the gun in the back of my waistband and take another running leap at the wall. Again, I scale my way up, throw a leg over the top and drop down on the other side.

A second later, Avery throws herself against me. "Oh, my God, I thought you were dead," she cries.

I pull back and see the absolute terror in her blue eyes. "I'm okay," I reassure her.

Avery grabs my head and yanks my mouth down for a savage kiss. I don't think a woman ever kissed me like that before. It's hard and intense and so full of raw emotion. "You scared me half to death," she says and pulls back, gaze roaming over my body for bullet holes.

"Baby, I'm fine. But, we gotta go."

We take off at a run, headlong into the jungle. It's probably around noon now so the light isn't going to help cover our escape. I'm picturing the overall map of the compound in my head and remember that the nearest town is Northeast of our current position.

"That way," I say and Avery keeps right up with me, our strides long and even over the jungle floor. We don't slow down until we put a couple of miles between ourselves and Castillo's compound. Then, I feel it's okay to take a quick break.

"You a runner?" I ask, breathing hard, impressed with her stamina and quick-thinking.

"Liberty and I run every day," she says. She puts her hands on her hips and leans forward, trying to catch her breath.

"You did good in there, Ave," I tell her. *I'm so damn proud of her.* "You stayed calm, cool and collected. I'd have you on my team any day."

"Coming from you, that means a lot."

We exchange smiles.

"So, I think we should make our way over to the closest town which is about 18 klicks Northeast of the compound."

"That's about what? Eleven miles?"

"Yeah. And, the faster we move, the better."

"Do you think he'll send anyone after us?" she asks.

"Possibly. But, let's not hang around and find out. C'mon."

The farther out we travel, the thicker and more precarious the jungle becomes. My boot slides in some mud and vines slap against my face, but we press on. Avery is such a trooper and I glance back over my shoulder where she marches along behind me, head up, face stoic.

Suddenly, I freeze and Avery slams right into me. I hold up a hand and put a finger to my lips. Some sixth sense of mine is going off. I scratch the tingling at the back of my neck, listening to the sounds of the jungle.

Seemingly out of nowhere, two of Castillo's UFOC paramilitary soldiers crash out of the brush and attack. One jumps on me with a barrage of punches to my chest, almost knocking me off my feet, but I manage to slam an elbow in his face. Blood spurts from his now-broken nose. I spin and kick his leg then chop him hard against the base of his neck.

As he drops, I turn and see the other soldier has Avery pinned to a tree, hands around her neck. *Fuck no.* I grab the back of his shirt and yank him away from her. He releases her and she drops to the ground, gasping for breath, hands around her neck.

Holding him up by his collar, I pull my fist back and slam it into his face. I let go and he hits the ground with a thud. I'm on him in a heartbeat throwing punch after punch, making him regret ever laying a hand on Avery.

"Ryker!"

Her voice pulls me out of my tunnel vision and I stop pummeling the guy, lift my hands and see my knuckles are covered in blood. I lean back, flick it off and stand up. I'm breathing hard and glance down at the guy who I just beat to a bloody pulp. I don't even know if he's still alive. Then, I look over at Avery. "Are you okay?" I ask.

She's trembling and I take two long strides over and catch her in my arms. I gather her against me and place a kiss on her blonde head. When I pull back, I check out her neck and see red marks where he tried to strangle her. That's two near-strangulations in less than 24 hours. *Shit.*

"I'm okay," she says and straightens up, a fiery determination in those blue eyes.

"Let's keep moving," I say.

We continue on, pushing through the dense foliage and Avery's spirits seem to lift. "This is probably just a typical day on the job for you, huh?" she teases.

"How so?" I ask.

"Oh, you know. Crawling through the jungle, neutralizing bad guys, running for your life. Just another day in the life of a frogman."

"I guess it resembles some missions I've had, but don't forget, I've been retired for two years now. So, this is not a typical day anymore."

"What is?" she asks, keeping pace beside me.

"Totally boring."

"Tell me," she presses.

I sigh, legs pumping. "On a good day, I get up, drive over to Platinum Security and see if Jax has any new jobs for me. He, Griff and I shoot the shit for a while. Then, I go to work. Thrilling, isn't it?"

"You said on a good day."

"If it's a bad day, I probably wake up from a nightmare and can't get my shit together. I stay home, drink too much and get sucked into the dark memories and guilt that just won't fucking go away."

She stops, looks up at me. "One day, they'll go away, Ryker. I really believe that."

"I wish I did."

I look around at all the thick greenery and let out a weary sigh. "I can't believe I'm back here. Once again running for my life."

"Well, if it makes you feel any better, there's no one else I'd rather be on the run with," she says.

My mouth edges up and I swipe a hand over my stubbled jaw. "Ditto."

In the distance, I think I hear rotors.

"Is that a helicopter?" Avery asks.

Every muscle in my body tenses. *Unfriendlies incoming.* "Yeah. C'mon."

We start moving at a fast pace and moments later stumble out into a clearing. *Perfect,* I think in annoyance. Just when I'm about to pull Avery back into the jungle's edge and out of sight, guns on the helo begin firing down, tearing up the vegetation at our feet.

"Run!" I yell above the whirling blades above.

The helo drops lower and as a soldier peppers bullets all around us, several others rope down and hit the ground.

Shit. "Go, go, that way!" I point toward a patch of jungle, ready to dive in and disappear. But, the moment we stumble into the undergrowth, I see water. I grab Avery's arm and drag her down just as more bullets fly past us. As we slide down and through the mud, a hot sting slashes my upper arm and I curse. Bullet graze, I think, and glance down to see blood blossom on my shirt sleeve.

Avery and I race along the water, still at the edge of the jungle for cover, and I can see that it gets rougher and turns into mini rapids.

Oh, shit. A little farther up, we skid to a halt and realize we've hit a dead end. The ground abruptly drops and we stand at the top of a cliff. To our left, the water cascades down over the side in a stunning waterfall. The drop looks to be a good 100 feet and falls into a deep, *hopefully deep*, pool below.

Gunfire bursts all around us, shredding vegetation, inches away from shredding us, and I know there's no choice but to go over the falls. I look over at her and see the fear on her face.

"We have to jump!" I yell.

For me, this is nothing. I've done HELO jumps out of planes too many times to count and the water is like a second home to me. If I didn't have any bad guys on my tail, this would be fun. But, Avery isn't used to this kind of thing.

"You can do it, Ave. C'mon!" I grab her hand and before she can think too hard about it and psych herself out, my brave, beautiful woman, jumps into the rapids with me. They sweep us up and pull us apart, propelling us closer to the drop. I feel Avery get swept away from me and then I'm flying over the edge of the falls.

Soaring over the waterfall and down through the air, I see her for a moment and then lose sight of her when I hit the foamy water below. It's about 15 feet deep and crystal clear. I flip my feet like fins and make my way to the surface.

When my head breaks through the water, I look around for Avery. I don't see her right away and panic makes my gut churn. I've always loved the water and excelled at all my aquatic training-- from surf torture to drown proofing to surf passage and ocean swims. While so many guys panicked underwater, I turned into a fucking frog. Literally. I could hold my breath for 3:45. Beneath the surface, my world disappeared. I focused on the sound of my heart beat and visualized time stopping. I loved it.

But, Avery hasn't been through the extensive training that makes you comfortable in water. And, as far as I know, she never jumped off a cliff over a waterfall before. Worry tears through me when I still don't see her. My eyes scan the river and the shoreline, panic nipping at my gut.

Finally, I spot her blonde head. *Thank God.* She's pulling herself up on the muddy river bank and I swim over. "Ave! You okay?"

"I didn't drown so, yeah." She swipes her long hair back and gives me a lopsided grin.

"I'm making you an honorary frog after that," I say and pull myself up and out of the water.

Suddenly, the helo swoops into view above us.

"God, these guys just don't give up," she says and I help pull her up over the muddy bank and onto grass.

"That way!" I point to a section of dense jungle and we race toward it at full speed. We crash through the foliage, out of the helo's sights, but I know the soldiers who rappelled out earlier are still somewhere out there.

Unfortunately, they catch up quicker than I'd like.

We push forward, vines slapping our faces and thick undergrowth tripping us along the way. I hate the goddamn jungle. Put me in the ocean any day.

Right when I think we put some distance between us and the UFOC soldiers, a grenade comes flying out of nowhere. I grab Avery, hurl her out of the way and land on top of her. Boom! The ground rumbles and debris flies everywhere.

I scramble up and pull her with me. We run as fast as we can, but this part of the jungle is treacherous with lots of mud and vegetation. Avery slips and goes down hard. I spin around and pull her up, but when she steps on her ankle it goes out. *Shit.* I sweep her up and keep going.

Avery wraps her arms around my neck and I charge forward. Not too far behind, gunfire breaks out. Bullets zing past us, tearing off chunks of tree bark, and I dodge to the right, trying to outrun these assholes. Or, at least lose them.

They're fucking persistent, though, so I pick up my pace. At this point, I'm running so fast that I pray I don't wipe out. Last thing I want to do is land on Avery. I'd probably crush her.

I keep moving to the right, hard and fast, so they don't have the opportunity to flank us. If I let them surround us, trap us in, then it's game over.

All of a sudden, the ground gets extremely muddy which forces me to slow down. It sucks at my boots, trying to drag us down. I pause, breathing hard, and feel the ground beneath me start to slide away.

Oh, shit.

I realize we're standing too close to the edge of an embankment and the muddy ground collapses beneath my feet. "Mudslide!" I yell. Avery's arms tighten around me and then we drop, caught up in a vortex of mud, dirt and debris.

19

AVERY

Oh, for the love of God! First a waterfall, now a mudslide. I decide I hate the jungle.

My arms tighten around Ryker and my stomach drops as we plunge down the side of an embankment. Ryker holds me in front of him so his backside takes the brunt of the trip down. It's like a huge, filthy slide and we plummet down finally dropping into a pool of mud, twigs and leaves.

I swipe the mud out of my eyes and realize I'm sitting on Ryker's lap. "Well, that was quite a ride," I say.

He groans, wiping mud off his face.

"You okay?" I ask and stand up on wobbly legs.

"I think my backside got scraped off on the way down."

"Oh, shit." I reach down and help pull him out of the suctioning mud. "Lemme see." I move around to take a look. His shirt is shredded and his pants are pretty torn up, too. I can see plenty of scratches and cuts where skin is visible. "We need to clean you up."

"Too bad we didn't go over the waterfall second."

"I'm serious. You've got some good cuts."

"I'm fine," he says. "Except that I lost the gun. My phone, too."

I slide a hand over my now-empty pocket. "Shit, me, too." I look out into the endless green jungle ahead. "How close are we to that town? Any idea?"

Ryker looks down at his watch, wipes mud off the large face with his index finger, and checks the GPS. "If we head that way, we should make it in an hour or so." He glances down. "How's your ankle?"

"I'll let you know once we get on solid ground."

We pull ourselves out of the mud pit and I take a few steps. I try not to wince, but it's definitely sore. Probably twisted it. "I'll be fine," I say.

"You sure?"

I nod. "So, what's the plan once we get to town?"

"Call Gray. Hopefully he can pick us up."

We continue forward and all I can think about is getting out of this hellhole. "I'd kill for a hot shower right about now," I say.

"Soon," Ryker promises. "Though, we're going to have to find a new place to stay. I don't think it's safe to go back to the hotel."

"What about all our stuff?"

"Might have to leave it. Or pick it up later."

I nod and we continue forward. It seems like hours later, but we finally stumble onto the small town. Caked in dry mud and completely bedraggled, we look like a sad sight. I also feel a little exposed now that we've left the cover of the jungle and know that Ryker lost his gun.

We find a telephone near the small town square and Ryker grabs the receiver and dials Gray. How he remembers the phone number is beyond me. People, including me, are so dependent on everything being programmed into their cell phones nowadays that no one really knows anyone's information anymore. It's just hit a button and here you go.

Once again, I'm impressed by him.

They talk for a few minutes and then Ryker hangs up. "Gray's on his way. He's booking us on the first flight out in the morning. Meanwhile, he knows a place we can stay tonight. An old safehouse of his."

A safehouse. Wow, I may have been CIA, but this is operative stuff. And, Ryker was right, even though I'll probably never admit it to him.

There is a big difference between sitting at a desk and being out in the field. And, that difference is life and death.

I've gotten a small taste of what his SEAL experience must've been like. Going away to far off, foreign lands, dealing with enemies who want you dead and being able to make split second decisions and adapt when your well-crafted plan blows up in your face.

No wonder only a handful of men make it and have the honor of wearing the Trident pin.

I glance up at Ryker and even though he's covered with mud and numerous scrapes, he's never looked so good to me. The attraction curls low in my belly and I get the urge to jump on him. Then, my roaming gaze spots the bullet graze.

"Jesus, Ryker, were you shot?" My eyes widen and I grab his arm.

"Ow," he growls.

"Sorry." I make a face. "Let me look."

"Avery, it's fine."

"No, it's not. Now come here and sit down so I can check it out." I guide him over to a bench and make him sit even though I can tell he doesn't want to be fussed over.

Well, too bad.

I roll up the sticky, bloody, muddy sleeve of his shirt and cringe at the filthy wound. "We need to clean this out," I say.

"We can do it at the safehouse," he says and tries to push the sleeve back down.

But, I disagree. "No. Do you know how many germs and infections are out in that jungle? I'm going to at least rinse it off right now. Hang on."

Ryker lets out a long-suffering sigh while I approach a local selling fruit at a cart. I tell him that my friend and I got lost in the jungle, lost all our money and charm a couple of bottles of water from him. I head back over to the bench. "Give me your arm," I order Ryker.

"How many times did you bat your lashes at him?" Ryker asks in a dry voice.

"Why? Are you jealous I might run off with the local villager?"

He chuckles as I unscrew the cap and drizzle some water over the dirty graze. I wish I had something to wipe it off better, but nothing on us is clean. It will just have to do for now. "Does it hurt?" I ask him.

He just shrugs the other shoulder. "I've had worse."

That's for sure, I think, remembering the scars beneath his shirt.

"Do you know how brave you are?" I ask him.

"No, I'm really not."

"Seriously? Don't be so modest."

"I'm no braver than you, Ave. We both went over a waterfall today."

"And, down a mudslide," I add and grin.

The late afternoon sun warms us up and a ray of sunshine falls perfectly across Ryker's face, making his whisky-colored eyes appear a shade lighter and threaded in gold. I lay a hand along his muddy cheek and look into his beautiful eyes. "Thank you," I whisper. When he opens his mouth, I interrupt him. "And, don't even ask for what. The level of skill and bravery you displayed today deserves a damn medal, Ryker Flynn. And, I'm so grateful that you were with me when things turned bad. I wouldn't be sitting here right now if it weren't for you."

"Avery-"

"I'm serious. What kind of medal does a SEAL get for bravery, anyway?"

Ryker looks down at his clasped hands, starts brushing the dried mud away. "The Navy Cross," he says in a quiet voice.

Even though I start out teasing him, it suddenly occurs to me that Ryker probably received this medal after Operation Armageddon. "You have one, don't you?"

He nods. "For extraordinary heroism in combat with an armed enemy force." He forces a laugh. "They also threw in the Medal of Honor. I would've declined except that you can't. The President himself awarded them to me."

My eyes widen. The Medal of Honor is the highest and most prestigious military decoration awarded to those who have distinguished themselves by acts of valor. Luke received one, too. Of course, he was awarded posthumously and now resides in a curio cabinet in my parents' dining room. "You should be proud. Not wanting to decline the highest and most prestigious awards you can receive."

"Luke is gone. My team is gone. But, hey, I have a bunch of medals so all is good in the world."

"Ryker-"

"Gray's here," he says and stands up.

I let out a sigh and follow him to Gray's car, a rugged SUV. We get inside and Gray raises a brow. "What the hell happened to you two?" he asks.

"Sorry about the mud," I say.

He shrugs my apology off. "When I got to your hotel this morning and you weren't there, I didn't know what to think."

"We took a walk and ended up getting kidnapped."

Gray's eyes widen. "Don't tell me Castillo."

"Castillo," we both say.

"How did he know?" Gray wonders.

"I think someone at the bar overheard us talking and ran straight to him," Ryker says.

"Shit. I'm sorry. I thought it was a safe place to meet. Especially that early."

"We were taken to his compound and the man himself showed up," Ryker says.

"He wanted to know what we were doing down here and why we met with you," I add.

"Damn," Gray says. "How did you get out of there?"

"Your drawings helped," Ryker says.

I turn and glance at Ryker in the backseat and roll my eyes. He needs to stop being so damn modest. "It also helped that Ryker kicked everyone's ass. Do you think Castillo found his pit viper?"

Ryker finally smiles. "Maybe it bit him."

"Pit viper?" Gray echoes. "Sounds like you two had quite a day."

"Oh, and we also went over a waterfall," I say.

"And down a mudslide," Ryker adds.

"What is this? An Indiana Jones movie?" Gray asks, looking from me to Ryker in the rearview mirror.

"We haven't found any supernatural artifacts yet, so no," I say.

"Well, I'm just glad you're both okay. A little beat up maybe, but you're still in one piece and that's what counts."

"So, you don't think it's safe to go back to the hotel?" I ask.

"After what you just told me? No way. I'm taking you right to my old safehouse. There's some canned goods, a medical kit and you both could use a long, hot shower."

"Sounds like heaven," I say.

"It's off-the-grid so you'll be safe." Gray nods to a bag on the floor by my feet. "I grabbed your keys and i.d. from the hotel and there's some other stuff in there for you-- some clean clothes, your plane tickets, a burner phone, a gun and a couple other things that may, ah, be helpful. Just in case."

"Thanks," Ryker says. "We lost our phones and weapons so that's perfect."

Gray shakes his shaggy head. "I just can't believe how this all blew up like it did. I had no idea Castillo was keeping tabs on me."

"No doubt about it," Ryker confirms. "Better that you know, though. Don't underestimate him."

"I wish you would've had the opportunity to put a bullet in that bastard," Gray says.

"Yeah, me, too," Ryker says.

A few minutes later, we turn off the main road and drive down a dirt path. After another turn, Gray finally pulls up to a nondescript house tucked back from the road. Trees and some greenery surround it and it looks like nothing special. Definitely a place that no one would look twice at.

Gray shuts the car off and I drag myself out. I don't know about Ryker, but I'm exhausted. My adrenaline has finally crashed and I feel like I could sleep for a week.

Ryker grabs the bag out of the front seat and we follow Gray to the house. He gives us a quick tour and there's not much to it. The main living room is pretty sparse with a couch and coffee table. There's also a small kitchen with table and chairs, basic bathroom and one bedroom with a large, comfy-looking bed.

We're safe and I couldn't be happier, I think.

Gray opens a cupboard and pulls out a large first aid kit while Ryker rummages through the bag. I notice them exchange a look. Then, Gray opens the fridge and tosses us a couple of bottled waters. "Make yourself at home," he says. "If you need anything else, my number is programmed in the burner."

"Thank you so much, Gray," I say and give him a big hug. I don't think he expects it, but he awkwardly hugs me back.

Then, he and Ryker shake hands. "We really appreciate everything," Ryker says.

"My pleasure," Gray says. "I guess I'll see you when I see you."

I give a little wave goodbye and watch as he disappears out the front door. Then, I turn to Ryker and cross my arms. "Strip," I order him.

20

RYKER

"Aye, aye," I say and yank the filthy shirt off and drop it on the floor. "Gonna have to burn that."

While Avery digs through the medical kit on the counter, I peel off my grimy pants and kick them aside. When she turns, I notice her gaze skim down my body. I know I'm a dirty mess, but she looks mud-splattered and beautiful. And, despite how tired I am from our jungle adventure, my groin tightens.

Avery walks over, trying to appear all business, and examines the graze on my arm and the various cuts, scrapes and bruises down my back and thighs. "You're filthy," she announces. "Probably should wash off first and then I can clean your wounds better. C'mon."

I follow her down to the bathroom and instead of leaving, she leans over the tub, turns the water on and hits the shower. I watch her delicious ass move as she adjusts the water. Then, she turns and crooks a finger at me. "Get in."

"Are we doing this together?" I ask. Her gaze drops and there's no missing the thickening ridge pressing against my boxer briefs. "Because you're just as filthy."

In answer, she starts pulling her muddy clothes off. I strip off my boxer briefs and step into the tub. The warm water feels so good, washing the grime down the drain. I let the water pound down, loosening the debris stuck in my hair, washing away the dried blood on my arm and back and wherever else.

When Avery steps in behind me, I move over and pull her under the spray with me. She moans when the clean water hits her and I reach for a bottle of shampoo. I squeeze some over her head and she laughs. Then, I throw some in mine.

It takes me about 20 seconds to wash my short hair, but Avery's long blonde hair is full of jungle muck. I help her pluck out some leaves and slide my fingers through the wet strands, detangling them. As she finishes rinsing her hair, I pick up a bar of soap and lather it up in my hands.

"Turn around," I tell her. Avery turns and I soap up her back, running my hands all over her smooth, slippery skin. My hands glide over her shoulders and I massage them for a minute. When her head falls back with a little moan, I drop my mouth to the delicate curve where her neck and shoulder meet and kiss it.

She lets out a shaky breath, reaches up and slides a hand through my hair. Then, she turns and right when I move in for a kiss, she presses a hand against my chest. "Your turn," she says, grabbing the soap.

"So bossy," I tease.

Avery swirls the bar over my chest, around my flat nipples, down my abs, around my navel. When I feel her hand and soap dip down, brush my groin and move over a thigh, my cock turns to steel.

"God, you're so big, so beautiful," she says. She moves behind me and runs the soap over my shoulders and back, down over my ass and legs. I feel her lather up my calves, glance down and absorb the tantalizing sight of her bent over. As she makes her way back up, I feel her teeth graze my rear end.

"Fuck," I hiss. My self-control goes down the drain and I spin around and hike her slippery body up against mine. Her arms wrap around my neck and I grasp her hips and lift her up so she's straddling me, back against the tiles.

I kiss her and it's hot and deep. She thrusts her tongue into my mouth and I thrust my hips up in answer. *God, this woman is everything to me.* The thought fills my head and I can't think about it too hard. It terrifies me. For the last two years I've kept everyone at a distance because the more people you let in, the greater the chance you will lose them.

And, I've lost too many people that I love.

It's safer and smarter to maintain my distance emotionally. *Yeah right,* I think. *Go ahead and try, Flynn. Do you really think you'll be satisfied with just fucking her and walking away?*

As hard as it'll be, I don't have an option.

Tomorrow, we go home and everything will go back to the way it was because it's safer that way.

But, tonight, I'm going to forget about everything but us. I am going to give and take as much pleasure as possible and make this amazing woman come until she's screaming. *God bless, Gray,* I think, remembering the condoms I saw in the bag he packed for us.

God, is it that obvious?

I don't even care. Avery wraps around me like a cat and it's making me crazy. I lean an arm against the wall, massage one of her breasts and lick up the side of her face. When she pushes down, settling over the tip of my pulsating cock, I scoop my hands under her ass and lift her up a bit.

"Ryker. I need you."

"Hang on, baby" I whisper. I hit the water off, step out of the tub and grab a towel on my way to the bedroom. When she reaches down to touch me, I drop her on the bed. "Patience."

I pad out to the kitchen, grab the condoms and go back into the bedroom. "Compliments of Gray," I say and toss them on the bed.

A flush rises in Avery's cheeks and I grab her ankles and drag her over, right to the edge of the bed. She squeals and I lower to my knees, spread her legs and drag my rough, bristled cheek up an inside thigh. Her body tenses and I place steamy kisses up, up, up. Until I reach her wet core and lick up her folds. A cry rips from her mouth and I suck her clit into my mouth, working the little bud until her hips buck up off the bed.

Avery's hands dig into the sheets, and she's twisting and moaning as I lick and suck. I slide one, two fingers up inside her and blow softly. As my fingers move in and out, stroking her, I lean back on my haunches and soak up the rapturous look that moves across her gorgeous face. "Come for me, Ave."

For a moment she hovers at the edge of her climax, but the slightest amount of pressure from my thumb on her clit pushes her over. "Oh, God, Ryker," she cries. I revel in the way her entire body seems to roll with pleasure.

Then, I get up, move onto the bed, and shift her onto her side. I grind up against her delectable behind and nip her shoulder. Little hellion rubs her ass against my cock and I'm done. I grab one of the condoms, tear it open and roll it on. My hand grasps the top of Avery's hip, still laying on her side, and I hold her in place. Then, I slide up into her wet warmth with a groan.

"You're so fucking wet. For me," I hiss.

"Only you," she says, pressing her back into my chest.

My top leg moves over hers, trapping it, and I thrust up hard. I set a ruthless pace and reach around to rub her.

"Ryker, God!" Her voice is raspy, desperate, and she grabs a pillow in her fist.

I need to see those cornflower eyes roll back in an orgasm so I pull out, flip her onto her back and plunge back inside with one, deep thrust. Her nails dig into the backs of my shoulders and I grunt, picking up the pace, slamming into her.

We almost died today. The thought makes me work harder and I tilt her up and sink to the hilt. *Jesus Christ.* Nothing ever felt so good and I'm on the verge of exploding. "Look at me, Ave," I say. My voice sounds raw and desperate.

Avery meets my gaze, her blue eyes melding with mine. As we move together, it's just not our bodies that are in perfect sync. It's our hearts and souls, too. *They have to be,* I think, *because when I'm inside her, it's like I see God.*

We both scream out at the exact same moment. The orgasm that rocks my body is more powerful than any I've experienced before and the normal shudder is like a full-blown fucking seizure that shakes my body down to my toes.

"*Jesus*," I hiss and drop down beside her. What the fuck? Why is it so damn intense with her?

Because you love her, a small voice whispers.

No. I can't afford to love anyone. Not anymore. Especially not someone who is so good and so goddamn wonderful. If I ever lost her, I'd lose my mind.

Enjoy tonight, Ryker. Because tomorrow you have to walk away. You don't deserve her and you can't give her what she wants or needs. *I'm broken.* Avery deserves someone whole.

I roll away from her, go to the bathroom to get rid of the condom and take a few deep breaths, trying to collect myself. Whatever it is between us...it's too powerful. And, that scares the shit out of me because I am always in control.

Strong, disciplined and focused. Until I smell that sweet sugary smell of Avery's. Then, I don't know up from down and all I want to do is kiss her all over. When I walk back into the bedroom, she's sitting up with the sheet wrapped around her. She slides out of bed and motions for me to follow.

"C'mon, I want to bandage your arm."

I follow her into the kitchen, pull out a pair of shorts from the duffle bag and slip them on. I'm bigger than Gray so they're not quite as roomy as I'd like, but they'll do. Avery glances down and smirks.

"Nice shorts."

"I can take them off," I say and sit down in a chair.

"Keep them on. For now," she adds with a wicked smile.

As she starts to put some antibacterial cream on my shoulder where the bullet grazed, I look down and study her cute toes painted with pink nailpolish. "I miss your little pink slippers with the poof on top," I say and slide a hand around her waist.

"Ryker," she admonishes and wiggles out of my grasp. "I'm trying to tend to your wounds."

"So serious," I tease and pinch her ass.

Avery jumps with a squeal and swats at my hand. "Will you please behave yourself?"

"For now," I say, echoing her words.

I sigh and let her wrap my arm in a bandage and then fuss over the endless scrapes. Her fingers trail over the tattoo on my upper arm.

"Luke had the same tattoo," she says.

"We got them together."

"My Frogmen," she says with a small smile.

I like the possessive tone in her voice. Am I hers? Is she mine? For now, yes.

"Did you guys have funny call signs?" she asks.

"They were cool, not funny."

"Tell me."

"Well, you know we had a love for all things Star Wars."

"Oh, no," she says and fights back a grin. "Were you Leia or Yoda?"

I reach out and pull her down onto my lap. "You are hysterical," I say and nuzzle the back of her neck. Then, I nip her shoulder. "Luke was Skywalker, obviously, and I was Solo."

"Oh, Han," she says, pulling the sheet up, and straddling me. "I'll be your Princess Leia any day." When she begins kissing my neck, my eyes slide shut, and I dig my fingers into her hips.

"Will you put your hair in puffs for me?" I ask on a breathless whisper.

"I'll even wear the gold bikini."

I let out a husky laugh and sit back, enjoying the feel of her soft lips moving up along my jaw. She presses butterfly kisses along my cheek, at the corner of my eye and above my eyebrow.

"I think you missed my lips," I tease.

"I'm getting there," she says and continues to trail languid kisses down the other side of my face.

Finally, she finds my mouth and the kiss is slow and steamy.

I slide my hands under her, stand up and carry her back to the bedroom. I've had enough first aid and it's time to enjoy the rest of our night.

Our last night together in Columbia.
Our last night together forever.

21

AVERY

The flight back to Los Angeles goes way too fast. Way faster than the flight down to Colombia. Every moment sitting beside Ryker, stealing glances at his handsome profile, makes my heart flutter. I flush when I think about last night and parts of my body still ache from the things we did.

Ryker Flynn is everything I ever imagined and more. He's a consummate lover, thorough and attentive, but there's something else, something powerful that happens when we're together. When he's holding my gaze with those whisky-colored eyes and moving deep inside me, I feel things I've never known existed.

I am falling so in love with him, I think. Why even deny it?

And, now that we're heading back to L.A., I have no idea what he's thinking or where we go from here. Even though he's being polite and considerate, I can already feel him pulling away. Those damn walls of his are so hard to penetrate. The moment I think I'm making some kind of progress, they shoot up all over again.

And, that breaks my heart.

But, I'm going to fight for my man. And, I'm going to show him that we are better together than apart.

Ryker is a man who has sacrificed things his entire life. He's always focused on his work and, in the process, sacrificed his personal life. I don't get the feeling he's ever been in love and if you'd ask him, he'd probably say he doesn't deserve it. Always the martyr.

For once, I want him to start thinking about what he wants and needs. And, I hope, that's me.

After we land at LAX, we head straight for a taxi since we don't have any luggage. We both wear a pair of cargo pants and t-shirt from Gray so it'll be nice to get back home and slip into my own clothes. And I can't wait to get Liberty back.

We decide to stop at my place first so I can change and then head over to his condo. It's strange to be home, I think, as I unlock the door. But, I'm glad to be back. The last week has been an absolute whirlwind and my time is all off since Columbia is three hours ahead.

I change into a pair of leggings and a light sweater. Then, I spritz some of my Pink Sugar perfume across me and head back out to the living room where Ryker waits on the couch. "Are you hungry?" I ask.

"Starving," he says.

"Want to grab some food on the way to your place?"

"In-n-Out?"

"You read my mind," I say.

We hop in my Jeep, grab some cheeseburgers and animal-style fries from the iconic Cali burger joint and head over to Ryker's condo. We devour our food then he heads down to his room to change into something that suits him a little bit better. Even though it was kind of cute that his cargo pants were a few inches too short.

Ryker looks much more comfortable in his own clothes when he returns and I pop up off the couch.

"I just called Jax and he, Griff and Harlow are still at the office so let's head over. Liberty is there, too."

"Oh, I missed her so much," I say.

"He said he's got a couple of new cell phones for us, too."

Ryker's condo is super close to the Platinum Security office and we get there in no time. I pull my Jeep up to the curb and we hop out. He guides me over to the front door and opens it for me. A moment later,

Liberty comes rushing out of an office, bounds down the hall and jumps up on me. The pure joy on her face is priceless.

"I missed you, baby girl," I say and Ryker bends down and pets her. I love that he loves animals so much, especially mine.

"You should get yourself a dog," I say, watching the way he lights up when he pets Liberty. Ryker is the perfect candidate for a service dog, but I know he'd never do it. He's too stubborn and has too much pride. After everything that happened, I'm willing to bet he never even spoke to anyone about it. Just suffered in silence.

He scratches behind Liberty's ear. "I will. One of these days."

"Flynn! Down here," Griff calls.

"C'mon," Ryker says and places a hand on my lower back. He guides me down to the back corner office, Liberty trailing behind us.

Griff and Jax stand up and they all do this hand slide and knuckle bump that makes me smile. "Welcome back, bro," Griff says.

"Good to see you both," Jax says.

"Thank you for watching Liberty. I hope she was good for you and Easton."

"She was very good. So much so that we're talking about adopting a shepherd."

I rub Liberty's furry head. "You should. They're the best."

"So, fill us in," Griff says, his bright blue eyes mischievous as he looks from me to Ryker. "Anything we should know?"

I glance at Ryker and feel a wave of nerves kick in. I'm not even sure what's going on between us, but Griff seems to approve.

"Where should we start?" Ryker asks me.

"How about when we got kidnapped?"

Both Jax and Ryker straighten up. At the same moment, Harlow appears in the doorway. "Did you say kidnapped?" she asks.

I look up and get my first look at Harlow Vaughn, P.S's super smart computer genius and hacker extraordinaire. She's gorgeous with her dark brown hair swept up in a ponytail and she possesses intuitive bluish-gray eyes. "You must be Avery," she says and smiles.

"It's nice to finally meet you," I say and shake her hand.

"You, too. Now what the hell? Who kidnapped you?"

"Castillo," Ryker answers.

"Oh, shit," Griff says.

"Are you fucking kidding me?" Jax exclaims.

"Unfortunately, no." Ryker starts telling them the story about how we were buying souvenirs at a local market when we got tazed and snatched off the street by some of Castillo's men. He tells them how we were taken to his compound instead of having to break into it.

"He's a complete ego maniac," I say. "He has all these poisonous animals in aquariums and threatened us with them."

"We're lucky we made it out of there before he brought out the pit viper," Ryker says.

"Pit viper?" Harlow echoes with a shiver. "God. This is why I'm a hacker. I can stay safely inside, behind my computer."

"But, my girl was very brave when she came face to face with the poison dart frog," Ryker says.

My girl. I like the sound of that.

"That's because I like frogs," I say. We share a little smile and I'm pretty sure everyone else in the room notices.

"So, how'd you escape?" Griff asks.

"They called Castillo out and I cut our zip ties-"

"Knife in the boot?" Griff confirms.

"Always," Ryker answers. "We made it outside, got Avery over the wall and then I ran into a little trouble with an AK-47. But, I made it over and we had to trek through the jungle for awhile."

"Castillo sent his men after us. And, if that wasn't bad enough, we went over a waterfall and got caught in a mudslide. That's when we lost our phones. Oh, and, Ryker's arm got grazed by a bullet."

"Jesus," Griff says.

"We made our way to a small town and called Gray. He let us stay at a safehouse of his and then we flew out this morning."

"And, here we are," I say. Liberty presses her long snout against my leg and I stroke her head.

Jax reaches into his desk and pulls out two new phones. He slides them across the desk and we each scoop one up and say thanks. "So, what's the next step?" Jax asks.

"We need to find her old source," Ryker says. "The only person other than Castillo who knows Valkyrie's true identity."

"He's like a ghost, though. It's going to be impossible," I tell them.

"What's your old source's name?" Harlow asks.

"John Miller," I say. "As if that will help."

"I'm on it," she says and stands up. "Soon as I find anything out, I'll let you guys know." She gives me a big smile. "And, besides, I like challenges."

"Thanks, Harlow," I say.

"Don't worry. I'll dig up something. No one can stay a ghost for long." With a swish of her ponytail, she heads back over to her office.

"I'm glad I hired her," Jax says.

"Because I told you to," Griff reminds him.

"Right. Well, either way, she's exactly what we needed around here."

When I stifle a yawn behind my hand, Ryker immediately notices. "We should get you home," he says. "It's been a long 24 hours."

I nod and grab Liberty's leash off the edge of Jax's desk. "Tell Easton hello," I say and clip the leash on her collar. "And, thank you again for babysitting."

"Any time," Jax says.

"I would've offered, too," Griff says. "But Lexi has a cat. I don't think Whimsy would approve."

I laugh. "No problem. I'm going to go load Liberty in the Jeep."

Ryker nods. "Okay. Be out in a second."

I give the guys a little wave and head out to my car. Suddenly, I feel like I'm half asleep on my feet. The adventure, danger and excitement from the last few days hits me hard and I'm ready to climb into my bed and go to sleep.

I help Liberty into the car and slide into the driver's seat. A minute later, Ryker opens the door and gets inside. On our way back to his place, the ride is pretty quiet. Then, I'm pulling up in front of his condo.

I don't know what to do or say and I tighten my grip on the

steering wheel. Finally, I turn to him and he's watching me closely, his gaze intent. "Thank you," I whisper. "For everything."

Suddenly, he leans forward, tilts my chin up and kisses me. It's soft and sweet. "Goodbye, Avery," he says. Then, he slips out, shutting the door behind him.

My eyes slide shut and my heart stops mid-beat.

Goodbye, Avery.

His words sound so final. Like everything that happened between us is over.

With a heavy heart, I drive back to North Hollywood and return to my quiet apartment. I change into a nightshirt, wash my face, brush my teeth and crawl under my covers. Liberty jumps onto the bed and curls up beside me.

And, I've never felt so utterly alone.

I wish Ryker was lying next to me. God, I miss the warmth of his hard body pressed to mine. I miss his kisses and caresses.

How am I supposed to just continue on with my life as though we never slept together in Columbia? As though I never fell in love with him? As though I don't want him by my side every day for the rest of my life?

I know he's pulling away because he thinks it's for the best. He thinks his demons and the things he's done in the past make him somehow unworthy of love.

But, that couldn't be any further from the truth.

I've never known a man who deserves love as much as Ryker does. Time and again in Columbia, he risked his life for me. He's honorable and brave.

I just wish he could see what I see.

It isn't over yet, I think, and that gives me a flicker of hope. We still have to track down John Miller and find out Valkyrie's true identity. Only then will my name be cleared.

And, maybe then Ryker can find some sort of peace with his past.

I'll do anything in my power to help him forgive himself and bury his demons. I know better than anyone what it's like to live with guilt and blame. But, for the first time in a very long time, I see a light at the end of the tunnel.

I let out a small sigh and reach over to pet Liberty.

I'm going to figure that man out, I decide. I'm going to help him realize that he deserves love and tear down his walls. And, in the process, I only hope he realizes that he cares for me as much as I care for him.

Because, at this point, I realize that a life without Ryker Flynn is going to be a lonely, lonely existence.

2 2

RYKER

I watch Avery drive away and feel terrible. I basically just said goodbye to her and it doesn't feel right. I know that doing the honorable thing is hard sometimes, but this is more than that. This is like half my soul just got ripped away.

Dammit.

Am I wrong? I wonder. Instead of pushing her away, should I be fighting for her? *No.* I can't be selfish. I have to put what's best for her above all else. Including my own needs and wants. Avery called me a martyr before and maybe I am, but I have to be.

I flip a light on and look over my cold, empty condo. I know there's always a crash after the mission, but I just feel depressed. A huge part of me wishes I had invited Avery home, but that would've only led to sex. And, I'm trying to keep my distance, not fall harder for her than I already have.

God, this is going to be hard. Avery is the one woman I always wanted and, for a short time, I had her. And, our short time together was so sweet. Utterly incredible. Now, I have to go back to how it was before. And, it fucking sucks.

With a sigh, I wander over to the fridge and pull out a beer. I twist the cap off and take a long swig. Sometimes drinking helps, but several minutes later, I know that it won't help tonight. The only thing that will make things right is having Avery back in my bed.

But, she's back off-limits and I just have to suck it up.

I set the empty beer bottle on the counter and think back to after Avery and Liberty walked out of Platinum Security. Jax and Griff instantly pounced, demanding details like a couple of gossipy women.

"Well?" Griff asked.

I looked from one to the other and rolled my eyes. "Yes, okay," I said. There was no point trying to deny it. These two would just find out because that's what they do. Dig shit up on people.

Griff gave a whoop and punched his fist in the air like a frat boy and Jax just smiled. I didn't tell them that I was planning to end it with her, though.

I wish I could just figure out a way to make peace with my past and accept the stains on my soul. To feel worthy of love.

To deserve Avery Archer.

I may as well just wish for a million dollars to fall into my lap while I'm at it.

After taking my usual five minutes in the bathroom to get ready for bed, I wander down to my room and fall into my big, empty bed. Soon, being with Avery in Columbia will just seem like a dream and I try to convince myself that I'll eventually forget all about it.

But, deep down, I know that's not true. More than likely, once this case is over, I'm going to spiral into the darkest and deepest depression I've ever experienced.

After a long night of tossing and turning and missing Avery's body beside mine, I roll out of bed and go for a brisk early morning run. I like running when the sun is just coming up on the horizon and before most people are up and about. There's something nice about the quiet and peace.

My arms and legs pump as I push myself. I always time my runs and challenge myself to maintain what I was expected to do during my BUD/S training-- four miles in 32 minutes or less. I'll probably beat my usual time today, though, because I'm running like the hounds of hell are nipping at my heels.

After my run and coming in under the 32 minutes, I hop in the shower. And, instantly remember the shower Avery and I took together. *God.* Thoughts of soaping her up make my pulse pound and my dick hard.

I shake my head, trying to shove the erotic thoughts out of my head and slather my face with shaving cream. It feels good to lose the beard from Colombia. We always kept a beard during missions, especially to the Middle East, and nowadays, other than a little scruff now and then, I prefer to be clean-shaven.

Having a beard takes me back to darker times and feelings.

I get out of the shower, dry off and throw on a gray t-shirt and black cargo pants. When my cell rings a minute later, I grab it and see Harlow's name.

"Harlow," I say.

"Hi, Ryker," she says. "I found some info on John Miller. I'm heading over to the office now. Can you come by and I'll fill you in?"

"I'm on my way," I say.

Ten minutes later, I walk into Platinum Security. It's quiet except for the tapping of a keyboard and no one else is in yet except Harlow and me. We're both the early birds of our little group. "Hey," I say and step into her office. I hand her a coffee, sit down and sip mine.

"Thanks, I needed this," she says and takes a long drink. "I've been up most of the night tracking this asshole down."

One of the things I've noticed about Harlow is she swears like a sailor. I find it amusing and hide a grin. "What have you got?" I ask and lean forward.

"John Miller is one of the aliases for Brian Little. Forty-five years old and a former CIA turned hacker. Apparently, he leaked some classified information and his days at the agency ended. Forced retirement so to speak. Though they never proved he got paid for the information, I'd be willing to bet my last dime that he did, liked the feeling and proceeded to supply highly-classified info to others. Anyway, I did some digging and have a Reseda address for you."

Perfect, I think. *Today, I'm going to pay a visit to John Miller.* "Thanks, Harlow, you're a lifesaver."

149

"Easy peasy," she says.

As a plan starts to formulate in my head, Harlow studies me over the edge of her laptop with inquisitive bluish-gray eyes. "I really like Avery," she says, gauging my reaction.

I'm not sure where she's going with this so I just nod.

"I want to invite her to go out for drinks with me and Lexi. If that's alright," she adds, eyeing me closely.

Lexi Ryder is Griff's fiancée and Harlow's good friend.

I shrug, trying to play it off. "Avery is allowed to hang out with whoever she wants," I say. "It's none of my business."

Harlow arches a dark brow. "Hmm. I kind of got the feeling you two are an item."

I shake my head. "No, we're just-" *What are we?* I wonder. *Hell if I know.* Again, she lifts that brow and I frown. "I have to go," I say and stand up.

"Sorry," she says quickly. "I didn't mean to pry. It's just…"

Her voice trails off and I pause.

"You two look really good together." Harlow smiles then looks back down at her keyboard and begins tapping away. "If I find out anything else about Miller, I'll let you know."

"Thanks," I mumble and walk down to my office. I sit down at my desk, fire my computer up and stare at the screen, thinking about Avery and wondering if we really do look good together. I picture her blonde hair and pretty blue eyes. She's tall, nearly 5'8", with a slim, yet deliciously curvy build. I'm so different with dark hair and brown eyes. Dark to her light.

I have no idea how much time I spend daydreaming about Avery, but at some point, Jax pokes his head in the doorway.

"You're in early," he says. "Got a lead?"

"Yeah, Harlow got an address for John Miller. I'm planning to take a trip there." I reach for my coffee, take a sip and realize it's ice cold.

"Why don't Griff and I go with you? In case he gives you a hard time."

"Sure," I say. "Back up is always appreciated."

"Griff probably looks the least threatening of the three of us so why don't we have him approach Miller first. Then, we'll push our way in and give Miller an ultimatum. Either give up Valkyrie's identity or get his ass kicked."

"Have I mentioned how much I enjoy working for you, Jax?" I ask.

"Hey, whatever gets the job done. Guys like Miller are scum, anyway."

"Truth," I say.

Two hours later, Jax, Griff and I head over to Reseda in my Expedition. The address leads us to a small house which makes me think John Miller isn't making too much money selling classified information anymore or he's trying to stay off the radar and not attract attention.

Probably the latter. *Once a rat always a rat*, I think.

I park a block away and the three of us head up the street. We go up the walkway and Griff knocks on the front door while Jax and I stay out of sight, off to the side. For a moment, it's quiet. Then, we hear someone move inside. I signal Jax and we split, each making our way around the house and to the back. Meanwhile, Griff holds his position up front to make sure our target doesn't escape that way.

I reach for my SIG Sauer, my backup since the other was lost in Columbia, and keep low, my back against the side of the house as I circle around to the rear yard. The moment Jax and I spot each other, the back door opens and a man runs out.

I take off after him and bring him down in a tackle before he even gets halfway across the yard. Then, I yank him up and Jax moves in, his Glock 22 aimed at the guy.

"What the hell?" the guy sputters.

"Let's talk," I say and shove him back toward the house.

"Who are you guys?" he asks.

"The better question is who're you, John Miller?"

He curses under his breath and I push him inside. "Anyone else home?" I ask.

"No," he grumbles.

"Are you lying?"

"No, okay? It's just me."

We step into the kitchen and I shove him down into a chair, my fingers digging into his shoulder. Jax lets Griff in through the front and they do a quick sweep of the one-level home.

"Clear," Griff calls.

"Clear," Jax calls.

A moment later, they step into the kitchen.

"No one else here," Jax confirms.

"I told you," John Miller says.

"Shut up," I say and squeeze his shoulder. The guy looks like a rat and I hate him on sight. Weasels like this who profit off selling classified secrets put this country in danger and make me sick. I hope he gives me a reason to fuck him up because I'm itching to do it.

Jax and Griff must notice how pissed I look because they move in and quickly take control of the situation. Jax puts a zip tie around Miller's wrists and Griff leans against the counter, arms crossed. Both have more experience interrogating prisoners so it's fine by me. I'll just stand by and be ready to kick his ass.

"We have a few questions for you, Mr. Miller," Griff says. "Or, is it Mr. Little? Brian Little, right? Former CIA who was booted for selling classified intel."

Griff's voice is low and even, but there's a veiled threat present.

"I don't know what you're talking about," Little says in a snarky tone.

That's all I need. Without warning, I aim my fist for his jaw and let it fly. The hit slams his head to the side and the good thing is that the sucker is attached or I think it would've spun all the way around on his shoulders. Blood trickles down his lip. "Try again," I growl.

Little's eyes widen and now he knows we aren't playing. We mean business and if he doesn't give us answers, I'm going to enjoy beating the shit out of him. The rat lifts his zip-tied hands up to block his face from more punches. *As if that's going to help,* I think.

"Okay, okay," he mutters. "I don't want any trouble."

"We want to know about the intel you provided Avery Archer regarding Operation Armageddon," Griff says. "Where'd you get it?"

Brian Little thinks for a minute then shrugs. "That was years ago. I mean, how am I supposed to remember-"

Bam! My fist connects with his cheek and it's going to leave a nice bruise. "Wrong answer."

"Shit, alright, stop hitting me," Little cries.

"All you have to do is tell us the truth," Griff says.

Little sighs. "I was paid to feed Avery bad intel. Someone didn't want that mission to succeed."

"Who didn't?" Griff asks.

"There was a rogue agent getting paid to protect Antonio Castillo. When he heard about the mission to take his bread and butter down, he had to make sure that didn't happen."

"Who is this rogue agent?" Griff presses.

"I don't know. Just went by the code name Valkyrie."

We all exchange a look. Most likely, Little is telling the truth and he and Valkyrie never met in person. Only took care of business through burner phones and other untraceable means.

"You never met Valkyrie?"

"No. We communicated online and with burners."

"Any guess about Valkyrie's true identity?"

"No clue. He used a voice distorting machine when we spoke."

"You keep saying 'he'-- are you sure about that?" Griff asks.

Little frowns. "I mean, I guess Valkyrie could be a woman. I told you I don't know."

Griff looks over at me and Jax. I don't think we're going to get any more information out of this asshole. I squeeze my hand into a fist and know that five of the best and strongest men in the world died because of this man's greed.

Five good men with families who loved them.

My nostrils flare and I see red like a bull. I need to inflict some of the pain that I've felt over the last two years on this fucker.

"Let's go," Jax says to Griff. Then, he looks at me. "You've got one minute, Flynn. If you're not out by then, we will drag you out."

I give him a sharp nod, all of my anger, frustration and pent-up guilt and misery directed toward Brian Little, aka John Miller. The moment Griff and Jax turn to walk out, I grab Little by his shirt and haul him up out of the chair.

"Stand up, you coward," I growl. I pull my knife, slice the zip tie off and attack. Blind rage propels me and Brian Little doesn't stand a chance. I'm here to deliver justice for the death of my best friend and the others on my team.

As I punch Little into the ground, I don't think he even tries to fight back. "Fucking weak coward," I hiss between blows. "Do you have any idea what you did?"

Thirty seconds into the beating, Little stops trying to block my blows. I think he's out cold. I huff out a breath, lean back on my haunches and wipe my bloody knuckles off on his shirt. I stand up, deliver a final kick to his ribs and stalk out.

Jax and Griff wait outside on the front lawn.

"Ready?" Jax asks.

I nod.

"Feel better?" Griff asks.

"I thought I would, but…" I let out a breath. "He didn't even fight back."

"Well, that takes the fun out of it."

I don't say anything. Just head down the block back to my Expedition. Even though I just beat the pulp out of the guy who led my team into a slaughter, I feel no satisfaction.

In fact, I've never felt more empty.

23

AVERY

The next morning, after a long night of tossing and turning, I go out for a run with Liberty and then return and decide to check my emails. I have some work-related jobs that I need to respond to and also set up some new client photo shoots. After everything that happened, it seems strange to be doing the same old mundane thing. Like everything is back to normal.

Because it doesn't feel normal. Not having Ryker in my life feels all wrong.

I reach for my phone, wanting to call him, but hesitate. What if he doesn't want to hear from me? I think. There was no missing the finality in his goodbye last night. Remembering that makes my heart hurt.

If he has any important news, he will call me.

In the meantime, I have to keep living my life and not mope around and cry over a man who doesn't want me.

With a heavy heart and mind, I pull up the photo shoot of the couple I shot last week before we left for Colombia and begin to go through the pictures. The love in their eyes is clear and I feel a sharp prick of envy. They chose each other and now are planning to spend the rest of their lives together.

I've never had anyone choose me.

I ignore the wave of self-pity and organize and edit the best photos. A few hours later, I write a note to the couple and email the pictures to them. I glance at my watch and see it's barely noon. What am I going to do with myself for the rest of the day?

For the rest of my life? I wonder.

It seems like time moves so much slower without Ryker around. I've cared about him for so long and, over the years, those feelings only intensified. But, they never reached the level they're at currently because now I know firsthand how amazing he is and, God, I want him in my life.

Okay, Ave, so what are you going to do about it? I think. *Sit here and dwell on what could've been or get your ass up and fight for your man?*

I'm going to fight for my man, I decide. I'll get ready and stop by Platinum Security and see if they have any new leads. This is my case, after all, and I want to find out more about John Miller and Valkyrie.

I put a little extra effort in my appearance and hope it makes Ryker look twice. I curl my hair, put on some makeup and slip into jeans and a fitted t-shirt that says US Navy. Then I spritz myself with my Pink Sugar perfume and tug on a pair of black boots.

I toss Liberty a treat and head out the door. The day is sunny and warm, a perfect 75 degrees. North Hollywood may not be the most happening spot in LA, but I appreciate the quiet neighborhood. My Jeep Wrangler is parked at the curb and as I head over, I notice a fancy car slow down as it passes.

I'd hardly consider myself a luxury car fanatic, but something strikes me when I look at the sleek, black car. *Unease*, I realize. It's low to the ground and the rumble of the engine promises extreme horse-power. I unlock my car and watch the sports car pass. It's an Aston Martin.

I slide into the Jeep and snap a photo of the car with my phone. I'm not even sure why. Just a gut feeling and I'm always taking pictures of things, anyway. No one in this neighborhood can afford a car like that. Probably someone from Beverly Hills who wandered over the hill and got lost looking for Ventura Boulevard with all of its upscale boutiques and shopping.

With thoughts of Ryker in my head, I pull out and head toward the 101 N freeway. Traffic is moving and I hit the gas, merging between cars. I'm going to play it casual when I get to the office. See if Harlow turned up any information yet. I really like her and hope we can be friends. God knows, I could use a friend.

Right as I hit the first exit for Hollywood, an SUV comes out of nowhere and cuts me off. *Shit.* I hit the brakes and honk. People drive like idiots here, I think. Then, the SUV slams on its brakes and I almost rear end it.

What a dick, I think, and check my mirror, getting ready to switch lanes. But, I can't because another SUV pulls up alongside me, blocking me in. Out of the blue, the driver veers into me and runs me off the road. The other car is still in front and, together, they force me into the breakdown lane beneath an overpass.

What the hell?

When I see the SUV doors open and two masked men get out, I reach over and lock my doors. I have no idea what's going on, but I know these guys are bad news. I glance around, searching for a weapon, wishing I had Ryker's SIG Sauer.

The first man stops beside my window and motions for me to roll the window down. *Like hell,* I think. When he reveals a gun, my stomach plummets. He taps on the window with the end of the gun and I roll the window down a tiny amount.

"If you dig into Operation Armageddon any further, you die. Understand?"

I nod my head.

"Say it," he demands.

"I understand," I force out.

Then, he lifts his gun and fires.

Oh, shit. I hit the deck, covering my ears, my last thoughts of Ryker's handsome, smiling face. But, he's not shooting at me and, instead, blows out all four of the Jeep's tires. Curled up, half my body under the steering wheel, I hear the SUVs squeal off.

My heart thunders, but the fear quickly turns to anger. *Assholes.* Now, I'm stuck on the side of the freeway. And, of course, I never renewed my AAA card. I pull myself up, reach for my cell phone and call Ryker.

It takes him about 15 minutes to find me and when he sidles up alongside my car and sees the wrecked tires, a murderous look darkens his face. I open the door and he pulls me out and into his arms. "Are you okay?" he asks, face lost in my hair.

"I'm fine," I say. "Just pissed about my tires."

Ryker pulls back, presses a kiss to my forehead and studies me closely. "Did you get a look at them?"

I shake my head. "They were wearing masks. And, they warned me to stop digging into Operation Armageddon."

"What did they say exactly?" When I tell him, Ryker's whisky eyes turn thunderous with rage. "C'mon," he says and takes my hand.

We head over to his Expedition and he pulls out his phone and calls AAA. Of course, he would keep his auto membership current. The man is always prepared. After telling them to take it to a nearby garage and put new tires on it, he hangs up and drives us to Platinum Security.

Once there, we all head into Jax's office and they have me relate what happened.

"Seems like our buddy Brian Little reported back to Valkyrie," Griff says.

"Brian Little?" I ask.

"Harlow found out John Miller's real identity is Brian Little," Ryker says. "We paid him a visit this morning."

"Why didn't you tell me?" I demand, feeling a spike of annoyance. "I would've come."

"That's why we didn't tell you," he says.

I place a hand on my hips and narrow my eyes at the three of them. "I can handle myself just fine, thank you very much."

"We have no doubts," Jax says, "but, we wanted to keep you out of it. For this very reason."

"Well, I'm in it up to my eyeballs so keep me in the damn loop. Understand?"

The three of them exchange looks after I scold them. A moment later, Harlow walks in. "I heard what happened," she says. "Are you okay?"

"Fine," I say between gritted teeth. "I just wish these three would understand that I'm not some porcelain doll. I can handle myself and I don't need their constant protection."

"We understand, Ave," Ryker says. "I should've called you this morning after Harlow filled me in. I'm sorry."

His apology catches me off-guard and I feel my anger melt away. He's being completely sincere not just trying to placate me and I appreciate it. I know he only wants me to be safe, but he also needs to understand that this is ultimately about clearing my name. I need to be involved and I need to know everything in detail that they uncover.

I sigh and give a small nod. "I don't mean to sound ungrateful because I appreciate everything you guys have done. I just need you to understand that it's important that you keep me involved. Not on a need-to-know basis."

"Roger that," Ryker says and Griff and Jax nod their agreement.

"So, what happened this morning?" I ask.

Again, they all exchange a look and I hope they don't plan to keep anything from me. I wait and Griff says, "Harlow tracked down an address in Reseda for Brian Little, aka John Miller. We conducted a little interrogation and he confirmed feeding you bogus intel."

My heart speeds up. "And, Valkyrie?"

"Claims he doesn't know his true identity."

"And you believed him?" I ask.

"We do."

This takes me by surprise. "Why? He's a liar and a traitor. He-"

"He told us everything he knew," Ryker says, eyes and voice flat. "I made sure."

Oh. That means they used force. My gaze drops to Ryker's knuckles and, for the first time, I notice how raw and swollen they look. I just nod.

"So, let's review what we know," Harlow says and lifts her tablet. "John Miller, your source, had a secret contact, aka Valkyrie, who went rogue and was on Antonio Castillo's payroll. Paid to keep the drug lord off the CIA's radar. But, Castillo practically runs the entire Columbian drug trade so let's be realistic-- he's on everyone's radar. When Castillo was tied to selling arms to the Middle East, the US government decided to do something about it. CIA intel showed Castillo had a meeting with an ally out in the jungle and only a handful of his men would accompany him. No more than 15-20 people total."

Harlow looks up and everyone waits for her to continue. "Ryker's team was tasked with going in and neutralizing Castillo. But, the mission, Operation Armageddon, was a complete clusterfuck. Intel was wrong and there were nearly 80 guerillas waiting to take the six-man SEAL team out. Because Valkyrie was protecting Castillo."

I look over at Ryker and see a storm of emotion in his eyes. Without thinking, I move closer and lay my hand over his. He laces his fingers through mine and squeezes.

Harlow taps on her tablet then flips it around to show us an image of a warrior woman in full armor and a winged helmet. "It's interesting to note that Valkyrie are the beautiful warrior maidens of Norse mythology. Their job is to choose which soldiers will die in battle. I wouldn't rule out our target as being female."

I glance down at the other image that popped up when Harlow searched for Valkyrie and see a sleek-looking car. The same one I saw earlier today. "Oh, my God. Harlow, what kind of car is that?"

Harlow taps the screen, enlarging the image, and shows me. "Aston Martin Valkyrie. Why?"

"That same exact car drove by my apartment earlier. I remember thinking it was weird because it rolled right by me and almost came to a stop. Right before I got in my Jeep and ran off the road."

Ryker's gaze snaps over to me. "Did you get a look at the driver?"

I shake my head. "Windows were too dark."

"I don't suppose many people drive that kind of car in North Hollywood," Jax says.

Harlow pulls up the car's stats. "I'd say probably not, considering its price tag is $3.2 million and it packs a V12 engine that has 1,160 horsepower."

Griff whistles under his breath.

"But, I'm willing to bet someone on a drug lord's payroll can afford it," I say. "Someone like Valkyrie." Then, I remember the photo I took. I pull my phone out and hand it to Ryker. "I forgot, I took a picture of it."

A huge smile lights his face. "We have partial plates," he says. "Harlow?"

"On it," she says. "Can you email me the pic?"

I nod and Ryker hands me the phone back. "Good job, Ave," he says. He looks so proud and I can't help but glow at his approval. I email the picture to Harlow then let out a breath. We have something to go on now. A lead that could give us Valkyrie's true identity.

It has to be Valkyrie. This can't just be a coincidence.

I feel a wave of relief knowing that we're one step closer to bringing this person down and clearing my name. I just wish there was a way to bring Ryker's team back.

I notice his face suddenly darken. "If this is Valkyrie then they know where you live," he says.

"It's not safe for you to go back," Jax says. "You're more than welcome to stay at Easton's."

"She's staying with me," Ryker says. He slants a possessive look my way. "You and Liberty. Okay?" he asks me.

"Okay," I say.

God knows, there's nowhere on Earth I'd rather be.

24

RYKER

The more I think about it, the more angry I get.

My scabbed knuckles turn white around the steering wheel, and my thoughts are consumed by the fact that Avery could've been in serious danger today. She could've been hurt, kidnapped or even killed. I'm going to track this asshole down and when I'm through, Valkyrie will never take another breath again.

From the corner of my eye, I look over at Avery in the passenger seat. We just picked up Liberty and an overnight bag for Avery. Originally, I planned on putting her in the guest room, but after realizing that I could've lost her forever today, that's not happening.

She's sleeping next to me where she'll be safe. Well, safe from everyone but me.

No, I think. You know the deal. *Hands off.*

It's going to be hard, but I need to behave myself. Avery's safety is my top priority. But, she needs to behave herself, too, because I'm only so strong when it comes to resisting her charms.

When we get to my condo, she feeds Liberty her dinner and we order a pizza. I keep looking over at her and something seems different. Avery always looks beautiful, but for some reason, she looks extra beautiful tonight. When my cock twitches, I grind my teeth together.

Here we go, I think.

"Thank you for letting us stay with you," she says.

"Of course." When I meet her gaze, she's watching me with those cornflower baby blues and the twitch turns into a full-blown erection. I look away and my eyes slide shut. *Dammit.* The idea of potentially losing her today makes me want to pull her into my arms, carry her down to my bed and make love to her all night.

I pop up off the couch and head toward the kitchen. "Want something to drink?" I ask. I open the fridge. "I've got Corona and water."

"Corona works," she calls back.

"Great," I say and try to adjust the heavy bulge in my pants. I take my time, hoping things below my belt will calm down, and open the beers and pop a slice of lime in each opening. No one has the power to affect me like Avery does. Normally, I have a lot of self-control, but when it comes to her, I have very little.

God, all I want to do is walk back in there, push her down and slide up into her warm, wet body.

I scratch my hands through my short hair and focus on something else. Like the guy I almost beat to death this morning. Actually, that's a bit dramatic. I could have, but I didn't. Not even close. When I hear Avery move up beside me, I turn and hand her the beer.

"Thanks," she says.

I nod, take a long swig.

When the doorbell rings, I swipe up my wallet and jog to the front door. I need to keep my distance, but, fuck, it's hard. I pay the delivery guy and walk back into the kitchen. I open the lid and we each take a slice smothered in pepperoni.

I lean a hip on the counter and she does the same, eyeing me closely as she chews. I try to avoid her gaze, but it's getting harder and harder. "What?" I murmur and swallow.

"Nothing. You just look extra handsome tonight."

My pulse kicks up a notch. She's going to make this so damn difficult for me. I need to lay down the law. "Nothing can happen between us tonight. You know that, right?"

But, Avery only shrugs.

"Ave-"

"Why is the decision solely yours?" she asks.

I hear that spark in her voice. I guess she has a point.

"You're so used to giving out orders to others, but I'm not one of your soldiers," she says and tilts her chin up. "I am a woman who has needs and wants. And, I want you, Ryker." She drops the pizza slice back in the box and walks right up to me. Takes my face in her hands. "In my bed and inside of me," she adds in a low voice.

Christ, she's killing me. Wearing down my resistance, making me want her so badly that it physically hurts.

"Don't you want me, Ryker?" she asks.

"Of course, I fucking want you," I hiss. I slam my mouth down and capture hers in a heated, demanding kiss. My hands move around to cup her ass and then yank her up against my steel cock. When she writhes against me, I groan into her mouth. "I can say no to anyone but you," I whisper and scoop her up, spinning her around and sitting her on the counter.

"Good," she says and reaches down to pull my shirt up and off. Her hands slide over my chest and my breath hitches. I look down, watching as her fingers glide over my pecs, upper arms, ribs and abs. She swirls a finger around my navel then lifts it to touch the scar on my shoulder. Her index finger moves down to touch each scar from the five bullets that hit me. "Who is able to survive being shot five times?" she asks, furrowing her brow.

I rub the frown away between her eyebrows. Some might say I was lucky, but luck had nothing to do with it. I was just able to hang on a little longer than the others because I would've died out there, too. No doubt about it.

Avery leans forward and places a kiss on each scar and my breathing increases. The feel of her warm lips against my skin is more than I can bear. Then, her fingers unsnap my cargo pants and slip inside.

Fuck. Those slim fingers stroke from base to tip and I push my hips forward. She shoves my pants down further and I kick them aside, giving her full access to do whatever she wants. "Sit," she says and pushes a hand against my chest.

Without a word, I drop down in a chair at the table and she gives me a long, heated look before hopping off the counter and strolling over. The sway of her hips is too good, too tempting, and I reach out and grab the loopholes in her jeans and pull her closer. Her breasts are right in front of my face and strain against her US Navy t-shirt.

"I like your shirt," I say and nuzzle my face against her chest.

Avery slowly lowers between my spread legs. She drags a hand down my taut abs, gaze holding mine, and runs her tongue between her lips. Then, her hands and mouth start to work their magic. My head drops back and my hips jerk.

The feel of her warm, wet mouth sliding up and down my cock is almost too much to handle. I lift my head back up and watch her, sucking, cheeks hollowed out, and I groan long and hard. Then, she hums. "Holy shit, Ave," I hiss and wrap my fingers through her long blonde hair.

She keeps going and I don't have the strength to stop her. I'm throbbing, pulsating, and she's sucking me into a frenzy. Pleasure slams through me and I come hard, my body lifting off the chair. Avery moves up, straddling my lap, and licks her lips. "God, you know just how to do that. So good," I say, still panting and barely able to string a complete sentence together.

"I'm glad you like it," she says and starts to pull her t-shirt up.

I help Avery slide the shirt up and over her head. I catch a glimpse of pink satin before she leans into my naked chest and kisses me. It's slow, but demanding. As our mouths part, she catches my lower lip between hers and sucks.

My hands move up and cup the soft satin bra, molding her breasts. As pretty as it is, I want it out of the way. I reach around, unsnap it and watch it slide down her arms. "God, you're beautiful," I say and dip my head to worship one of her perfect, full breasts with my mouth. She arches back as I suck and tease the nipple into a pointed crest. Then, I swirl my tongue over to the other one.

Avery's hips gyrate against me and I reach down and crook a finger in the waistband of her pants. "Jeans off," I say.

She pulls back and gives me a saucy smile. "I thought we weren't doing this."

"Off. Now."

Avery slides off my lap, then makes a big production out of unzipping and sliding off her jeans. Her little show is getting me hot and hard all over again. Her gaze drops down to my lap and she smirks.

Finally, she kicks the jeans aside and stands before me in those tiny pink satin panties. Something in me snaps and I pull her forward, rip the panties off and yank her down on my lap again. Legs spread, she straddles me and wraps her arms up and around my neck. I reach down between us and find her swollen center.

"So wet," I murmur and stroke her folds.

"Yes," she sighs and pushes up against my hand. When I slip a finger inside her, she grinds and writhes. "Please," she begs. "Get inside me."

My mind is a blur, hazy with want. Desire pounds through me and I grip her hips, line her up with the tip of my cock, and surge upward. As I slide up into her wet warmth, Avery slams down and what was slow just became fast.

Our bodies move together, meeting, slamming, grinding. "Harder," she cries.

I reach down and rub her clit until she's digging her nails into my upper arms and making mewling sounds in the back of her throat. God, it's sexy. "Come for me, Ave."

We move fast and hard and when she explodes in an orgasm, I'm a second behind her. It's like a blinding explosion and our bodies surge up. I feel her body contract around me and a shudder rips through me as I empty into her.

The afterglow is bright and the pleasure that washes over me makes me wonder why I keep trying to push her away. Why do I keep trying to run from the best thing that's ever happened to me?

Fuck. I forgot protection. The thought hits me and brings me back

166

to reality. I slide out and curse myself for being so careless. I have never forgotten before. Ever. "Ave, I forgot-"

"It's okay," she says, reading my mind. "I'm clean if that's what you're worried about."

"No. I mean, I'm clean, too. But, you're not on birth control. Are you?"

"No, but I keep track of my cycle. We're fine."

I let out a breath and kiss her. And, it's weird, but a part of me wonders what it would be like to have a baby with her. To get married and have a family with this amazing woman. The thought doesn't scare me at all. Quite the opposite, in fact.

Shit, a morbid part of me hopes I did just knock her up. Because being with Avery is like finding an anchor in a storm-tossed sea. There's something about her that grounds me, makes me feel safe. Going to bed each night with her and waking up each morning beside her...I can't think of anything that I'd like more. It sounds like a perfect way to spend the rest of my life.

And, even though I know my soul is stained and full of dark sins, I can't seem to stay away from her no matter how hard I try.

I'm in love with her. Completely and totally in love with Avery Archer. I think a small part of me has always loved her.

Obviously I can't tell her, but I can show her. I plan to spend the rest of the night showing her.

I stand, pull Avery up into my arms and head down to my bedroom.

25

AVERY

od, I love this man, I think.

But, I know if I tell him, he will run. Already, he keeps trying to push me away because he thinks he isn't good enough. I just want to yell in his face that he's a goddamn hero. But, of course, he doesn't want to hear it. He's not used to praise for his actions. Only receiving orders, doing his job and coming home.

I grasp his face in my hands and kiss him senseless as he carries me to his bed. I can't get enough of him. His big, strong body makes me feel safe and he has such a sense of honor. When we're together, I feel the goodness inside him. I just wish he did, too.

I fall back against his pillows and his sheets smell like him. Like pine-scented soap. *Mmm, delish.* He starts to kiss his way up my body and I squirm out from under him and push him back. "Lay down, soldier," I order.

His bed is big and I watch him lay on his back, stretching out all 6'4" of himself, eyes watching me with keen interest. *Those eyes.* Brown with flecks of gold that always remind me of expensive whisky and all I want to do is drink him. Every last drop.

I straddle his waist and splay my hands across his rock-hard abs.

Dented grooves, the result of thousands of sit-ups, rise to meet my fingers. "I love touching you," I say and trace up over his granite pecs.

"You can touch me all you want," he says and digs his fingers into my hips.

"Do you know what I thought the first time I saw you?" I ask.

I feel him tense beneath me and his gaze holds mine.

"That you were the biggest, strongest, most handsome man I'd ever seen."

His nostrils flare and his large hands glide up and over my breasts. "I thought you looked like an angel," he whispers.

A small smile curves my mouth and I lean into his caresses. "Ryker," I purr. "You're the angel. An archangel to be feared. A warrior who defends and protects." I lean forward and swirl a tongue around a flat nipple.

He reaches for my face and pulls me down for a long, heated kiss. I slide my tongue against his and feel the desire building again. God, I could spend a month in bed with this man and still crave more.

"I can't get enough of you," he murmurs, rounding his hands over my ass and squeezing. "You're like...sunlight."

I reach down and wrap my hands around his long, hard length. Then, I guide him right where I need and want him. As I start to slide down, I watch the expression on his face change from desire to need. He lifts his hips, sliding up, and I take him to the hilt, grinding down.

"Christ," he murmurs.

I tilt my body, positioning myself just right, and start to rock my hips, setting a slow and burning rhythm. He thrusts up, moving with me, and my head drops forward, hair cascading over his chest. He grabs a fistful, twining his fingers through it.

"Ride me, baby," he murmurs. "Ride me hard."

I squeeze my thighs and move faster. One of Ryker's hands drifts down and when he starts massaging my clit, I throw my head back and ride him harder, faster. The friction increases between our bodies and I drag my nails down his chest, feeling the swell of pleasure build.

My gaze drops down and he watches me intently with passion-glazed eyes, one hand digging into my hip and the other doing unbelievably delicious things that make me clench harder around him.

"Oh, God," I cry, slamming against him. It's all too much now and his circling finger pushes me over the edge. My climax is intense and powerful waves ripple through my lower body all the way down to my toes.

Ryker surges up with a groan and spills deep inside me. I drop down on his chest, hair spread all around us, and take a moment to catch my breath. Then, I press a kiss to the scar on his shoulder.

His hand strokes my hair out of my face and skims down my back. I slip off him and he pulls me into his arms. His lips press against my forehead and then I snuggle down deep against his chest. He pulls the sheet up over us and I smell pine all around me, lulling me to sleep.

A few hours later, my eyes flutter open and Ryker is watching me. We're facing each other, sharing a pillow, noses practically touching. I smile shyly and pull back. "What?" I ask.

He runs a finger down my nose and gives me a crooked grin. "I love looking at you."

My heart thumps harder. "Not as much as I love looking at you." I slide a hand over the tattoo on his upper arm. "Do you miss being a SEAL?"

"I'll be a SEAL til the day I die."

"I mean, do you miss going out on missions?"

Instead of answering, he reaches over and touches the hollow above my collarbone. "Your heart is pounding," he says.

"Because you're touching me," I whisper.

A mixture of emotions flashes across his face. "You like when I touch you?"

"I *love* when you touch me, Ryker."

His hand glides up the curve of my neck and cups my jaw.

I lay my hand over his. "You had doubts?" I ask.

He glances away, worries his bottom lip for a second. "Sometimes I feel..."

"What?" I whisper.

"I don't feel worthy of you. I've done things..." He heaves out a sigh. "I have blood on my hands and sometimes I think if I touch you then I'm making you dirty, too. And, I hate that."

"I want your hands on me, Ryker. Nothing feels as good as your big, strong hands on my body." I see a slight wave of relief flicker through his eyes and I lace my fingers through his. "If you ever stop touching me, I'm going to kick your ass."

Ryker lets out a low, half-laugh and buries his face in my hair. "It's just hard, Ave. I try, but..." He huffs out a breath. "I'm so fucking damaged. I wish every day that I was good enough for you."

His low voice sounds tortured and I pull him close, cradling him against my chest. It's not fair, I think, and feel tears prick my eyes. Ryker has been through so much and my heart bleeds for him.

I want to tell him I love him. So fucking badly. I let out a long, low breath and run my fingers through his cropped hair. "Ryker..." I whisper, gathering my courage. "Do you have any idea how much I love you?"

His entire body tenses against me. *Oh, God,* I think. *What did I do?*

I don't feel him breathing. He's just...frozen. But, after a minute, he pulls back and looks deeply into my eyes. "You love me?"

I'm so nervous and suddenly all my words are lodged in my throat. So, I just nod.

He lets out a shaky breath then leans in and kisses me. It's soft and tender. But, I still have no idea what he's thinking. When the kiss ends, I pull back and search his eyes. "Do you care for me? At least a little bit?" I ask.

Multiple emotions flick over his face and he gazes at me like he's seeing me for the first time again. "It's always been you, Ave," he says in a raw voice.

The air whooshes out of me and I press up into him, relief and love pouring through me. Ryker drags me up and kisses me again, his lips devouring mine, and I kiss him back with every ounce of love I have for him.

"I feel like I'm dreaming," I say.

Our gazes lock and he smiles. "If this is a dream, I don't ever want to wake up." Suddenly, he sits up, dragging me onto his lap.

"Tell me again," he says and nuzzles his face into the curve of my neck.

"I love you, Ryker," I say, unable to believe the words are actually coming out of my mouth.

His arms tighten around me. "Ave...God, I love you." He holds me for a long moment and then presses a kiss to my temple. "I think you're the reason I'm alive," he says in a voice so low that I have to strain to hear him.

"What do you mean?" I ask. Even though I want to turn around and face him, I stay how I am, curled into his chest. I think it makes it easier for him to talk to me.

I feel his warm breath at my ear, rustling my hair. "I remember laying on the ground just numb from the pain. There was so much blood and I thought I was going to die. And that maybe it was okay. Then, I saw your face. It gave me strength...something to live for."

His arms are still wrapped around me and I pull his hands up and kiss them.

"I carried Luke for almost five miles then collapsed. Too much blood loss. I remember telling him I was sorry. I just couldn't go any further. And, he made a joke about dying together in some crummy jungle when we should've been on our way back to civilization and getting ready to go out on a double date he had set up with the Rizzo twins."

"That sounds like Luke," I say, a small smile touching my lips.

"He died beside me not long after."

I hear the sadness, guilt and regret in his voice. "It's not your fault," I say. "You did your best, but you were hurt, too. It's a miracle you didn't die beside him. And, don't you dare say you wish you had."

"I used to wish I had. I used to wish it every day."

"And now?" I ask.

He hesitates, runs a finger up my arm. "For the first time in a very long time, I feel like I have something to live for."

I turn my face and look up at him. His mouth dips and he kisses me with a sweet fierceness.

"I hope that means me," I say.

"It's 110 percent you, baby."

I turn in his arms and raise a brow. "So, who are these Rizzo twins?" I ask.

Ryker bursts out laughing and flips me over, his large body covering mine. "Darla and Deena Rizzo. They were quite a pair."

My eyes narrow and before I can say another word, he crushes his mouth to mine.

"Just so you know," he whispers, "they're nothing compared to you."

"Good recovery," I say and place a hand along his jaw. It's scratchy and I love the feel of it against my palm. When I trace a finger up and around his ear, he flinches. Like he did in Columbia. "What's wrong? Every time I touch near your ears, you pull away."

He lets out a breath. "Sorry. Habit, I guess," he says.

"What do you mean?"

"When we were fighting Castillo's men, one of them used an RPG to launch a grenade. It shot right past me and exploded way too close. It fucked my hearing all up so now I have to wear these mini hearing aids."

I just blink. I had no idea. "I never knew."

"Nobody really knows. Except Griff, I guess. They're tiny and custom made to fit inside my ear canal. Other than having to change the batteries every once in a while, they're pretty much in there and don't move."

My big, strong warrior wears hearing aids. The thought pulls at my heartstrings and I realize he's not as invincible as he seems. I pull him down and place a kiss against first one ear, then the other. "Thank you for telling me," I whisper. "You can tell me anything, you know."

"You're obliterating my walls. You know that?"

"I hope so," I say. "You can trust me, Ryker."

"I love you, Ave."

"I love you, too," I say.

He lowers his face and when he kisses me, I can feel how very much he loves me.

26

RYKER

I 've never confide in anyone the way I confide in Avery tonight. It's like a weight lifts off my shoulders and, for the first time in years, I can breathe. Deep, full breaths of fresh air instead of shallow gasps of fetid air.

I lay on my back, one hand tucked beneath my head and my other wrapped around Avery. She nestles down in the crook of my arm and nothing ever felt so right.

She told me she loves me.

God. Avery loves me.

My heart soars and I feel this crazy wave of giddiness. *When did I turn into such a sap?* I wonder. I don't even care because I haven't felt this good in years. It's like this unbelievable high that's indescribable.

Almost a little like when I used to do HALO jumps. High altitude-low opening jumps out of a perfectly good plane at 35,000 feet is the ultimate rush. The free fall is crazy intense and there's no way to accurately describe the sensation.

Kind of like love, I realize.

I've never been in love before. There were women over the years, of course, but I never let any get close and certainly never let my emotions get involved. It was always purely physical for me. But, Avery was different. From day one. She always held a piece of my heart and I knew she was special. But, now, it's like full-blown, can't-function-without-you feelings that scare the shit out of me.

Even so, I'm not going to mess this up. I'm going to give it 110 percent. Like it's a mission that I will succeed accomplishing. Because I'm a goddamn SEAL and we're winners. Failure isn't a word in our vocabulary.

Avery and I are going to work-- have to work-- because she's the best thing to ever happen to me. I tilt my face into her hair and breathe in her sugary sweetness. She smells like a cloud of cotton candy and I want to eat her up until I'm left with a sugar high.

I'm going to protect her and help clear her name. Valkyrie is going to pay for all the damage that he or she inflicted on me, Avery and my team. And, I'm going in hot. It's time to finally settle the score and I'm looking forward to it.

Maybe I am a little like an archangel, I think. Because Armageddon is coming for Valkyrie and it's judgement time. And, I am the Judge, the Jury and the Executioner.

No mercy.

There will be no forgiveness for my dark sins and I accept that. I have no doubt that when my life here is over, I'm not going anywhere nice. I have a pretty good feeling that the Devil is waiting for me, rubbing his hands in gleeful anticipation.

So, I may as well get my revenge.

In the meantime, the Devil's going to have to wait a little bit longer because right now I'm going to enjoy every moment I have with this blonde angel.

I hear a soft mewling and look down and see Liberty lay her long nose on my side of the bed. "You gotta go out?" I ask quietly. I scratch her nose then carefully move away from Avery, doing my best not to wake her up. "C'mon, pretty girl," I say and Liberty follows me.

I leash her up and take her out to use the bathroom. A strange feeling settles over me. Like this is what it would be like living with

Avery and Liberty. Waking up next to her, taking the dog out...domestic fucking bliss.

I like it. A lot.

The sun is rising and a beautiful orange glow begins to brighten the sky. I sit down on the steps leading up to my condo and pet Liberty. Together, we watch the sun rise and, for me, it almost feels cathartic. Like one chapter of my life closes and now a new, much better one is opening.

All of a sudden, my vision blurs with hot tears. "I'll take good care of her, Luke," I say under my breath. "I promise." I swipe a hand across my eyes, stand up and take Liberty back inside.

I'm used to getting up early so I wander into the kitchen and make some coffee. I assume Avery will sleep for a couple more hours, but as I take my first sip of coffee, I hear her get up and start moving around. When she walks into the kitchen, I hand her a mug and she accepts it with a small smile.

"Thank you," she says.

I wrap a hand around her waist and pull her in for a kiss. "Good morning," I murmur between kisses. She tastes like peppermint toothpaste and, as always, smells like a bakery.

"Morning," she replies.

"You're up early."

"I was going to take Liberty out."

"Already did," I say and lean down to stroke the shepherd. "We watched the sun come up."

Avery takes a sip of the hot coffee and watches me over the rim of her mug.

"What?" I ask and squeeze her side.

She shakes her head. "I'm just trying to figure out if last night was all just a dream."

"It better have been real," I tell her.

A smile curves her mouth. She sets the mug down and wraps her arms around me. "So, what's the plan for today?" she asks.

"I'm thinking of a run and then head over to the office. See if Harlow has any new information for us."

"How about a run, then a shower, and then head over to the office?"

"Even better," I say.

And, that's exactly what we do.

27

AVERY

When Ryker and I get to the Platinum Security office, Harlow is already there and probably three coffees into her day.

"Do you ever go home and sleep?" I ask.

"I run on caffeine," she says. "And, after working so long in my dark hole of an apartment, it's nice to get out and have somewhere else to go. I swear, until I worked here, I hadn't seen sunshine in years."

"Any news on Valkyrie?" Ryker asks.

Harlow's gaze slants down to his big hand at my waist and a small smirk curves her mouth. "Not yet, but I've got several programs running so as soon as something pings, I'll let you know."

"What kind of programs?" I ask.

"Those that I designed. With enough time, I can pretty much find out anything about anybody," she says with a flick of her long, brown ponytail. "People inevitably leave trails and my programs find the breadcrumbs and piece them together."

"That's pretty amazing."

"It's all just coding. I've always enjoyed it." She taps away on her keyboard.

Ryker slips his hand into mine and pulls me over to the doorway of her office.

"Oh, Avery," Harlow says and glances up. "Lexi and I are going out for drinks this weekend. You should come."

"Yeah, sure," I say. "That sounds fun." As Ryker leads me down to his office, I can't help but smile. It would be really nice to have some girlfriends in my life again.

While Ryker sits down at his desk and opens his laptop, I flip my tablet open and start looking up anything and everything I can find on "Valkyrie," Antonio Castillo and the United Forces of Colombia. I don't expect to find much, but I want to help.

An hour or so passes before Jax shows up. He comes in, all tall, dark and brooding bad boy, and sits in the chair next to me, stretching his long legs out. He and Ryker start reviewing the case, going over every angle and detail. I'm listening closely when Griff saunters in, wearing shades and chewing gum, a lazy smile on his face. He reminds me of a famous actor and finally it hits me-- a cross between Chris Pine and Chris Hemsworth. And, a dash of Brad Pitt.

He's really too good-looking, I think. Lexi definitely has her hands full with this one.

They all do their little signature hand greeting then Jax and Ryker exchange smirks. "You seem awfully...relaxed," Jax comments.

Griff tucks his sunglasses in the neckline of his shirt. "That's because I just got laid," he drawls and snaps his gum. His bright blue eyes flick over to me and he tosses me a grin. "Sorry."

"I think it's safe to say we all got laid last night," Jax says in a dry voice.

I feel my cheeks burn and look up at Ryker who smiles at me.

"Yeah, last night, and also like just now in the car. Lexi dropped me off on her way to the library."

Jax rolls his eyes and Ryker chuckles.

"Hey, guys," Harlow says and pokes her head in. "I got a hit on Valkyrie's identity."

Ryker sits up straighter and we exchange looks.

Harlow carries her tablet, walks in and props a hip on Ryker's desk. Her fingers fly over it, bringing up data. "Remember how I said we shouldn't rule out a woman? Well, it looks like Valkyrie is Freya Singer, ex-CIA operative turned rogue. Her dossier is a mile long, none of it good."

"Freya Singer," Griff repeats. "That name sounds familiar."

"When did she officially leave the CIA?" Jax asks.

Harlow taps away on her tablet. "Not long after Operation Armageddon went down. It's like she just disappeared."

"Probably retired on Castillo's payments," Ryker comments darkly.

"I found an address for her in Las Vegas. Under an alias, of course, but if you do enough digging and have the right programs..."

"You can find anything," Jax says.

"That's right," Harlow says with a smile.

"Anything yet on the wire transfers between her and Castillo?" Griff asks.

"Not yet, but if transfers happened, which I'm sure they did, then I'll find them. Just need a little more time." She does some more tapping. "I have a few programs running right now searching for that."

Jax nods. "So, we have a couple of options. To bring Freya Singer down legally, we wait for the proof of the wire transfers and then report her. In the meantime, we could take a trip to Sin City. Check the place out."

"Let's go," Ryker says and stands up.

I don't know how I feel about him confronting Freya. She's a trigger for the terrible things that happened two years ago and he's going to need all the support he can get. "I'm going," I say and stand up next to him.

Ryker shakes his head. "No. You need to stay here."

"For all we know, Freya *is* here. I'm safest with you."

"If Freya is here then this is the perfect opportunity to search her home in Vegas," Griff says. "I can get us in and out without her ever knowing." He glances at Harlow. "As long as you handle shutting down any security she has."

"Let me see what I can find," she says and starts digging.

Jax looks at me. "You can stay with Easton while we go to Vegas.

You'll be safe there. Griff and I installed a state-of-the-art security system for her awhile back."

I grit my teeth, but don't say anything. Yet. This conversation is far from over. I want to be with Ryker and the guys, helping them search. Not stuck in some Hollywood Hills mansion doing nothing. I hate feeling useless.

"When do we leave for Vegas?" Griff asks and glances down at his watch.

"As soon as you're ready," Jax says. "We'll take the helicopter, depart from Burbank Airport and arrive at McCarran Airport in just over two hours."

"One of the perks of having a rich fiancée is getting a helicopter as an engagement gift," Griff teases.

"Correct me if I'm wrong, but didn't you and your fiancée just find a treasure worth millions?"

"We let her brother take the credit," Griff says with a grin.

"Besides, Easton knows how much I love to fly," Jax says with a shrug. "I still wish I would've joined the Air Force instead of being a cop."

"You would've been a good leader," Ryker says.

"Thanks," Jax says.

We all know, coming from Ryker, that's a huge compliment.

"Okay," Jax says. "Let's meet at Burbank in an hour."

They guys nod their approval and I follow Ryker out to his car, completely quiet. Until we get inside. Then, I turn and announce, "I want to come with you."

I can tell he knew this was coming by the look on his face. "This is a recon mission, Ave. We're going to be in and out and back before you even know it. I'm not saying I don't want your help, baby. I just think you can better use your time here."

He scoops my hand up, kisses its back and makes it really difficult for me to want to argue with him. "How?" I ask.

"Harlow has a lot of information we need to sift through. If you can help with that it would make a huge difference."

I'll do anything to help, I think. "Okay," I say. "When I'm at Easton's, I'll bring my laptop and do whatever Harlow needs me to do."

"Thank you," he says and gives me a charming smile.

We head over to Easton's, but I leave Liberty at home. She'll be fine for the afternoon. As we pull up the circular driveway, I see Jax's Norton Commando motorcycle already there. Ryker and I walk up to the front door and Easton pulls it open before we even knock.

"Hi," she gushes and envelops me in a hug. "I hear you're staying with me while our guys fly to Vegas." Easton links an arm through mine and ushers me inside the massive foyer. Her home is beyond stunning, all floor-to-ceiling glass and various levels, all open and airy. The back opens up to a large patio with a barbeque pit, outdoor furniture and a crystal blue swimming pool near the glass wall that sits right at the edge of a hill that drops into the canyon below.

"Yes. I wanted to go, but got relegated to some desk work instead," I say and nod to the laptop under my arm.

"Well, first things first," she says, her raven curls bouncing. She wears her signature red lipstick and looks ready to walk a red carpet even though she's in yoga pants and a t-shirt. Easton Ross is a first-class star, no doubt about it.

I glance over at Jax who sits with Ryker and love that these two opposites got together. All elegance and manners, Easton resembles a long-ago actress from vintage Hollywood. While Jax is more of a rebel without a cause, bad boy to the bone, with his dark, scruffy good looks. They are going to have some beautiful children, I think.

Griff arrives not long after, always the last one to stroll in with a lazy smile on his face. While the three of them have a pow-wow in the living room, Easton and I go sit at the island in the kitchen.

"So are you two official?" she asks, her green eyes shining bright.

I can't help but smile. "Kind of," I say. "We just haven't announced it to the world."

Easton nods and moves a manicured hand across her lips making a "my mouth is zipped and I'm throwing away the key" motion.

"I'm glad," she says. "You're going to be really good for him."

"Are you two sharing secrets?" Jax asks, coming up behind Easton and wrapping his arms around her waist. He kisses her temple.

"Just some girl talk. Nothing you need to worry yourself about," she says and turns in his arms. They kiss for a long moment.

Then, Ryker moves up beside me, pulls me up into his arms and captures my mouth in a slow, heated kiss that makes my knees weak.

"I'll wait outside," I hear Griff mumble.

When Ryker finally pulls away, I reach up and lay a hand against his face. A face that has become so very dear to me. "Be careful," I say.

He nods, kisses me again and then he and Jax leave.

I let out a sigh and drop back down on the tall stool beside the island. Damn, I love that man. In such a short time, he's become my world. Though, in all fairness, I've had feelings for him for years.

"So," Easton says and places her porcelain face in her hands. "I want to know all about you and Ryker."

"Like what?" I ask.

"Do you love him?"

I nod. "So much. I think I've loved him for years. I guess that's why it's so surreal that we're finally together now."

Her bright red lips curve into a huge smile. "I'm so happy for you both. Ryker…" her voice trails off.

"What?" I ask.

"Well, ever since I've known him, he always seemed so sad and distant. This is the first time I'm seeing him actually smile. And, the fact that he just kissed you like that in front of everyone…" her voice trails off. "It means something really huge."

"I'm glad. We've both been through a lot these last couple of years and I really hope we can find closure," I say.

"You will," Easton says. "And, then you'll find the happily-ever-after you both deserve."

"You sure did with Jax," I say.

"And, Griff with Lexi."

I smile, knowing there's nothing that I want more. Maybe she's right. After this is all over, maybe Ryker and I will finally find the peace we so desperately need and we will be able to move forward together.

God, I really hope so.

28

RYKER

The flight to Las Vegas' McCarran Airport is smooth and uneventful. As I watch Jax bring the bird down with expert precision, I think he's right. He missed his calling as a pilot. He would've made a great Night Stalker. The elite aviation unit flies special operators like Navy SEALs and the Army's Delta Force into the most dangerous and secretive missions the US conducts. The 160th Special Operations Aviation Regiment, its formal name, operates religiously by their creed which says they'll be there within plus or minus 30 seconds of any operation time and they'd "rather die than quit."

My kind of guys.

Once we have boots on the ground, we hop in the rental car that Harlow has waiting for us. Again, I think about how lucky I feel to be a part of this team and how we work together so seamlessly.

After we leave the airport, Jax drives us North of the city to Tule Springs where we track down the address Harlow provided. It's a sprawling house in the middle of the desert and, unfortunately for us, there aren't a lot of places to hide.

"Let's stash the car up the road," Griff says. "Then, circle around the back. According to the drawings Harlow sent, there are a few back entrances."

Jax pulls up behind some cactus and other brush. Dressed all in black, guns in holsters at our hips and knives in boots, we're ready. We get out and double check our respective weapons.

We each place tiny comms in our ears and I have to use a specially-designed hook that wraps around my ear because of my hearing aids.

"Comms check," I say. We each check in through our earpiece then start down the dusty road, doing our best to stay off to the side and ready to drop down and out of cover at the slightest sound of an approaching vehicle. Luckily, the road is lonely and quiet.

I text Harlow and let her know our ETA to the house. She responds back and tells me all cameras and alarms are down. "Harlow says it's a-go," I say. "We're clear to move in."

The three of us circle around the large house, staying low. A fence circles the entire property and helps provide cover as we make our way to the rear part of the property. So far, so good. No sign of anyone.

Jax lifts a closed fist and we stop. There are several entrances-- one on either side of the house and large sliding doors in the middle which lead to a great room. We plan to breach a side entrance with Griff's lockpicking skills and separate from there, clearing rooms as we go.

Together, we jog over to the side door and Griff drops down in front of the lock. In less than 30 seconds, he picks both locks and the door swings inward. Guns ready and close to our bodies, we slip inside. Jax gives another hand signal and we split off.

I move right and head into what looks like a library, sweep the area and find no one. "Clear right," I say in a low voice.

A moment later, Griff's voice comes through the earpiece. "Clear left," Griff murmurs.

"Clear front," Jax adds a moment later.

No one's home.

"I've got an office over here," Griff says.

I holster my SIG Sauer and make my way over to the left side of the house. At the same time, I get that prickling feeling at the back of my neck and scratch. *Shit. Not a good sign,* I think.

When I walk into the office, Griff is already in the chair at the desk and copying the hard drive with some fancy little CIA gadget. Meanwhile, Jax is pulling open drawers, searching for anything that looks important.

I have a bad feeling that just isn't going away. "Something's not right," I murmur.

They both look up. "What do you mean?" Jax asks.

"I don't know. Just a gut feeling."

Griff looks down at his large watch. "Be done in three minutes."

"I'm going to search the bedroom," I say and head out. The master bedroom on the far side of the house is decorated in muted blues and grays with pops of silver. I skirt around the huge king-sized bed and glance into the attached bathroom. All looks normal so I head over to a closed door and pull it open to reveal a giant walk-in closet.

A painting on the far wall catches my attention and I walk over and lift the edge. *Yep, I thought so.* I pull the painting off the wall and eye the safe hidden behind it. "Griff," I say. "I found a safe. Can you take a look?"

"Be there in 30 seconds," he responds.

"Roger that," I say.

Lucky for us, the CIA taught Griff a bunch of useful skills when he was an operative and one of those just happens to be safecracking.

Griff and Jax appear exactly 30 seconds later. Griff walks up to the safe, blue eyes narrowing. "It's top of the line," he says. "Biometric safe. Needs her fingerprint to open it."

"Shit," I swear. "So, you can't open it?"

"No, I can open it," Griff says with a confident smile. Jax and I watch over his shoulder as he pushes the fingerprint reader in and, using that hole, he inserts his picking tools. "Just have to move the solenoid," he explains.

I have no idea what he's talking about, but I'm damn glad he's on my team. We each have our own unique skill set and it has come in damn handy time and time again. Suddenly, there's a click and the door opens.

One glance reveals the safe is empty. A second later, an alarm goes off.

"Fuck," Griff hisses. He slams it shut. "Time to go."

We all spin around and head out the way we came at the back of the house. When we reach the side door, we file out and Griff tugs the door shut behind him.

"I thought the alarms were off," I say.

"House alarm," Griff says. "Safe must run on backup batteries."

"Why was it empty, though?" Jax asks.

It doesn't make sense and I scratch the back of my neck. As we jog back down the road to the rental car, my phone vibrates in my pocket. I pull it out and see "Unknown Caller" on the screen. "Ryker Flynn," I say.

"Well, hello, Ryker Flynn," a female voice says. It's low and smoky.

I don't recognize the voice and frown. "Who is this?"

"Oh, come now. You can't even take an educated guess?"

"I have no idea who this is," I say not in the mood to play games.

"That's disappointing. I suppose I could put Avery on the line and she can tell you."

My heart fucking drops. I stop walking, hit the speaker and hold the phone up for Griff and Jax.

"Or, I can have Easton tell you."

Jax's head snaps up.

"Did you find what you were looking for at my house?" she asks.

Oh, God, this isn't good. Jax looks like he's ready to murder someone and I can't get my thundering heart to slow down.

"Where are you, Freya?" I ask.

"At Easton's, of course," she replies, completely nonchalant. I can almost hear the taunting smile in her voice. "We're having a fabulous time. Aren't we, ladies?"

In the background, I can hear feminine murmurs. It sounds like Avery and Easton are gagged and I feel my blood pressure skyrocket.

We have to get to them as soon as possible, I think. Freya Singer is a murderous bitch and every moment they are with her, they are in danger.

Terrible and extreme danger.

29

AVERY

fter the guys leave and Easton arms the security system, she pulls her favorite champagne out and pours us each a glass. The Taittinger's Blanc de Blancs is an exclusive French champagne that's absolutely delicious.

We head into the large, open back area of the house and sit down on the couch. "Are you ready for your wedding next week?" I ask her.

Her green eyes sparkle. "I've never been more nervous and excited for anything in my entire life," she admits.

"When did you and Jax meet?" I ask.

"Back in July. It's a crazy story. I hired him because I had a stalker," she says and takes a sip of champagne. "Turns out it was some asshole I used to date. But, I'm grateful or else we never would've met. I was America's Sweetheart, the actress who seemingly had it all together, and here he comes on his motorcycle with his sleeve of tattoos, scruffy face and leather jacket." She gets this starry-eyed look on her face. "Until then, I always fell for the pretty boy types like Griff. But, there was something so mesmerizing about Jaxon Wilder. After our first meeting, I couldn't stop thinking about him."

"Sounds like love at first sight," I say.

"Oh, definitely not," she says with a laugh. "We got under each

190

other's skin quite a lot. He used to smoke like a chimney and swear like a sailor. I got him to quit smoking and he got me to start swearing." She tosses me a playful wink.

I chuckle and sigh. I know what she means. As much as you adore someone, he can drive you bonkers.

"So, tell me about you and Ryker," she says.

"Well, we met through my brother Luke. He and Ryker met during Navy SEALs training and became best friends. Over the years, he'd come visit with Luke. From the moment I met Ryker..." I swallow hard and hear the dreamy tone in my voice.

"You knew?"

"I knew no one else would ever measure up to him. Every guy I dated was nothing compared to Ryker. He literally ruined dating for me. But, he was worth the wait," I add with a small smile.

"If he's the one then it's always worth the wait," she says.

"Is it always just easy with you and Jax?" I ask.

"Absolutely not," she says with a laugh. "But, you learn to compromise and choose your battles. The thing is, I can't imagine my life without him. It's like he gives me a reason to wake up each morning. A reason to breathe. Nothing else did that until him."

I understand exactly what she means. "Our past is a little rocky," I admit. "After his team died, he blamed me. I blamed myself, too. That's why this is so important," I say. "Proving Freya set the team up and clearing my name would be so healing for both of us."

"Things seem to be going well, though."

"They've never been better," I say. "But, the last thing I want to do is scare him off."

"You've said you love each other?" she asks.

I nod and feel a flush rise in my cheeks. "Last night."

"Well, he didn't bolt," she says. "So, that's a good sign."

We both laugh.

"Trust me, Avery, when I say the man is smitten. He's not going anywhere."

"You think?"

"I know. Whenever he looks at you, you can practically see the cartoon hearts popping out of his eyes."

I burst out laughing. It's all I want. Just Ryker to love me as much as I love him.

"Seeing these macho Alpha men find love is such a treat," she says. "It hits them upside the head and knocks them on their ass. They run from it and don't think they're worthy, but these three deserve it so much because they've all been to hell and back"

I don't know Jax or Griff's story and my ears perk up.

Easton's voice lowers. "Jax's sister was murdered and he blamed himself because he couldn't save her. He had demons just like Griff and Ryker. He has a younger brother, too, but he never comes around. I've never met Sebastian, but I'm hoping that'll change next week and he'll come to the wedding."

"I'm sorry to hear about Jax's sister."

She nods. "It really tore him up. He met Griff when he needed help tracking down the drug dealers who murdered her. They hit it off and when Jax opened Platinum Security he brought Griff on board. And, Griff introduced him to Ryker."

"What's Griff's story?" I ask

"Former CIA operative. Things went bad on a mission and his partner died. That's really all I know. These guys remain pretty quiet about their pasts. They suffer in silence with their demons. That's why it's up to us to help them forgive themselves. To bring some light and love back into their lives."

"I haven't met Lexi yet, but Harlow invited me to get drinks with them this weekend. You should come! Unless you're going to be doing the wedding stuff."

"I'd love to," she gushes. "Lexi is so sweet and I'd love to get to know Harlow better. Oh, and I'm keeping the wedding super small so Jax doesn't have a heart attack. So, it's pretty much all set." She jumps up. "Want to see my dress?"

"Yes!" I pop up and follow her down to the master bedroom. Even though she's a celebrity, I love how easy it is to talk to Easton. Like me, I think she doesn't have many close girlfriends so getting to spend time together is fun for both of us.

Easton steps into her huge walk-in closet and points to a covered dress hanging up. She unzips the protective cover and pulls out an ivory gown. "It's a 1954 Chanel evening gown."

"Oh, wow," I say. The bodice is completely beaded with a scalloped neckline and short, off-the-shoulder sleeves. The tulle skirt, covered in more beaded patterns, flares out and hits the floor. "It's absolutely gorgeous."

"I figured if I'm going to marry the most perfect man in the world then I need to be wearing the most perfect dress. And, nothing compares to vintage Chanel."

"You can say that again. You're going to make a stunning bride, Easton."

"Aw, thank you," she says and gives me a quick hug. Then, as she hangs the dress back up and re-zips it, I hear a noise behind me and turn.

A woman all in black stands there, a gun in her hand.

When I gasp, Easton turns, green eyes widening.

"Congratulations to the bride-to-be," the dark-haired woman says.

She looks to be about 30 and maybe an inch shorter than me. Her dark eyes flick over to me. "And, you must be Avery, my little scapegoat."

I feel a chill move through my body. "You're Valkyrie," I say.

"Very good."

"How did you get in here?" Easton demands, hands on her hips. "My security-"

"-was easy to circumvent. Next time, tell your boyfriend to do a better job."

Easton's green eyes narrow and I take a step forward. "What are you doing here?" I ask.

"Maybe the better question is why are you digging up the past?"

"Because you made me take the fall for something that wasn't my fault. You fed me false information and protected a drug lord and arms dealer. And, that bad intel led my brother and his team into a slaughter. You're the reason Luke is dead," I say, clenching my hands into fists. I want to slug the bitch, take her down and beat the crap out of her.

"Down, Avery," she says in a low voice. "Your brother and his team were collateral and they shouldn't have tried to interfere. It was my job to protect Antonio from prying U.S. eyes and that's exactly what I did."

"They had orders. SEALs don't refuse orders," I snap.

Freya shrugs a slim shoulder. "Guess they can't win 'em all."

I've had enough of this cow, I think, and take another step forward. If I can just catch her off-guard then maybe-

But, Freya lifts her gun. "Don't move," she orders. She studies me for a moment then smirks. "You're feistier than I thought you'd be. Maybe you should've gone rogue. I didn't think you had it in you, but maybe I was wrong."

I glance over at Easton who wears a dress and heels. As much as I adore my new friend, I have a feeling she isn't going to be very helpful in a fight. I decide to bide my time and wait for the right moment to strike.

Freya points her gun toward the door. "Let's go to the kitchen and chat," she says.

Easton and I walk out of the closet and into the master bedroom, Freya on our heels. A part of me is glad she's here and not in Las Vegas. This means the guys are probably searching her empty house right now and not in any sort of danger.

When I slow down, she shoves me. "Move it, blondie."

I glare at her over my shoulder. "Don't touch me," I hiss.

Her dark eyes flash. A moment later we reach the kitchen and she waves the gun, pointing to a couple of chairs. "Sit," she says and pulls out a handful of zip ties.

Dammit. It's now or never, I think. I move over to the chair and pretend to start to sit, but at the last moment, I spin and sweep her leg. Freya stumbles, off balance, and starts to fall backwards. I shove her arm up, trying to twist the gun out of her hand, and we drop down to the floor. I roll, ducking an elbow and manage to slam my palm up against her chin with a resounding whack.

She's holding onto the damn gun like it's glued to her hand. I see her swing a fist, too late, and she whomps me upside the head. *Shit.* I see stars, but instantly fire back with a punch of my own. My knuckles crack against her cheek and when I jerk my knee up to hit her in the stomach, she manages to kick me hard in the thigh.

Ugh. With a groan, I roll onto my side and see Easton standing there with a large kitchen knife clutched in her hands. I wish she had a gun, I think.

Freya scrambles up and orders Easton to drop the knife. Without much of an option, Easton lays the blade on the counter. "Sit," Freya snaps and zip ties Easton's hands.

I can see Freya's really pissed now and she swipes blood off her face. I didn't even realize I'd drawn blood.

Good, I think, and pull myself up into a sitting position.

"In the chair," Freya snarls at me.

I get up and sit down, eyeing her bloody cheek. I must've got her with my nails, I realize happily. She wraps the tie around my wrists and pulls hard. I want to wince, but I don't give her the satisfaction.

"Big plans, Freya?" I ask.

Her dark eyes narrow. "You're a pain in the ass," she says. "I'm glad you took the fall for your brother's death. And, I'm glad Ryker hated you for it. Because he did, didn't he? Hated and blamed you for years."

I feel like she just dropped acid in my wounds. *Bitch.* "Ryker loves me," I say through gritted teeth.

"Ryker loves me," she mimics then laughs. "Sure he does. He may be fucking you, but he doesn't love you. A man like that, a man who killed for a living, doesn't know the meaning of the word love. He's a mindless machine who only knows how to take orders and complete missions. Wake up, Avery. He's a warrior built by the U.S. government."

"Don't listen to her, Avery," Easton says.

"Oh, what the hell do you know, Miss I-live-in-a-Hollywood-fucking-bubble? You don't know anything about the real world."

"She knows more than you'll ever know," I say. "She knows how to be a friend and care for others."

"Oh, Jesus Christ, enough of the theatrics." Freya tucks her gun in its holster and pulls her phone out of a pocket. "What's your boyfriend's number?" she asks me.

I shake my head.

"Better give it to me, blondie, or I'll put a bullet in your new bestie."

Shit. I glance over at Easton and grit my teeth. *Dammit.* Ryker is going to be so worried. I let out a sigh and rattle off his phone number.

Then, Freya shoves a kitchen towel in each of our mouths. My nostrils flare and I'm so angry that she holds the advantage right now, I could spit.

Freya punches the number into her phone, hits the speaker and I hear it begin to ring.

Please, don't answer, please don't answer, please don't-

"Ryker Flynn."

His deep voice fills me with confidence. And, even though it's only been a few hours, I realize how much I miss him.

"Well, hello, Ryker Flynn," Freya says and smiles at me and Easton.

"Who is this?" he asks.

"Oh, come now. You can't even take an educated guess?"

"I have no idea who this is," he snaps.

"That's disappointing," Freya says. "I suppose I could put Avery on the line and she can tell you." Stunned silence comes over the line. "Or, I can have Easton tell you."

When there's no response, Freya sighs. "Did you find what you were looking for at my house?"

"Where are you, Freya?" Ryker asks and the murderous tone in his voice gives me chills.

"At Easton's, of course," she replies, completely nonchalant. She smiles at us again. "We're having a fabulous time. Aren't we, ladies?"

When she kicks my shin, I give a small murmur.

"I have a few demands," Freya announces. "And, if you and your friends aren't willing to meet them then Easton and Avery will end up as collateral. Just like your SEAL team," she adds in a nasty voice.

30

RYKER

I exchange a look with Jax and Griff and realize my hand shakes. My grip tightens on the phone and I try to steady it.

"What do you want?" Jax growls.

"The better question is what do *you* want?"

To take you fucking down, I think. Make you pay for all the heartache and deceit that took innocent lives and destroyed people I loved.

And, now Freya has Avery and Easton hostage and I'm about to lose it. *Fucking lose it.*

I force myself to focus and take four deep breaths.

"We want you to let them go," Jax says in as calm of a voice as he can muster.

Freya laughs. "Jaxon Wilder, I presume? The groom-to-be, if I'm not mistaken. You have a lovely fiancée, Jax. She's not much of a fighter, though. Now, Avery, on the other hand. What a hellion."

I struggle to keep my cool, but it's getting harder and harder with each passing moment. "If you hurt either of them, I will hunt you down and slit your throat," I growl. Griff lays a hand on my arm and slants me a warning look.

"Why am I not surprised?" she asks. "At ease, soldier. We only tussled for a minute and I'm the one who's bleeding."

Good, I think, and release a pent-up breath.

"You obviously want something, Freya," Jax says. "So, why don't you stop wasting our time and get to the point?"

"Very perceptive of you, Mr. Wilder. I'll tell you exactly what I want and if you don't deliver it then one of these two lovely ladies dies."

A menacing silence radiates over the phone line.

"What?" I grit out.

"Two things. First, drop your investigation into Operation Armageddon. It's over and let's just let the blame lay with Avery like it has the past two years. Second, I was told by my friend Antonio Castillo that you visited his compound recently."

"Yeah, so?" I say.

"So, he has something that I want. You may have seen it when you were in there sneaking around. A priceless Columbian emerald called La Rosa Verde. I want you to steal it for me."

"You want me to steal from your friend?"

"Castillo owes me. I figure the emerald, the pride of his little stolen collection of artifacts, should cover it."

"His compound is too heavily-guarded," I say.

"You got in and out before, so you can do it again."

"And, what if we can't get it?"

"Either break into the compound and steal the emerald for me or your girlfriend dies. I think it's pretty clear. I'll be in touch."

Click.

When Freya hangs up, my heart drops. I glance from Jax to Griff and haven't felt this helpless since I laid wounded on the jungle floor two years earlier.

"C'mon," Griff says, taking lead since Jax and I are consumed with worry and dread. "They'll be okay. Freya won't hurt them. Not when she still wants us to do something for her."

I nod. "He's right. As long as we get the emerald, she's going to be willing to bargain."

"Then, let's go get that fucking emerald," Jax hisses.

"First things first," Griff says. "Back to the helicopter. Jax, are you okay to fly us back?"

He nods. "I'll be fine."

"Okay then. We need to get back and make sure your women are okay."

"If she hurt them in any way..." Jax's voice trails off and he's dangerously pissed.

The flight back is tense and over two hours of not knowing what happened to Avery and Easton is gut-wrenching. We land at Burbank Airport and hightail it out of there. I drive like a bat out of hell and make it to the Hollywood Hills in record time.

The Expedition screeches to a halt and we jump out and run into Easton's.

It's dead quiet and I feel that prickle at the base of my neck. I draw my gun and we move forward, clearing each room fast. When we reach the kitchen, I freeze. Easton sits in a chair, zip tied to it and gagged.

Jax pushes past us, drops to his knees and pulls the gag out. "Are you okay, Princess?" he asks, running his hands all over her, making sure she isn't hurt. He notices a cut on her arm and inhales sharply.

"I'm fine," she says and he cuts the ties loose.

"Where's Avery?" I ask, feeling a sick wave of dread pour through me.

"She took her," Easton says, green eyes shining with tears. "Said she was her insurance."

"Goddammit," I swear and kick a chair across the room. I run my hands through my short hair and spin around. Oh, God, it feels like my whole world is crumbling and spinning wildly out of control at the same time.

"We'll get her back, Ryker," Griff says.

Jax lifts Easton's arm and frowns at the bloody slash where a blade cut her. "She cut you?" he asks, tone deadly.

Easton nods. "She said...she said that I was too perfect and needed a scar." Jax pulls her into his arms. "She was going to mark my face, but Avery managed to hit her. A few times, actually."

My eyes slid shut and I let out a ragged breath. My girl's so brave, I think. *Hang in there, baby.*

"Jax, go take care of Easton," Griff says. "Ryker, let's come up with a plan."

I nod and slump down in a stool at the island. "I have to get Liberty," I mumble. "She's alone, waiting for Avery."

"I'll have Lexi get her," Griff says. He pulls out his phone and launches into a quick explanation of what's going on and she instantly offers to help with Liberty. He tells her he has to go to Columbia and all I can think is here we go again.

I don't want to go back to that hellhole, but I don't have a choice. Time is of the essence and we don't have the luxury of dicking around at airports and waiting for connecting flights. I yank my phone out and call an important man that I haven't spoken to since my team died. Since he visited me at the hospital and I decided to retire.

When I'm finally connected to my contact, Captain Joseph Cutler, I stand upright and feel like I should salute him even though we're talking over the phone. "Captain Cutler," I say. "It's Lieutenant Commander Ryker Flynn."

I know I'm probably the last person he expects to hear from, but he used to be my Commander and is one of the best leaders and men I know. He was promoted to Captain and if anyone can help me, it's him.

After a quick, yet detailed explanation of the current situation and my need to get down to Columbia as soon as possible, Cutler is quiet. "There's a KC-135 heading out on a training mission. You can hop on a ride. Thanks to that Medal of Honor you have," he adds.

Relief floods me and Cutler gives me the details. "When you get back," Cutler says, "I want a full debrief."

"Yes, sir," I say. "Thank you, sir."

After I hang up, I glance down at my watch. We leave in a couple of hours and will be jumping when it's dark. I'm pretty sure Griff has done night jumps, but probably not Jax.

KELLY MYERS

Griff hangs up with Lexi and arches a brow.

"I got us a ride down to Columbia and we leave in two hours on a military transport plane. They're headed down to South America to drop off some equipment and do some training exercises. Only thing is they're not stopping and we need to jump. Does it work for you?"

"It's been awhile, but, hell yeah," Griff says, his blue eyes lighting up.

We both look up when Jax walks in and he frowns. "Tell me I didn't hear that right."

"It's a HALO jump," I say. "High Altitude/ Low Opening."

"Fuck." He looks from me to Griff. "How high are we gonna to be?"

Griff and I exchange smiles. "Does it matter?" Griff asks.

"I fucking hate heights."

"You don't have to come. Honestly, Jax, it might be better if you stay here. You can keep an eye on Easton and Lexi and act as our comms support."

"Harlow is comms support."

"If you've never jumped out of a plane, this probably isn't a good time to start," Griff says. "Hell, I've never done this kind of jump. It can be nerve-wracking in the dark and that fucking high, a lot can go wrong. And, don't forget you're getting married next week."

"I can't let you two go in there alone. We have no idea how many guards will be there."

"We'll have Harlow do a heat scan," I say. "And, I'll call Gray. He's familiar with the compound, too, and two ex-CIA ops is better than one."

"Are you sure?" Jax asks. "I'll jump out of the goddamn plane."

"Stay here," I say. "You and Liberty can protect Easton and Lexi."

"And, you can work with Harlow to get us in and out of that compound."

Jax gives a sharp nod and I put a call in to Grayson. After I explain the situation, he's only too happy to join our little assault team. He plans to meet us at the Drop Zone and I promise to send him the coordinates as soon as I know.

Staying focused on the mission at hand is good for me because it doesn't give me time to obsess about Avery. I'm sick with worry, but if I had no plan right now, I'd be losing my damn mind.

We don't have much time, but I email all the information I have about the compound and Antonio Castillo to Jax and Harlow. Then, it's time for Griff and I to leave.

"We'll be in and out fast," Griff says. "Hopefully, before anyone realizes the emerald is gone."

"And, we're going to have you and Harlow guiding us," I add.

Griff and I exchange our signature handshake with Jax. It's a bittersweet moment and I hope to God, we make it back safely for his wedding next week.

"Be careful," Jax says, dark eyes intense. "I can't run P.S. without you two idiots. And, I certainly can't get married without my two best men, either."

"See you soon, bro," Griff says and I nod.

After leaving Easton's, we make a couple of quick stops to my place and his apartment to change and organize the supplies and weapons we need to bring with us. We each wear Tru-Spec Quarter Zip Combat shirts, bullet proof vests, cargo pants and boots. Underneath, we wear polypropylene knit undergarments to prevent frostbite since it could be as low as -45 degrees when we jump out of the plane. Our backpacks contain the necessities-- weapons, night vision goggles, extra ammunition, water, our comms and GPS and other assorted gadgets.

Then, we head to the Los Angeles Air Force Base in El Segundo. We have about 45 minutes before the large military plane takes off and we talk to the pilot for a few minutes. When he finds out I was a SEAL, he instantly warms up. "My cousin's a Frogman," he says. "It's an honor to have you onboard."

The pilot explains where we're going to jump and since he has no plans of landing in Colombia, this confirms it's going to be a high altitude jump. It's been awhile and I'm looking forward to it. Griff looks a little nervous, though.

After I text the DZ coordinates to Gray, Griff and I make our way into the bowels of the enormous KC-135. We greet some other military guys who come onboard, but no one asks any questions. We all know the drill and everything is classified from here on out. We find a couple of seats and buckle up.

The large plane takes off and we settle in for our ride down to Colombia. We discuss the plan and go over each detail for hours. I also give Griff the rundown of how to do a high altitude jump without dying. About 45 minutes from our DZ, we start breathing in pure oxygen.

"Never jumped from 35,000 feet before," Griff says and manages to pop a stick of gum into his mouth between breaths.

"Don't worry," I tell him. "We'll have oxygen bottles. Right now, just pre-breathe and focus on your breaths."

We inhale the 100 percent oxygen which will flush the nitrogen from our bloodstreams and help us avoid decompression sickness.

"Good thing you quit smoking," I say.

"Why's that?" he asks, his voice wary.

"It can make you more susceptible to hypoxia."

"Great. And, remind me what that is again?" He breathes the oxygen in.

"When your body doesn't get enough oxygen. A jumper suffering from hypoxia may lose consciousness and then won't be able to open his parachute."

"Fuck," Griff hisses and breathes more deeply than before. "If I die, Lexi is going to kill me."

"You're gonna do great, CIA," I tell him and pat his shoulder.

Before we know it, we're slipping into our helmets, harness and parachute. Griff kisses his pack before sliding it onto his back. I check him over, make sure everything is properly fastened.

"Any last questions?" I ask.

He looks a little green. "Nah. Just tell Lexi I love her."

"You can tell her yourself in a little bit," I say. We pull our face masks on and I check my watch. "Almost at the DZ."

The cargo door lowers and a freezing wind tears in through the opening. The drop is 35,000 feet, the typical height a commercial airliner flies, and into pitch blackness. We stand at the edge of the ramp and prepare to jump.

"Motherfuck," Griff swears.

I give him the okay sign and he gives it back. Then, I throw myself out of a perfectly good airplane.

31

AVERY

Sitting now in the passenger seat of the Aston Martin Valkyrie, I glance over at Freya's profile.

Earlier, when she slashed Easton's arm, I lost it. At the time, only my hands were bound so I launched myself out of the chair and slammed into her. We both went down hard and I managed to hit her with my elbow before she turned the gun in my face. "You're coming with me," she hissed. "And, you," she said to Easton. "I want you to deliver a message for me."

Easton looked over at me and I nodded, trying to reassure her. I knew she was kidnapped by her stalker not long ago, but Freya Singer was about as evil as they got. I could tell Easton was scared and I wanted to give her a boost of confidence.

"It's okay," I said. "Jax is coming."

"Shut up," Freya snapped and kicked my leg. "I have no doubt your men are hustling back right now, worried out of their little minds. So, when they return, you tell them they better deliver La Verde Rosa in 24 hours or I will kill Avery. And, I will enjoy it thoroughly."

After zip tying Easton to the chair, Freya grabbed me by the hair and yanked me up off the floor. Damn, I tried not to squeal, but it hurt. She shoved me toward the front door and I was so grateful she decided to leave Easton behind.

I'd never forgive myself if Easton didn't make it to her wedding next week in that beautiful Chanel gown.

Now, I glare at Freya. The second I get the opportunity, I am taking this bitch down. *Just hang in there, Ave, and bide your time.* She'll slip up at some point. They always do.

And, I'll be ready.

My gaze wanders over the car's sleek interior and I'm not impressed. *What a waste of money,* I think. The engine roars and a car like this is meant for show-offs, I think. "In my opinion, three million dollars for a car is a little excessive," I say.

She slants me a look. "It was a drop in the bucket. Protecting a Columbian drug lord paid awfully well."

"You said he owed you," I remind her.

A darkness settles over her face. If she wasn't so evil, she'd be pretty. Her features are rather striking with high cheekbones and dark, cat-shaped eyes. But, the rottenness in her soul erases any potential beauty.

"Antonio Castillo is a bastard," she says and starts driving us down the hill toward Sunset Boulevard.

Hmm, interesting. I can't help but wonder what happened between the two of them that terminated their relationship. Not that I think she'll tell me, but I ask anyway. "What did he do?"

"None of your business," she snaps.

So much for bonding over our mutual dislike of Castillo. I look out the tinted window. "Where are we going?" I ask.

"Do I need to gag you again?"

I roll my eyes and pull at the zip ties. She drives for about 45 minutes then tells me to drop my head down into my lap. With a sigh, I do as she says. I'm still paying close attention to where we're going, though, and it's somewhere North of the city, in the mountains by Santa Clarita.

The fancy car doesn't do too well on the back roads, but we drive for another ten minutes or so after exiting the freeway. Finally, we pull to a stop and I lift my head. I see a small house in the middle of a dusty yard.

Freya gets out and circles around the car, gun in her hand. She opens the door and motions for me to get out. "Let's go."

When I slide out, she grabs my arm and tugs me toward the house. "Move it," she barks.

I can feel her impatience and annoyance, but I'm extremely patient. Just like Luke and Ryker had to be when they were out on certain missions. I remember Luke telling me that sometimes they spent 90 percent of their time lying in wait for the enemy.

Eventually, Freya would slip, mess up somehow. Then, I'll strike.

Freya opens the door and pushes me inside. The place is dusty and dark. It's obvious no one has been here in quite some time. She yanks a chair away from a table. "Sit," she orders, pulling out more zip ties.

With a sigh, I drop down in the chair and watch as she secures my ankles to the wooden legs. Then, she pulls her knife, slashes through the tie binding my wrists and refastens each wrist to the armrests of the chair.

Well, if I couldn't escape before, I sure as hell can't now.

Freya moves over to the counter and lays her weapons down. "If you try to move out of that chair, I'll shoot you."

"I couldn't move if I wanted to," I assure her and strain at the tight bindings. The plastic just cuts into my skin and I stop pulling.

"Good. Because I really don't want to get blood on my floor."

With another sigh, I slouch down in the seat. "I still don't understand why you want them to go down there and break into Castillo's compound."

"For the emerald," she says. "I already explained it."

"But, why? Obviously you have more money than you know what to do with."

Freya studies me for a long moment with eyes as black as obsidian. "You're smarter than I gave you credit for. When I had Miller feed you that bogus intel about Castillo's army, I assumed you were the perfect scapegoat. A dumb blonde trying to impress her boss."

"Dumb blondes don't work at the Central Intelligence Agency," I tell her in a tart voice.

"Apparently not. I underestimated you." She folds her arms across her chest. "I never thought I'd hear your name again, much less learn that you and your boyfriend were digging for the truth."

My boyfriend. The thought of Ryker makes my heart swell. And, this woman standing in front of me sent him into a jungle full of Castillo's forces, fully expecting him to die like the rest of his team.

But, he didn't. He survived and thank God for that, I think. Not only did Freya rob me of my brother, but also she tried to take Ryker away from me. I feel my anger at the whole situation begin to build into a burning fury.

I want her to pay.

And, I have no problem being the Angel of Death who swoops in and serves justice.

"You never answered my question," I say, straining against the zip ties. "Why do you need some crummy emerald when you already have millions and millions of dollars?"

I have the impression that she and Castillo didn't end on good terms and I'm hoping to pull as much information out of her as possible. Who knows? It could help later.

"First of all, you can never have too much money," she says. "And, second…"

When her voice trails off, I look up, unable to miss the expression on her face.

Sorrow.

Freya shrugs and the moment passes. "Tale as old as time. He hurt someone I cared about."

I raise a brow. "Really? Well, then I guess you know how it feels. I feel like we've come full circle."

"Not some stupid guy I had a crush on," she snaps. "It was someone much more important than some man."

I study her closely. From her words, I'm guessing it was a family member. "Who?"

I don't expect her to respond, but after a moment of hesitation, she does. "My sister," she says in a low, haunted voice.

Well, if that's not karma then I don't know what is and I probably should've thought it through before I blurt out, "Karma's a bitch isn't it?"

Eyes flashing, Freya stalks over and slaps my face so hard that I think I feel my brain rattle in my skull. My head snaps to the side and my vision fills with stars.

"Shut your mouth," she hisses.

No, not gonna happen, I think. "You're the reason my brother is dead," I remind her.

She releases a pent-up, furious breath, grabs an empty vase off the table and smashes it against the floor. Then, she spins around to face me and I see hellfire in her eyes.

Shit. I pushed her too far.

Suddenly, an eerie calmness settles over her. She swipes her phone up, turns it toward me and hits record. "Say hello to Ryker, Avery."

My stomach clenches as she moves closer, but I put on a brave face. "What're you doing?" I ask.

"Making a video to send to your big, strong man."

When she pushes the camera into my face, I turn my head, trying to ignore her. Then, she moves fast, like a bolt of lightning, and before I even realize it, she's behind me and slipping something around my neck.

I try to duck and pull away, but I can't move too far since my wrists are secured to the chair. Freya pulls the rope tight and I cry out as she begins to strangle me. The pressure on my neck is increasing and I thrash my body, trying to escape the tightening rope.

"Stop," I gasp.

All the while, she records.

Oh, God, please don't let Ryker see me die like this. Just when I feel like I'm going to pass out and darkness starts closing in at the edge of my vision, Freya releases the pressure on my neck and whips the rope away. I fall forward, choking and gasping for air. I want to rub my neck, but can only pull against the zip ties and clench my fists.

"Get the emerald or next time I won't stop until she's dead," Freya threatens. "Don't contact me until you have it." She hits stop.

"Please," I say, my voice scratchy. "Don't send that."

When she hits send, my heart sinks.

Freya gives me a little smirk. "Too late."

"You're going to regret that," I rasp.

Freya circles back around, eyeing me closely, dragging the rope between her fingers. "I can't decide if you're really stupid or really brave."

I cough, still feeling the pressure of the rope against my neck. "I'm not stupid," I say between gritted teeth.

"Yet you believed John Miller's intel which led to the death of those brave, young men. Including Luke."

Whatever she says, I decide I'm going to let it roll off me. She's just trying to upset me, make me unfocused. "Their death isn't on my conscience any longer. The moment I learned what you did, I made my peace." Her eyes narrow. "But, I'm willing to bet you haven't made your peace with whatever Castillo did to your sister."

A vein pops in Freya's forehead and I know I've found her weak spot. Possibly, most likely, her only weak spot. And, I intend to take full advantage.

"Did he murder her?" I ask.

"Shut up," she says in a low voice.

"You said he hurt her. Did he torture her? Rape her? Punish her because of something you did?"

"I am done with this conversation," Freya says. She grabs her weapons off the counter and stalks out.

Good. I hope she's pissed and stays away from me for a while. I slump down in my chair and let out a breath. I need to come up with a plan. Figure out a way to escape. I wonder what she did with my phone.

I sit back up, pulling at the zip ties, and look around, a plan beginning to form in my head. Ryker and Griff won't be back from Columbia until tomorrow.

If they make it out, a small voice whispers.

Of course they're going to make it. Jesus. *Stay positive, Ave.* And, you're going to make it out of here, too.

In the meantime, I only have myself to rely on. At some point, I'm hoping Freya falls asleep. Or, at least leaves me alone like now. I just have to keep getting under her skin, drive her away and then that will give me the opportunity to try and get the hell out of here.

First things first, I think.

I need to get my hands on a knife and cut these damn zip ties before my circulation cuts off. Then, I'm going to find my phone.

I just hope Freya stays away long enough to let me do it.

32

RYKER

I launch myself out of the plane and somersault into the inky blackness. When I glance up, I spot Griff just above and to the side of me. I motion him over and we make our way to each other and grip wrists.

The sensation of falling through the wind and night is unreal. A high like no other.

We give each other a thumbs-up and let go.

I check my altimeter and after about 85 seconds of free fall, it's time to deploy my chute. A moment later, I see Griff's parachute billow out above him and we cruise through the night air, finally landing on the ground below.

I land smoothly and start removing the harness. Not far away, Griff comes in for his own landing and rips his helmet off.

"Holy shit!" he says. "That was one helluva ride, Flynn."

I smile. He's right. There's nothing quite like a HALO jump, especially at night.

"How many of those have you done?" he asks.

"Oh, hell, I don't know. A couple hundred maybe?"

"Christ, that's a lot," he says with a laugh and runs a hand through his mussed hair. "I think I swallowed my fucking gum."

I chuckle and suddenly, headlights flicker on and a car door opens. "Nice landing," Gray says and walks up to meet us. "Good to see you again, Ryker," he says and we slap backs.

"This is Griff Lawson," I say. "Griff, meet Grayson Shaw, also ex-CIA."

They shake hands.

"Have to say, I didn't expect to see you back so soon," Gray says. We start walking toward his SUV which is well-equipped to traverse the rough jungle roads, and I begin to fill him in on what's been happening.

"When we tracked down Avery's source, John Miller, he warned Freya Singer, aka Valkyrie, that we were on to them. She came after Avery and Easton, my friend's fiancée. She took Avery." My voice cracks and I clench my fists.

"Oh, shit," Gray says.

"She's holding her somewhere and will do an exchange for some emerald we're supposed to steal."

"Castillo's La Verde Rosa, I presume," Gray says.

We get into the SUV and Gray drives us back toward the road.

"Yeah, what do you know about it?" Griff asks.

"Just that it's worth millions. And, a hot property that he probably stole from one of his rivals."

"I saw it when Avery and I escaped his compound. It's in a glass case in a room at the back of the house."

"I brought a few CIA gadgets that should help me get it out of there," Griff says.

"Ah, the good 'ol days," Gray says. "Okay, so what's the plan?"

"We'll breach the rear wall by the guard tower, take the guard down. Once inside, we'll make our way to the room where the emerald is located, quietly neutralizing any tangos as we go. Harlow is analyzing heat signatures as we speak, but last looks showed approximately 20 bodies present."

"We're going to try to get in and out without alerting the whole damn compound," Griff says. "But, you know how that can go."

"Right?" Gray's silver eyes flash.

"While Griff secures the emerald, we'll keep a lookout for threats. Then, we'll go out the sliding doors and over the wall."

"Sounds pretty straightforward," Gray says.

My phone buzzes and I pull it out of a zipped pocket. "Hopefully Harlow has some info about-"

But, the message isn't from Harlow.

"Unknown" shows up on the screen and I scratch the back of my neck, dread filling every crevice of my body.

"Fuck," I hiss.

They both look over. "What is it?" Griff asks.

I feel like a rubber band stretched taut, ready to snap. "A video," I force out. I rub a hand across my face, take a deep breath and hit play.

The footage shakes as the camera moves up and down. Then, I hear Freya's voice.

"Say hello to Ryker, Avery."

The camera turns around and I see Avery, hands and feet zip tied to a wooden chair. She looks up and those cornflower blue eyes of hers flash.

"What're you doing?" she asks.

My heart clenches. She looks so damn brave.

"Making a video to send to your big, strong man."

Freya pushes the camera into Avery's face and she turns away. Then, Freya shoots around the chair and slips a rope around her neck.

Oh, my God, no. I stop breathing.

Avery tries to duck and pull away, but she can't because she's secured to the chair. When Freya pulls the rope tight, Avery cries out and begins thrashing.

"Stop," she gasps.

I can't look away from the video and a part of me feels like it's dying when Avery stops fighting and her eyes slide shut. My eyes fucking burn as I watch the woman I love with every shred of my being begin to pass out from lack of oxygen.

From being strangled to death.

Then, just as suddenly as she struck, Freya backs off, yanking the rope away. Avery falls forward choking and gasping for air.

"Get the emerald or next time I won't stop until she's dead," Freya threatens. "Don't contact me until you have it."

The video stops.

A rage like I have never known before rises up within me. I want to smash my phone into a million little pieces, but instead, I pound my fist repeatedly against the dashboard of Gray's car.

"Ryker! Ryker!" Griff says, leaning over the backseat, grabbing my shoulder. "Calm down. Avery's okay."

"No, she's not. She almost fucking strangled her!" I bite out in a savage voice.

Aw, shit. I think I cracked the dash. But, I'm so goddamn angry and frustrated right now because I can't help her. I'm so far away and all I want to do is storm into wherever she is and rescue her. And, I can't.

Fucking Freya Singer is a dead woman, I think.

I suck in a deep breath, count, swipe my palms over my eyes. I have to focus, get the emerald and then use it to get Avery back. And, I will get her back, safe and sound.

I have to, I think. If anything happens to Avery, I won't ever come back from it. I'll die.

"Avery is strong," Griff says. "We'll get the emerald and get her back. But, right now, you need to keep it together so we can complete this mission. Got it?"

I give a sharp nod, eyes on the cracked dashboard. Griff pats my arm and sits back. "Sorry, I'll pay for that," I mumble to Gray.

"I get it," Gray says. "When these assholes hurt the ones we love…" He lets out a low breath. "There's really no coming back from it."

"Your sister," I say, remembering when Avery connected the dots about Gray losing his sister.

"Yeah."

"I'm sorry." I swipe a hand through my hair, trying to rein in my emotions. It's time to concentrate, to be clear and present.

"How much further?" Griff asks.

"ETA ten minutes," Gray says.

"Let's go over Plan B," I say. "If the shit hits the fan, and it always fucking does, I want to make sure we have an exit."

216

As we go over the contingency plan, I get into warrior mode. Five minutes out, I check my weapons. In the backseat, I can hear Griff doing the same. Then, I pull the night vision goggles out.

I'm ready.

When Gray pulls up behind a cluster of trees and turns the engine off, I jump out and sling my HK416 over my shoulder. The assault rifle is heavily modified with a suppressor, custom stock, various optics and flashlight. The 30-round magazine is ready to go.

We each place tiny comms in our ears and I wrap the specially-designed hook around my ear. Then, we connect to Harlow.

"Hey, guys," she says in that low, breathy voice of hers. There's a soothing quality in her tone that inspires confidence and calmness. "I've got 18 heat signatures at the compound including the four guards in each tower."

"Six guys a piece. Better odds than we thought," Griff says and pops a stick of gum into his mouth.

"Love your optimism, 007," Harlow says.

Gray pulls up the GPS and squints in the darkness. "We need to head 2.6 klicks South."

"Roger that," I say.

I begin to march in that direction, pushing all thoughts of Avery into a separate compartment in my mind and shutting the lid. Soldiers who can't focus on the situation in front of them have a tendency to die.

That's not going to be me, I decide, and adjust the night vision goggles over my eyes.

We cruise down a jungle path and when we spot the wall around the compound, we stop. "ShadowWalker, we are in position. Deactivate cameras and alarms," I say.

"Roger that, Solo." There's the sound of faint tapping and I can't help but think of the last time I was down here and used my code-name. But, I quickly push those dark thoughts away and wait for Harlow's go.

"Cameras are on a loop and the alarm has been deactivated," Harlow confirms. "All set, guys."

"We're going in," I say.

I check out the corner guard tower and raise my index finger to communicate one guard. Silently, we stalk to the jungle's edge, I lift my rifle, aim and take the guard out with one shot.

The moment he drops, we hustle over to the wall and I boost Griff up first. At the top of the wall, Griff throws a leg over and hangs there, scoping it out. After about 30 seconds, he motions for us to follow.

I boost Gray and then take a running leap and jump up. Gray grabs my wrist and helps me up the rest of the way. Gray drops down beside Griff and I follow, swinging my rifle into position the moment my boots hit the ground.

It's quiet. *Almost too quiet,* I think.

We move over to the corner door that Avery and I breached last time. Griff works the lock open in 20 seconds and then we head inside. I'm in front, Griff in the middle and Gray brings up the rear, keeping an eye out behind us.

Halfway down the hall, one of Castillo's soldiers turns the counter and practically walks right into me. *Pop, pop.* He drops from my shots and Griff grabs him under the arms and drags him through a nearby open door. He pulls the door shut and then we start forward again.

We run into two more surprised guards and dispatch them quickly. When we reach the room where the emerald is kept, I raise a closed fist and everyone freezes.

The door is closed.

I reach a hand out, try the handle. Locked. I motion to Griff who moves in and we cover him, eyes on the hallway, as he picks the lock.

Thirty seconds later, the door opens and we all hurry in and shut it behind us. The room is empty and our gazes lock on the glass case containing the emerald. Griff moves over and starts to examine the setup while I move to the rear glass sliding doors and take up position. Gray keeps watch at the door we just came inside.

My pulse pounds in my ears and I glance from the dark night over to Griff. He slides his hands over the glass case, seemingly searching for something. Then, he pulls a device out of his backpack, attaches it to the glass and hits a button.

He explained the device earlier and told us how it will run through hundreds of thousands of number combinations until it finds the correct sequence that will deactivate the alarm on the case. The CIA sure has some fancy gadgets and I'm grateful my friend is in possession of a few. Whether legally or not.

As we wait for the descrambler to work its magic, Gray suddenly signals. The sound of heavy boots and a low whistle sound out in the hallway. *Shit.*

Griff ducks behind the case, I slide behind a long, heavy curtain panel and Gray moves to the side of the door, out of sight in case it opens. We all wait, on edge, and then the door swings inward.

The moment the soldier steps across the threshold, Gray swings his gun down hard. The guy drops and when Gray steps around him to shut the door, another soldier appears, lifts his weapon and fires.

Fuck. So much for getting in and out without anyone knowing. I push the curtain aside, swing my rifle up and shoot. Then, I drop down, using a couch for cover, and shoot two more times. Two more dead soldiers hit the floor.

"How's it going over there?" I ask Griff.

"Still waiting for the last two numbers," he says, eyes on the device.

"Incoming," Gray warns and moves behind the nearest chair.

Three more soldiers come running, one babbling on his radio. *Not good.* They begin taking shots, but stay just out of the room, making it harder for us to hit them. The bullets fly into the room and then a burst of gunfire shatters the large sliding door near me.

Shards of glass spray me and I turn away, covering my face. I feel a clusterfuck coming on just like before and I refuse to let that happen again. *We can't get trapped in this room,* I think. I spin around and begin shooting at the first couple of soldiers who storm inside the broken sliding door. They go down, but more are outside, waiting for the right moment to strike, lined up like ants.

Suddenly, one of the soldiers tosses a stun grenade. "Flashbang!" I yell and we all drop. The moment it detonates, it emits an intensely loud bang and a blinding flash. It's disorienting and made to cause temporary problems like confusion, flash blindness, loss of coordination and deafness.

Spots dance before my eyes and I blink hard, trying to clear my vision. My hearing is already shot to hell so I'm not overly concerned about that. But, I am concerned about Griff and Grayson.

And, then, I see a soldier moving in through the broken sliding doors, fast and low, and coming up behind Griff.

"Griff!" I yell.

Griff spins, kicks the gun out of the bad guy's hand and they start throwing punches. Meanwhile, Gray is busy fighting off the soldiers in the hall. A stream of bad guys pours in and I begin to pick them off. But, my vision is still messed up from the flash grenade and I don't move in time when a soldier shoots.

The bullet hits me in the middle of my chest and all the air whooshes out of me. I drop my rifle and fly backwards, roll over the couch and drop behind it on the floor. I lay on my back, dazed, and feel like I've just been hit by a semi-truck as I rip my vest open.

Shit. I pull in a few deep breaths and reach for the blade in my boot as I pull myself up.

Suddenly, two soldiers pounce on me at once. I manage to slice one across the neck and kick the other in the leg. But, then another appears and punches me hard in the arm and my blade goes flying. I jerk around, sweep a leg and take him down. As I spin around, I hit the other one hard in the kidney.

I stumble away, swiping up my knife and re-sheathing it, and see Griff's opponent out cold on the floor. And, Griff, God bless him, is pulling the emerald out of the case. Out of nowhere, another soldier appears and when he lifts his gun in Griff's direction, I pull my SIG Sauer and fire.

Griff slips the emerald into his backpack and I don't see any more bad guys outside. I think we got them all. For the moment, anyway. I turn toward Grayson and fire off a couple shots at the guys still hovering in the hallway.

"Let's go!" Griff yells.

We all start backing up, shooting, and slip out the back sliding doors into the night.

And, straight into a couple of armed soldiers who flank Antonio Castillo.

"I didn't think I'd see you again so soon, Señor Flynn," Castillo says and lifts his cigar. He takes a puff, dark eyes full of vengeance.

Sonofabitch.

33

AVERY

I try to slide the chair, but in order to move it, I have to put my whole body into it and the legs scrape louder than I want across the floor. *Damn.* I wait for Freya to come out and see what I'm doing, but she doesn't.

I must've really pissed her off. *Oh, well, let her have a taste of her own medicine,* I think. The important thing is that she stays away so I can get out of here.

My gaze moves over to the small kitchen area and I hope there's a knife in one of those drawers. Problem is, I'm not exactly sure how I'm going to reach it with my wrists and ankles secured tightly to the chair.

There's got to be a way. *Think, Ave.*

I wish she had tied me up with duct tape or something that I could manipulate and twist and tear. But, no, she used zip ties. If my wrists were still bound together, I could lift my arms and slam them down with enough force that the plastic would break. But, she's got each wrist secured to the arms of the chair which makes my job of escaping much more difficult.

I look around for a sharp edge or hard surface that I can use to rub the tie against. Friction should help to eventually break the tie. The only thing that may work is the edge of the kitchen table and the great thing is it's literally right next to me.

I scoot over just a bit, lean my weight to the left and balance on the balls of my left foot. This tilts my right side up just enough so I can start rubbing the corner of the table against the plastic tie on my right wrist.

You just need to get one arm free, I remind myself. Then, I can hop my chair over and find a knife.

Freya leaves me alone for about 20 minutes and when I hear her start moving around in the bedroom, I drop back down and check out my progress. It's not great, but I can see a mark. When she walks back in, she appears more in control.

"I hope you didn't toss my phone," I say, hoping she will reveal where it's hidden. "It's brand new. I lost my other one in Columbia."

"You can have your precious phone back when your boyfriend delivers the emerald," she says.

Good, so that means it's here somewhere.

It's time to try a new tactic, I think. Bond with my captor.

"I didn't mean to upset you earlier-" I begin.

"Sure you did," she interrupts.

"No matter what the situation was, the fact is you lost your sister and I lost my brother. I don't know about you, but I was close with Luke."

Her dark eyes narrow. "We were close, too," she says between gritted teeth.

I figure as long as part of her mind is on her sister then she's not 100 percent focused on me. "I blamed myself for his death. At least you don't have to live with that kind of guilt."

All of a sudden, Freya blows. It's what I was hoping for, but it's even more epic than I could have hoped.

"You have no fucking idea what I've been living with, blondie," she snaps and moves closer, getting right up in my face. Her face twists up into a nasty snarl. "Yesenia's death had nothing to do with karma and everything to do with Castillo."

I don't say anything, just wait and hope she will continue to vent.

"I failed to warn him about a rival. I got the intel too late and he lost a shipment of his precious drugs when it was stolen. He has billions. Big, fucking deal, right?"

"Sounds like a drop in the bucket."

"It wasn't even a drop. But, he wanted to teach me a lesson so I'd never miss anything again. A lesson that would hit home, he said."

I have a feeling that I already know where this story is going and I feel a wave of sympathy. No matter how evil this woman is, she's still someone who loved and lost her sister.

"The bastard kidnapped her. And, then gave her to his men. As a reward."

"Jesus," I whisper.

"I don't know how many times they raped her or how long they beat her until she died from a knife wound." Freya lets out a long sigh. Then, she looks at me with hard eyes that flash with vengeance. "I hope your little team kills him."

"I knew this was never about the emerald," I say.

She snorts. "I don't give a shit about that stupid stone. I just want Castillo dead. And, who better to do it than a former Navy SEAL and ex-CIA op with a score to settle?"

It pisses me off that her need for vengeance puts Ryker in danger, but I suppress my anger. "For what it's worth, I'm sorry."

Freya eyes me for a moment then shrugs. "He pulled the same shit with Grayson Shaw's sister, I hear. He's wanted revenge even longer than I have."

My heart sinks. *Poor Gray.* How many women has Castillo thrown to his men like scraps to wolves? God, I hope Ryker, Griff and Gray take care of that bastard so he can never hurt anyone again.

And, even though Freya Singer is a horrible person, I can empathize with her on a human level.

But, I still plan to take her ass down.

It's getting late and I stifle a yawn. I slouch down in my chair and pretend I'm going to sleep for a bit. With hooded eyes, I watch Freya wander over to the fridge and take out a bottle of water. She twists the cap off and takes a long drink. Then, she walks past me and disappears back into the bedroom.

Thanks for offering me some.

The moment I hear her lay down on the bed, my eyes pop fully open and I get to work sawing at the zip tie again. Yeah, Castillo is a disgusting human being, but Freya Singer is right up there with him. It's her sister, Gray's sister and Ryker's team that I feel bad for. Not to mention all the other victims handed over to his men.

Right now, Ryker is down in Columbia at that monster's compound and I pray to God he and the other guys are safe. I'm terrified for them and the fact that Freya sent him the video of her choking me could be enough to throw him off his game. Break his concentration.

I send up a quick prayer for them and continue to drag the zip tie back and forth along the sharp corner of the table. When I exert more pressure and go faster, my wrist slips and I get stabbed in my skin. *Ow.* I grit my teeth and start sawing again.

I'm probably going to end up rubbing half my skin off, but that's just the way it goes. I've got a plan in my head now and I'm ready to make it happen.

An hour and a half later, I think Freya is finally asleep or at least resting deeply. She'd been moving around in the bedroom and came out twice to check on me. But, I just dropped down in my chair and pretended to be sleeping. I want her to believe that I'm not a threat and have no plans to escape tonight. That I'm just going to ride this out and wait til Ryker comes riding in on his horse like a knight in shining armor and waving the emerald.

Yeah, right, I think. *I am so outta here.*

My wrist is raw and bleeding, but I keep sawing. Finally, it looks like a decent amount of the plastic has worn away so I pull as hard as I can. I grit my teeth as the sharp plastic slices my skin and then, I hear what I've been waiting for-

Snap!

My heart leaps when the zip tie breaks. Okay, now I've got my right arm free and three more ties to cut. Boy, she made this damn difficult. I could've escaped an hour ago if she'd just have bound my hands and my ankles only. But, separating them and securing each limb to this chair is making my job tedious and difficult.

I wipe my bloody wrist against my pants and look over at the kitchen drawers. *Please, let there be a knife in one of them.* If I were smart, I'd keep a blade in my boot like Ryker. Let's be real, I'm not even wearing boots, I think, and glance down at my tennis shoes.

While I'm looking at my shoes, I tilt my head and notice a pen under the table. *Perfect.* I lean forward as far as I can, stretching my hand out and trying to reach it. I scoot the chair just a bit and my fingers wrap around it.

Then, I waste no time wedging the pen in between the tie and the wooden arm of the chair. I push as hard as I can, biting my lip against the pain, until the damn thing snaps. I rub my raw wrist then drop forward and do the same thing with each ankle. With enough pressure both plastic ties break and I let out a sigh of relief.

I'm free.

Well, almost, I think.

Still no sound from the bedroom so I stand up and tiptoe over to the kitchen area, searching for something to use as a weapon. In the third drawer I open, there's a steak knife. Better than nothing, I suppose, and clutch it in my fist.

Okay, now I need to find my phone.

My gaze moves over the room and lands on a backpack Freya left on the couch. I walk over, my feet silent against the floor, and unzip it as slowly and quietly as I can. It's dark and hard to see so I slip my free hand inside and rummage around. No weapons, just some clothes, water, snacks and...my phone.

I pull it out with a triumphant smile. My happiness is short-lived, though, when I see the red "low power" warning. *Oh, God, just stay charged for a little bit longer,* I plead.

I set the knife down, hit the Maps app and wait for my current location to pop up on the screen. Then, I snap a photo and hurriedly text the image to Ryker. Just as I'm about to send another text of the image to Jax and Harlow, my phone dies.

Dammit.

I let out a frustrated breath and shove my phone into my pocket. At least, Ryker now has my location. Only problem is, he's almost 3500 miles away.

It's okay, I tell myself, *because I'm leaving. Right now.*

When I turn toward the front door, I hear the floor creak behind me. *Shit.* Before I can even look back or grab the steak knife, Freya bodyslams me and we drop, rolling across the floor. She moves hard and fast and gets a few good punches in before I slam my knee up into her gut.

With a groan, she drops to the side and I scramble up and race for the front door.

But, the gunshot stops me in my tracks.

"I suggest you get your ass back here unless you want a bullet in the back," Freya says.

My head drops back and I slowly turn around.

"Nice try," she says.

I roll my eyes. "Why am I even here? You don't need me anymore. By now, they're at the compound and fighting Castillo and his men. If you get your way, he'll be dead soon."

"Or, they're able to sneak in and out without anyone the wiser. And, if that's the case, then they're going back in to kill Castillo."

"That was never part of the original plan. You said you only wanted the emerald."

"Plans change, blondie. Thanks to you," she adds.

"What are you talking about?"

"With all your prying questions about my sister, I decided simply taking Castillo's prized possession isn't enough. I want him dead, too."

"You can't make them go back in. Just take the emerald and forget about it."

"Did you? Forget about your brother?"

"This isn't about my brother or your sister. They're gone and nothing will ever bring them back. But, Ryker, Griff and Gray are still here, God willing, and if they get out of there alive, and then you send them back in to die..."

I don't even have the words to finish. I clench my jaw and my nostrils flare.

"That's really not my problem," she says in a cold voice.

"Oh, it's going to be your fucking problem," I warn her.

Freya smiles. "Ain't love grand? It gets you all riled up and fills your heart with fear. Fear that someday you'll lose the one person you can't live without."

I glare at her.

"Now, sit your ass down," she says and nods to the couch.

With a huff, I drop down and cross my arms.

Freya walks over to her pack and pulls something out. "I didn't want to do this," she says, "but, your big escape stunt doesn't give me much of a choice." As she heads over to me, I see the syringe in her hand. My eyes widen and I draw my legs up, ready to kick out.

"Just a little cocktail to make sure you stay put for the rest of the night," she explains. And, even though I'm prepared to kick, she strikes from the side, quicker than a viper.

I feel the needle sink into my upper arm and I cry out and punch. My fist hits her shoulder, but then she's moving out of my reach again. "Goodnight, blondie."

"What did you give me?" I ask. The room begins to sway before my eyes and I press a hand to my head. When I open my eyes again, everything looks fuzzy and strange-looking like I'm gazing into a funhouse mirror.

Maybe if I just rest my eyes for a minute, I think, and lean my head back against the couch. All of a sudden, I'm so tired...

I hope to God that Ryker is having better luck than me.

34

RYKER

alk about shitty luck, I think, and watch Antonio Castillo release another puff of smoke.

"Didn't think I'd be seeing you *ever* again," I say.

We're at a standstill. The soldiers point their guns at us and we train our weapons on them.

"I don't see the lovely Señorita Archer," Castillo comments. "That's too bad. I'd be lying if I said I didn't want to get to know her better."

I feel a muscle twitch in my cheek and I want to pound this asshole into the ground. But, I struggle to maintain my composure.

"And, thank you very much for releasing my pit viper," he says in a dangerous voice and lifts a bandaged arm. "Luckily, I keep antivenom close."

Ha, I'm glad the damn snake bit him. Serves him right for keeping the poor thing locked up in that aquarium.

Castillo glances at Griff. "I don't know you," he says, "but, I've been waiting a long time for you, Grayson Shaw. It's a shame your sister couldn't be with us, too."

With a growl, Gray starts to move toward Castillo, but Griff and I hold him back with our free hand. "Don't," I warn him, keeping my gun on Castillo.

"Ah, Sabrina Shaw," he reminisces and reaches down between his legs. "Now, she was a wild cat. Right up until the very end."

"Fuck you!" Gray yells, trying to yank out of our hold. "Filthy fucking pig." But, we just tighten our grip and feel a wave of sympathy for Gray. Castillo is an even worse human being than I originally thought and I cast him a look of absolute disgust.

"I'm the pig? At least I'm not a thief." He looks at each of us long and hard. "Breaking into another man's home and stealing from him." He shakes his head. "I earn my money by working hard. I have a business, an empire, and don't take from others like you three."

Gray laughs. "You run a drug cartel. You're the lowest of the low. Fucking scum." He spits.

Oh, boy, here we go. The look on Castillo's face tells me all I need to know. He's done talking and if we don't move fast, we're dead. I exchange looks with Griff and we let go of Shaw's arm.

Then, everything happens at once.

Everyone opens fire and I dive out of the way and roll behind the nearest available cover. I peer around the tree and fire my SIG at a soldier and he drops. I see Griff not far away, crouching behind a boulder and shooting, and Gray is right out in the open slashing at a soldier with his knife.

Dammit, he's going to get himself killed.

In all the craziness, I see Castillo make a run for it with one of his guards, heading back toward his house. *No way, not gonna happen.* I chase after them, pick off the guard and then shoot Castillo in the leg. He screams and falls.

I glance back to see Griff finish off the last soldier. Grayson holds his arm where blood seeps through his fingers and his adversary lays on the ground with Gray's knife sticking out of his chest. As I turn back and look down at Castillo's shocked face, I feel Griff and Gray move up on either side of me.

"Shot him in the leg," I say. "For my brothers."

"Fuck you," Castillo grunts.

Gray lifts his gun and puts a bullet in his other leg and Castillo yells out a string of obscenities. "That's for Sabrina," he adds.

Gray and I exchange a look, aim our guns and the final two shots hit him in the heart at the same time. "And, that's for all the others," Gray says, staring down at the dead man whose eyes are frozen in wide-eyed surprise.

"Let's get the hell outta here," Griff says.

As we head toward the wall, Gray snags his knife out of the dead soldier, wipes it off and slides it back into its sheath.

"You need to wrap your arm," I tell him. "You're losing a lot of blood."

Gray grabs a soldier's shirt and tears the bottom part of it. Then, he wraps it around his arm. "It's fine. Over the wall."

Once again, I boost Griff, then Grayson and jump up last. When my boots hit the ground on the other side of the wall, I hit my comm. "It's done," I say.

Harlow's voice comes through my earpiece, loud and clear. And, full of relief. "Thank God," she says. "Everyone's alright?"

"Gray has a knife wound. Castillo is dead and we have the emerald."

I hear her report what I say.

"Jax there?" I ask.

"Yes. And, Lexi and Easton."

"Tell that redhead of mine that I'm on my way home to her," Griff says.

Harlow repeats Griff's message. "Lexi says you better be."

"We'll see you soon," I say.

As we make our way back to Gray's car, no one says much. I look up at the black, star-filled sky and vow never to return to this miserable country again. I'm glad Castillo is dead because now he can't hurt anyone else. But, Avery is still in trouble and I won't rest until I find her and get her far away from Freya Singer.

Gray drives Griff and I move straight to the US Air Force Base in Malambo where we're supposed to rendezvous with Captain Cutler's contact who will get us on the next flight out of here. When he pulls up to the gate, we all get out, gather our gear up and say our goodbyes.

"Good meeting you, Gray. Thanks for having our backs," Griff says.

Gray nods.

"Are you gonna be okay?" I ask.

Another nod. "You know, now that Castillo is gone there's no reason for me to stay down here. Might be time for me to head back home."

"You should," I say. "And, if you find yourself in L.A., think about coming over and working with us at Platinum Security. We'd be lucky to have you."

"Damn lucky," Griff adds.

"Appreciate it," he says. "Now, go get your woman, Flynn."

"Right," I say and turn toward the gate. *I'm coming, Avery. Hang on, baby.*

Luck is on our side because we manage to hop on a flight within an hour and arrive back in California by morning. It's been a long night and I'm on edge, desperate to make contact with Freya and swap the emerald for Avery.

Griff and I throw our gear in the back of my Expedition and before we leave El Segundo, I pull out my phone to send Freya a picture of the emerald. I purposely haven't looked at my phone since watching that video because I'm scared some morbid part of me is going to play it again. And, I can't handle that right now.

So, I'm shocked to see a text from Avery. "What the hell?" I open the message and Griff looks over from the passenger seat.

"What now?" he asks and runs a hand through his disheveled hair.

"It's a text from Avery." My heart hitches in my chest. "It's a map." I look over at Griff. "It must be where Freya is holding her."

I study the image and do a quick internet search. "She's near Santa Clarita, out in the hills."

"Let's move, bro," Griff says and pops a fresh stick of gum into his mouth.

"I have an idea," I say. "Where's the emerald?"

Griff reaches into his pocket and pulls out the bright green stone.

"Hold it out so I can take a picture," I say. The damn thing fills his entire palm and I quickly snap a close-up photo and text it to Freya.

We got it, I text. *But, still stuck in Columbia. Flying out within the hour.*

"Think she'll buy it?" I ask.

"I don't see why she wouldn't."

My phone buzzes with her response: *Is Castillo dead?*

"Shit. What do I say?" I look down at the text trying to figure out the best way to answer. "Lie to her?"

But, Griff shakes his head. "No. Tell her he's dead. She's bound to find out, anyway."

He's dead, I text. But, I hesitate, hoping it's the right answer. My eyes slide shut, I say a quick prayer and hit send.

Waiting for her response it pure torture, but it comes a minute later.

Good. Contact me when you land.

I let out a breath and turn the key. "We have 40 minutes to come up with a plan."

Griff calls Jax, puts him on speaker and we decide what the best course of action is for us to take. We have the element of surprise on our side which is good and we nail down a plan.

It's still fairly early and Sunday morning so traffic flows and, before I know it, I turn off the freeway and head into the stark hills of Santa Clarita. My nerves are on edge and I feel like I haven't seen Avery in forever.

And, I hate it.

I miss her so much it hurts. All I want is to pull her into my arms and smell her sugary scent. I want to kiss her hard and feel her heartbeat against mine. I never want to be without her again.

And, I'm never going to be, I decide, *because I'm going to marry my little hellion.*

Griff guides us as close as possible to our destination without alerting Freya that we're there. I park the Expedition and we get out. The sun shines in the perfect blue sky above and we gear up again. *God, I'll be glad when this is over,* I think. *I just need to go in and get my girl.*

After a quick weapons check, we make our way down a small hill and approach the location Avery sent from the rear. I see a small house in the distance and we move fast and low, using large boulders and cactus for cover.

The curtains are pulled tight over the windows and we jog up to the back of the house and press against it. I lift my hand, point to the rear entrance where Griff will go in and then circle my fingers around to indicate I'll bust through the front door. Griff nods, lifts his Glock.

As I skirt around the side of the house, I pull my SIG Sauer close to my body, elbows bent, grip tight. I'm ready to end this bullshit now. I spot a car in front and instantly recognize the Aston Martin Valkyrie. *Gotcha.*

I glance down at my watch and count the seconds as they tick down.

Three.

Two.

One.

I lift my foot and kick the front door in while Griff does the same thing around back. I race inside, expecting to see a surprised Freya. Hoping like hell to see Avery.

Instead, I run smack into Griff and we look around the empty house. I can tell they were here recently, but not anymore.

"Where the fuck are they?" I ask.

As if in answer, a gunshot cracks from somewhere outside.

35

AVERY

When my eyes flutter open, I have no idea if I've been out for an hour or a day. I blink and sit up, noticing sunlight seeping in through a curtain crack. I look down and see Freya zip tied my wrists together, but my ankles are free.

Where is she, anyway?

I glance around, don't see her and decide to make a break for it. Without much thought, I jump up, hurry to the back door, unlock it and race out into the bright morning. Three steps out, I hear a loud curse from back in the house.

I take off, legs pumping, and head up a hill. We're down in a valley and I'll have a better vantage point if I make my way up to the top of the hill. I need to figure out where the highway is and, at this point, my plan is simple. Just outrun the bitch.

Sweat drips down my temples, slips down my underarms and I run harder than I've ever run before, straight up the incline. I'm glad I'm used to running every day and, even with the experience, my legs and lungs burn.

Halfway up the hill, I brave a glance over my shoulder and see Freya closing in. *Shit.* When she lifts her gun and fires, I dodge to the side and move more evasively so she can't get a good target. Despite that, a bullet hits the rocky sand a foot away from me.

Jeez. I pick up my pace, but it's hard running through this sandy soil. Adrenaline spikes through me, though, and I'm almost to the top. *Just a little bit further, Ave.*

Another gunshot and I have no idea how close that one hit. All I know is thankfully, it didn't hit me. Finally, I reach the top and skid to a halt. Wow, I'm high and right at the edge of a precipice that drops down, overlooking the 5 North freeway.

My stomach sinks. I'm too high, I realize, and the hill's too steep to try to go down. I hear Freya, wait a second to judge her distance, then I spin around and, at the same time, launch my leg out with a power-house of a kick.

Not expecting the move or the force of my foot against her wrist, Freya releases the gun with a cry and it flies over the edge of the hill, dropping somewhere below in the rocky ravine. I waste no time throwing myself into her. We tumble down to the rocky ground and roll, right at the edge of the steep drop, all the while throwing and dodging punches.

I'm out of breath from the run, sweating in the dirt, the hot sun beating down on me and struggling against Freya with all my might. Nevertheless, she gets the upper hand and manages to pin me beneath her. I reach up, wrap my hands around her neck and begin to squeeze. But, then her hand finds a rock, grabs it and slams it upside my head.

Stunned, I see stars and my hands fall away from her neck.

Oh, God. I try to blink the blackness away that's threatening to consume me. *Don't pass out, don't pass out, don't pass out.* I repeat the mantra, but it's not helping and I feel my eyes slide shut.

This is it. I'm going to die up here in the dirt, under the beating sun.

And, then my mind conjures up Ryker. So tall, so strong. And, he's looking at me with those beautiful whisky-colored eyes. But, they're sad. And, then his words come back to me sounding just as raw and haunted as when he spoke them.

"I remember laying on the ground...and I thought I was going to die. And

that maybe it was okay. Then, I saw your face. It gave me strength...something to live for...I think you're the reason I'm alive."

The memory of his words infuses me with new strength and I muster up every last bit of fight I have left within me.

"It's always been you, Ave."

I am not leaving him alone in this world, I decide. I love him too damn much.

My eyes snap open and I slam a fist into Freya's face. She falls to the side and I scramble away, making a grab for the rock she hit me with. My fingers wrap around it and I turn to see her already lunging for me. She doesn't expect the rock in my hand and I hit with enough force to knock her off balance.

Freya's feet skid right over the edge of the ravine. With wide eyes, she slips over the side, fingers digging into the sandy soil, but it falls away, giving her nothing to grip. A scream rips from her throat as she drops.

Panting hard, I'm about to fall to the ground when I hear someone calling my name.

It's Ryker, I realize and turn. The sun hits him from behind as he comes up over the hill, and the backlight makes him look like he's glowing like some kind of ethereal being. Like a guardian angel.

I take a step toward him, arms out and then feel the rest of my energy drain. When I start to fall, Ryker swoops in and scoops me up into his arms. "I've got you," he whispers. I press my face into his chest and feel a million emotions tear through me.

When he tilts my chin up, I don't even realize tears stream from my eyes and down my dirty face. "Are you okay?" he asks.

"Just my head," I manage to say, unable to look away from his concerned gaze and the way the sunlight makes his golden-brown eyes sparkle.

He checks out the bloody gash at my hairline and grimaces.

Nearby, Griff looks over the edge of the ravine.

"Is she dead?" Ryker asks.

Griff nods. "No doubt about it."

Ryker's eyes slide shut and he kisses the top of my head. "Let's go," he says and starts back down the hill.

"I missed you," I mumble into his chest. I feel his arms tighten around me and then I pass out.

The next time I open my eyes, I smell soap and pine, and it takes me a moment to realize I'm in Ryker's bed. His arms are wrapped around me and I glance down to see I'm in one of his Navy t-shirts. I slide out of his arms and, the moment I move, my head pounds. I reach a tentative hand up and feel a bandage at my temple.

Ryker's eyes open and he slides up on an elbow. "How do you feel?" he asks.

"I have a raging headache, but other than that, I think okay."

He reaches out and lifts my hand, eyes narrowing at the scabs and chafed circles around my wrist. Then, he kisses the delicate skin and laces his fingers through mine. "Do you have any idea how worried I was about you?" he asks in a low voice.

"Probably as worried as I was about you," I say.

"You amaze me, Ave." He pulls me forward and kisses me. "So brave," he murmurs between kisses. "So strong."

I open my mouth and savor the taste of his mouth moving over mine. Our tongues slide against each other and I moan. I've missed this man so much. *My man.*

My hand curls into his hard, bare chest and my stomach flutters when his lips and tongue trail down my jawline. I pull back and stare into his liquid eyes. "I didn't know if I was ever going to see you again," I admit. My voice catches and I lay my hand over his heart, pressing my palm against his smooth, warm skin, and savoring the strong beat of his heart.

"I'm right here and I'm not going anywhere," he promises and covers my hand with his. "Feel that? It beats for you." He leans forward and brushes his lips over mine. "I love you, Avery."

Warmth pours through me and I smile for the first time in days. "Good. Because I love you so much." I run my hands along his smooth, dear face and I know I don't ever want to be away from him again.

Then, I tap his nose with my index finger. "For better or worse, I think you're stuck with me," I tease.

"Sounds perfect," he murmurs and pulls me in for another long kiss. Then, he glances at the clock on his nightstand and frowns. "We better get moving."

"Whatever it is, can't it wait?" I ask, trailing a finger down his chest.

He sucks in a sharp breath and grabs my quickly descending hand. "No. We actually have plans to meet your parents for dinner."

"What?" I jerk back and sit up straight.

"I hope you don't mind, but I called them."

I don't say anything just wait for him to continue.

"I told them a little bit about what's been going on," he says. "I know you haven't been close the last couple of years, but they need to know Luke's death wasn't your fault. And…"

His voice trails off and he swallows hard. He almost looks nervous which makes me nervous because Ryker Flynn is always the epitome of a confident Alpha male.

"What?" I ask in a soft voice.

"And, there's something else." He hesitates then lets out a breath. "I'm going to ask your father for permission to marry you."

My mouth drops and, after a stunned moment, I feel tears burn the backs of my eyes. I literally have no words. I'm just a mess of girly emotions.

His eyes search mine. "Is that okay?"

I've never seen him look so vulnerable and I break out into a huge grin. "Best thing since you saved me from rolling off a cliff."

"Baby, you saved yourself," he whispers. "And, I'm so proud of you."

I lean in, kiss my future husband and know that I'm the luckiest woman in the world.

That evening, we return to my apartment and Ryker cooks chicken and potatoes in my little kitchen while I get ready and straighten the place up. I pause in the doorway and watch him lean over the stove and taste something. He looks so damn sexy. I had no idea he could cook.

I love the idea that I still have so much more to learn about him. And, I'm going to spend the rest of my life doing exactly that.

I wander up behind him and slip my arms around his waist. "You look good in the kitchen," I say and nip the back of his shoulder.

He chuckles. "Let's just hope it tastes good."

"Oh, I have no doubts," I murmur, slipping my fingers under his t-shirt and gliding them between his hard, lower abs and the waistband of his cargo pants.

"Ave-"

"What time are my parents getting in again?" I ask, pushing up against his back.

As if in answer, there's a knock at the door.

He lets out a shaky breath, turns around and gives me a hard, quick kiss. "Hellion. Now go let your parents in and give me a sec to get myself together."

I smile and, when I turn around, he playfully slaps my ass. I squeal and hurry over to open the door. I haven't seen my Mom and Dad since Luke's funeral. We've talked on the phone, but nothing was ever the same after he died. They didn't know any specific details about Operation Armageddon, but details tend to leak, whether true or not, and when they asked me if what happened was my fault, I said yes. I took full responsibility for a burden that was never mine to bear.

"Hi," I say and give them each a hug. I motion for them to come inside and wave a hand over my place. "I know it's not much, but I like it."

"It's nice," my Mom says. They look around and I swallow hard, feeling awkward. I never wanted us to drift apart. Luke was always the glue that held my family together. But, I think there's hope for us to have a better relationship. That we can be closer.

When Ryker appears, I feel some of the tension ease from my shoulders. My parents love Ryker, always have, and they light up when they see him. My Dad pumps his hand and slaps him on the back and my Mom gives him a big hug. They begin to gush over him and say how much they miss seeing him.

But, me? Not so much. I can't help but feel like the prodigal daughter and bite the inside of my cheek.

Ryker looks a little embarrassed at the effusive greeting he gets and moves over to me, sliding an arm around my waist. My Dad's eyebrow shoots up and my Mom's mouth drops open. I can't help but smile, a wave of satisfaction flowing over me. *Yeah, we're together.*

If I'm good enough for Ryker then maybe they'll realize I'm good enough for them. It's kind of a childish thought, but I can't help it. Like any other kid, all I've ever wanted is their love and acceptance. For them to be proud of me.

"So, are you two dating?" my Mom asks carefully.

"Why don't we sit down?" Ryker suggests. "The food's ready and we have a lot of catching up to do."

I have to hand it to him-- Ryker knows how to take control of a situation. He manages to keep the conversation flowing and easy. Even when it gets hard and we have to talk about Luke and their mission two years ago. I immediately get tense, but then I feel Ryker's reassuring hand on my knee beneath the table.

Ryker reminds them that the operation he, Luke and the rest of the team went on is classified. But, he explains that we recently discovered information that ended up proving a rogue agent made sure I was fed bad intel that inevitably compromised the mission.

"We went to Colombia and found the proof we need to clear Avery's name," he says. "I want to make sure it's clear, once and for all, that Luke's death wasn't her fault. She was unknowingly set up."

I reach over and twine my fingers through his.

Then, my Mom bursts into tears. It's the last thing I expect and I'm not sure what to do. "Mom?" I frown.

"Oh, honey, we're so sorry. I just feel awful about everything that's happened the last couple of years."

I jump up, walk around the table and embrace my Mom. Tears burn my eyes and I feel my Dad lay a hand on my back. It feels so good to finally be communicating with them and I look over at the wonderful man who made it all happen.

Ryker gives me an encouraging nod, slips away from the table, and

I kneel down between my parents. We talk, we cry and we forgive. Things may never be perfect between us, but right now it feels pretty damn good.

After giving us some time to talk things out, Ryker comes back. We take turns heating our plates up in the microwave and then all sit down in the living room and talk and laugh like old times. At some point, Ryker and my Dad talk quietly between themselves while I chat with my Mom.

When he glances over at me and smiles, I know my Dad just gave his blessing. And, dammit, I feel the prick of tears again. I'm not sure when I turned into such a big baby, but one thing is for sure-- despite all my recent tears, I have never been happier.

36

RYKER

Avery's parents are supposed to fly back to Ohio in the morning, but they decide to extend their trip a couple more days and stay in Avery's guest room. And, I'm glad. While her parents are visiting, we take them around town, go to the beach and eat out. It's so nice to see the smile on Avery's face and to know that they're mending their fractured relationship.

I was extremely close to my parents so I wish the same thing for her.

On their last day, Avery's Mom helps her get ready and when she walks out of the bedroom, my stomach does this weird flutter-drop thing. She looks so pretty that I have a hard time catching my breath for a second.

I pull myself up off the couch and walk over, eyes moving down the white dress. I get the feeling it's something Easton would describe as vintage-inspired (I know, I've been hanging around too many women lately). The top is a fitted corset bodice and the full skirt flares out in Swiss dot tulle that hits her mid-calf (that's what I'm later told, anyway).

Honestly, the details don't mean a thing to me. All I know is she looks like an angel and I'm the luckiest bastard in the world because I'm about to marry her.

"You look so beautiful," I say in a low voice.

A blush highlights her cheeks. "And, you look extremely handsome," she says, eyeing my Navy uniform and all the medals on my chest. It's the first time I've worn my uniform since receiving my medals. It feels strange, but at the same time comforting. Like Luke and my lost brothers are right here with me for the most important day of my life.

We head over to the courthouse and, an hour later, we exchange vows and the judge declares us man and wife. *Holy shit. Talk about a whirlwind.* I pull Avery into my arms and kiss her.

And, nothing has ever felt so incredibly right.

We grab brunch and then drop her parents off at the airport. They cry and hug and promise to visit again soon. Then, I head back to her place, but on the way, I stop at a neighborhood bakery and we pick out a little wedding cake for later.

Well, that's the plan, anyway. But, once Avery steps into a bakery, all bets are off. We end up leaving with the cake and a pink box full of other sweet treats including cookies, brownies and I think she also picked out a cupcake and donut.

Liberty is still hanging out with Lexi, Griff and her very angry cat, Whimsy, but we promise to pick Libs up in the morning. I tell Griff something important came up and that we'll fill them all in tomorrow.

Because tonight is our wedding night and, as much as I love Liberty, I'd like some privacy with my new bride.

And, as much as I enjoyed her parents' visit, it's nice to return to a quiet apartment.

Avery kicks off her heels, drops her bouquet of pink roses on the table and turns to me with a mischievous smile. "We did it," she squeals.

I reach her in two long strides and lift her up. Her legs wrap around my waist as I dip my head and kiss her thoroughly. We haven't had any time alone in days and I'm looking forward to tonight like you can't believe.

The kiss turns hot and I push her back up against the wall, slipping a hand beneath all the fluff and ruffle, sliding it up her thigh and squeezing her ass. She moans into my mouth and I feel her nails scratch against the back of my neck.

My body responds to her every touch whether it's just the lightest flutter of her fingertips or the soft slide of her warm lips down my neck. No woman has ever had this kind of effect on me. I guess that's what happens when you love someone.

And, every inch of me loves Avery Archer-Flynn. She bewitched me from day one and now we officially belong to each other forever.

"We need to get you a ring," I murmur between kisses.

"You, too," she says, gliding her hands over my medals. "You better take your uniform off, handsome. I don't want to be held responsible for damaging it."

I chuckle and set her back down on her bare feet. Without the heels, she barely comes to my shoulder. "Same with that dress," I say.

"Speaking of which…" She spins around. "Can you unzip me, Mr. Flynn?"

"I'd be delighted to, Mrs. Flynn." I reach over and tug the zipper down, completely forgetting about my uniform. The dress slides down her curves and lands around her feet like a cloud. She steps out of it and stands before me in a lacey bra and panties the same color as her light pink bouquet. Her hair is still up, strewn with pink rosebuds, and I swallow down a lump in my throat.

A part of me still wonders if I deserve her. I guess old habits die hard. "You look like an angel," I whisper. I have this horrible feeling that if I blink she'll disappear.

Avery walks up to me and begins to carefully undo each brass button on my double-breasted jacket. She slides it off my shoulders and then hangs it up with the utmost care. Again, her fingers brush over the medals and something inside me twists. I came so close to dying out in that jungle and missing out on what is clearly becoming the best part of my life.

When she saunters back over to me, she grabs my tie and loosens the knot. "Strip, Lieutenant Commander Flynn," she orders with a devilish curve of her lips. I yank the tie over my head and while she works the buttons open on my stark white shirt, I unbuckle the belt and slide it off. Then, I kick off my shoes and work my navy blue, perfectly-pleated pants off.

Avery slides her hands over my chest and moves around to kiss the tattoo on my upper arm. "My hero," she murmurs, lips trailing around and moving across my back. My heart thunders when she slips a finger into the waist of my boxer briefs and then snaps the elastic band hard.

I spin around and yank her against me, capturing her mouth in a heated kiss. We devour each other like we're starving, trying to get our fill. But, we're both insatiable and nothing can quench the fire that consumes us.

I pick her up and carry her down to her bedroom. She keeps sliding her hand down into my boxer briefs and if she doesn't knock it off, I'm going to rip that pretty pink lingerie off her. Instead, I toss her on the bed and stand there, looking down at her, soaking in the image of her sprawled on the mattress with roses in her blonde hair and sheer pink lace barely covering the places that I'm about to lick.

"Come here," she says and motions me with a come-hither finger.

But, I shake my head, enjoying the view. "If you only knew how delicious you look right now. Like a pink-frosted dessert. Fucking edible."

I notice her breathing increases and her blue eyes take on a sultry, hooded look. When she lets her legs fall apart, I'm done just looking. I drop down on the bed between those tempting thighs and begin to kiss the tops of her breasts, skimming my tongue along the edge of pink lace. "You're like a piece of cotton candy. So sweet and all mine."

"All yours," she agrees and moves her hands up and down my back.

The light scratch of her nails feels so good and I bite the edge of her bra and tug. It's in my way and I want it gone. "Take it off," I say. "Before I rip it off."

While Avery slips the wisp of lace off, I get rid of the matching panties. I need to feel her naked body against mine, skin to skin, nothing between us. And, God, it feels good. She's so soft and smooth, like silk, and I sink my face into the curve of her neck and shoulder.

I feel her long legs wrap around me, drawing me closer, and I push up, rubbing the tip of my cock against her core. She moans, arching up, and I slide a hand down between our bodies. "You've never felt so wet," I murmur, sliding two fingers into her body. "So fucking tight."

Avery's hips grind against my palm and I drop my head down to worship her perfect, rosy-tipped breasts. I draw a nipple into my mouth and she runs her fingers through my cropped hair and down over my ears.

And, for the first time, I don't tense up. I lift my head and she's looking at me with inquisitive blue eyes, gauging my reaction. "Is this okay?" she asks in a tentative voice, fingers moving along the edge of my ears, circling my earlobes. "Can I touch you here?"

"You can touch me anywhere," I say. And, I mean it. After all the things we've done to each other and will do to each other, there's no reason to feel self-conscious about my hearing aids.

She smiles and her hands move away from my ears and down along my jaw. "Good. Because there are quite a few places I still want to explore."

I start to move my fingers again, in and out, then up along her folds, trailing her wetness up to the sensitive bud and then applying just the right amount of pressure to make her thrash and cry out. It's like a fucking magic button. Touch it just right and-

"Oh, God, Ryker," she purrs. I watch the pleasure roll over her face, the color high in her cheeks and her hips buck. The orgasm rips a cry from her throat and then I position myself at her slick entrance.

Her legs open further and I start to slide in, slowly, not wanting to hurt her, but also wanting to take my time. Push it to the limit.

"Ryker, please," she begs, arching up, trying to pull me deeper.

"Patience," I whisper and position my weight better on my elbows.

"Faster," she cries.

But, I don't rush it. Just move in then pull back, then go deeper then slide back, teasing her until she's writhing beneath me.

"Oh...God..."

She's on the edge and the moment I feel her entire body quiver, I thrust the rest of the way into her. Harder and faster now. I reach down, stroking just above the place where we're joined and our gazes lock.

Brown and blue, melting together.

Her breath comes out as little pants and passion glazes her eyes. Then, her head drops back against the pillow and I feel her inner body ripple around my cock. Every time she comes, she makes these whimpering noises and I love it. "I could watch you come all day," I tell her.

Her eyes flutter open, she reaches down and slides her hands over my ass. "Your turn," she says, squeezing around me hard, milking me.

The pressure begins to build and I feel my control slip. I plunge harder and after a few more thrusts, my entire body goes rigid, shudders and empties into Avery's warmth. I collapse, still deep inside of her, and then lift my head and find her mouth. After a slow, sultry kiss, I pull out and drop down beside her. "If we're not more careful," I whisper and place a kiss along her jaw, "you're going to get pregnant."

"Would that be so bad?"

My eyes meet hers and my mouth edges up. "Actually, nothing would make me happier."

She curls in to face me and lays a hand against my heart. "Same."

I let out a breath and stare into her blue, blue eyes. "What did I do to deserve you?" I ask.

"You deserve every good thing that comes your way," she says, her voice firm. "You've seen too many horrors. Experienced far more pain than anyone ever should in one lifetime. You're a warrior and a hero, Ryker Flynn, and don't you dare sell yourself short ever again."

The fierceness in her voice makes me wonder if she's right. Is it time to finally let go of the past and the dark sins that haunt me? Can I even do it?

As I snuggle down with Avery beneath her candy-scented sheets, I realize spending the rest of my life full of guilt is no way to live. And, it certainly isn't what Luke or my parents would want. They would want me to be happy and to forgive myself. They would want me to focus on Avery and be a good husband to her and start a family.

I rub my nose against hers, looking into those mesmerizing eyes of hers, and smile. "Have you always been this smart?" I ask.

"Always. And, don't you forget it, Mr. Flynn."

"Never, Mrs. Flynn."

EPILOGUE

AVERY

The next morning, we all go over to Easton's house high up in the Hollywood Hills. I still have a hard time believing I can call Easton Ross, America's Sweetheart, my close friend. It's kind of unreal and, at the same time, completely normal.

Everyone welcomes Ryker and me with huge hugs and Liberty can't stop woofing and licking me. Then, Easton grabs my hand and pries me away from Ryker. I give him a little shrug as she drags me off to chat with her, Harlow and Lexi. It's so funny to think that less than a month ago, my only friend was Liberty and now I'm sitting down next to three of the nicest, funniest and kindest women I've ever had the pleasure of meeting.

They ask me a million questions about everything that happened the last couple of weeks and I start at the beginning and tell them all about our adventure in Columbia-- which gets some smirks and knowing looks-- and how we went down to meet Grayson Shaw.

Of course, the mention of a potentially good-looking bachelor instantly sidetracks them.

"He sounds mysterious," Easton comments.

"Dark hair and gray eyes?" Lexi asks and raises her eyebrows. "Sounds like a striking combination."

When I nod and confirm that he is handsome in a rugged, shaggy kind of way, we all sort of look at Harlow, the single girl of the group.

"Oh, for Christsake, the man's in Columbia," Harlow says. "Besides, I don't do long-distance relationships. Especially when he lives on another continent."

"But, he mentioned maybe moving back to the states, didn't he?" Easton asks, all green-eyed innocence and curving red lips.

"He did and Ryker told him he should come work at Platinum Security."

"Hmm, well I guess we will see what happens with Mr. Shaw," Lexi says with a sly smile. "There's something a little exciting about former CIA men," she adds, her brown eyes drifting over to where Griff leans against the wall, drinking a beer with the guys. Feeling her gaze, he turns and tilts his bottle toward her with a devastating smile.

"Did you two pick a date yet?" Easton asks.

But, Lexi just lets out a dreamy sigh. "We're not in any rush," she says and runs a hand through her long red hair. "But, probably some time next year."

"What about you?" I ask Easton. "The big day is almost here."

"I could've married Jax yesterday," she says. "So, yes, I couldn't be more ready. I don't need an extravagant affair. Just him." She looks down at the huge diamond ring on her finger then over at her lanky, dark-haired fiancé.

"I can still do your wedding pictures, if you want," I offer.

"I'd love that."

"You still haven't told us where you're getting married," Lexi says.

"I know. Sorry about that but my publicist insisted that we shouldn't tell anyone until right before the ceremony if we want to make sure it stays quiet. Jax would probably leave me at the altar if any paparazzi show up."

"I seriously doubt that," I say. "Have you seen the way he looks at you?"

Easton blushes. "I just really hope his brother shows up to the wedding," she says in a low voice.

"Jax has a brother?" I ask. I'd never heard anything about a brother.

"A younger brother-- Sebastian. He's what you would call the black sheep of the family. And, a bit of a wild card. I haven't even met him yet, but I know Jax got ahold of him last week and invited him."

"He'll come," Lexi predicts. "It's an important day and he'll be there for his big brother."

"I hope so," Easton says. Then, she turns those green eyes on me. "What about you and Ryker?"

Now, it's my turn to blush.

"Are you finally official?" Harlow asks.

"You could say that," I say with a vague smile. We haven't told anyone yet about getting married, but I have a feeling everyone's about to find out.

Easton lays her perfectly-manicured hand over mine and squeezes. "I'm so glad you reached out when you did, Avery. He really needed you," she adds in a low voice.

"I needed him, too," I admit.

"So, tell us what happened with Castillo," Lexi says, getting the conversation back on track. "And, who is this Freya chick?"

I tell them the rest of the story and they listen intently, inter-rupting with a question from time to time, and looking spellbound when I reach the conclusion.

"God, that's almost as crazy as the adventure Griff and I had in New York," Lexi says.

"So, where's the emerald?" Harlow asks.

"Ryker and I decided to sell it. Then, we're going to divide the money up and give it to the families of his fallen teammates. Some had wives, kids...It'll help them."

"That's really sweet of you guys," Easton says. "I'm sure they'll appreciate it."

I nod, knowing that our decision to put Castillo's stolen prize toward something good gives Ryker a sense of satisfaction. Even possibly a feeling of redemption.

"What is it with those three attracting danger the way they do?" Lexi asks. We all look over where they stand, so handsome in their own way.

They all look over at once and we laugh.

"What's so funny?" Griff asks and saunters over. He grabs Lexi under the arms and she squeals as he scoops her up for a kiss.

Jax and Ryker also head over. Jax sits on the couch next to Easton and drags her into his lap, whispering something into her ear which makes her giggle.

I look up and Ryker reaches down and hauls me up into his arms. He pulls me close and presses his forehead against mine. "Do you have a kiss for me, Mrs. Flynn?"

I smile and brush my lips over his. Then, I pull back and we both realize that everyone is staring at us.

"Did I just hear that right?" Griff asks and shakes his head as though he misheard.

I glance back up at Ryker and we smile. "You heard right," he says. "We eloped last night."

Mouths drop and eyes go wide.

"Holy shit! Congrats, bro," Griff exclaims and slaps him on the back. Then, everyone bursts into congratulations and starts talking at once. The girls all hug me again.

Then, Easton grabs Jax and pulls him toward the kitchen. "We'll be back with champagne," she announces.

"What else?" Jax asks with a grin.

"I'm so happy for you both," Griff says, looking from me to Ryker, still absorbing the news.

"Thanks," Ryker says and then they do their secret handshake and hug it out.

Jax and Easton return with glasses of Taittinger's Blanc de Blancs for everyone and we all accept a glass of the expensive bubbly.

Ryker wraps an arm around my waist and then we all lift our glasses.

"As the only married man here, got any advice for me?" Jax asks.

"And, me," Griff adds and slants a glance at Lexi. "Shit, I'm not far behind you two."

Ryker thinks for a moment then looks down at me, his whisky-colored eyes shining. "Not really advice," he says. "More like wisdom maybe?"

"Marrying Avery has already made him smarter," Griff quips.

Ryker swirls the champagne in his glass then looks down at me. "I know I was living in the dark for a long time, but you showed me that's where the stars shine. And, that being broken is okay and that I shouldn't look at what I've lost, but what I have left." Ryker tips my chin up. "You loved me when I thought I least deserved it, but when I needed it most, and I love you so much, Ave."

My heart swells with love and whistles and claps fill the air as he leans in and kisses me. Then, he pulls back and lifts his glass again. "To the amazing woman who one day walks into your life and you can't remember how you ever lived without her," he toasts.

"Hear, hear," Jax says and kisses Easton.

Griff leans down and captures Lexi's mouth and I wind my fingers through Ryker's. "I love you," I whisper. As he kisses me again, I get a quick glance at Harlow. Though she smiles and drinks her champagne, I feel bad that she's the only one without someone.

But, Harlow Vaughn is smart and gorgeous. I have no doubt the right man will come along one day for her just as it did for Easton, Lexi and me.

As I wrap my arms around Ryker's neck and look deep into his eyes, the room and everyone around us seems to fall away. It's just me and him.

Then, Liberty walks up and gives a little yip. We look down and smile.

"I think she's happy you're her new Dad."

Ryker lowers a hand and pets her furry head. Then, he turns his attention back to me and tightens his arms. "And, I'm happy you're my wife, Mrs. Flynn." He pulls me up onto my toes and kisses me like a true Navy SEAL.

Focused, committed, relentless.

I remember Luke once telling me that they have a saying in the teams to act with "Extreme Violence of Action." What this means is that they go either 110% on something or not at all.

And, Ryker? Well, I can definitely attest that everything he does, he definitely goes above and beyond.

And, that makes me a very, very lucky lady.

The cliché claims that time heals all wounds, but I've learned that's not quite right.

It's love that does that.

***

If you enjoyed Ryker and Avery's story, you'll love reading about Sebastian and Harlow. He's Jax's wild card brother who's been MIA for over a year. She's Platinum Security's new hacker. Find out what happens when Bastian shows up at Harlow's door with a knife wound in *Dark Secrets*.

EXCERPT: DARK SECRETS

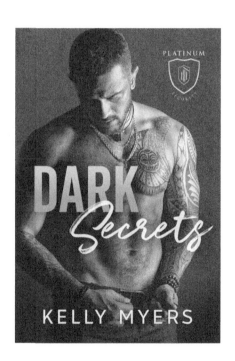

He's a bad boy in danger.
The same man I should stay miles away from.
I've got no intention of falling in love with Bastian.
But he's taking my heart... piece by piece every single day.
I want to trust him. I want to tell him how I feel.
But there's no way our reality will allow that.
Bastian is wild.
I know because I work for his older brother.
Little did I know that I would be dragged into his life.
But then he showed up at my doorstep with a knife wound.
And I only had one choice... to take him in.
Something tells me that he's out to harm me... If I can't trust him with my heart, can I at least trust him with my life?

Chapter One: Harlow

I sit in a satin-trimmed chair at the edge of a cliff in Malibu and feel a smile tug on my lips as the celebrity wedding of the decade begins. Despite everyone in town wishing they had an invite to beloved starlet Easton Ross's nuptials to her former bodyguard and bad boy Jaxon Wilder, only a handful of close friends are present.

And, I am lucky enough to be one of them because I recently began working at Jax's company, Platinum Security. There's no question he had a rough time getting the business up off the ground and nearly had to close, but when Easton hired him to protect her from a stalker, his reputation and clients increased dramatically. Enough so, that he could hire more people, including me. And, now, we're like a little dysfunctional family.

The small office in East Hollywood is dominated by alpha males with plenty of deadly government training that provides them with a certain skill set to work as bodyguards, locators, investigators, troubleshooters and any other shady job clients pay them to do. They consist of former Navy SEALs, ex-CIA operatives and Jax himself was

LAPD. Until he was let go for bad behavior. Although, in my book, revenge isn't necessarily bad.

Sometimes, it's deserved.

Until I came along, the ragtag group of anti-heroes was seriously lacking in one major area. Besides estrogen. And, that's someone with hacker skills. I had worked with Griff Lawson when he was CIA so he referred me to Jax and now here I am.

And, lucky for them. I don't mean to brag, but I'm the best of the best. I can find anything by digging deep online. The Dark Web is my best friend and coding keeps me sane.

Lately, the estrogen in the office has increased, though. These macho men have been falling like dominoes and meeting their matches. Love is definitely in the air and I glance over where Lexi Ryder sits next to me. Her fingers are entwined with Griff Lawson's and they are next in line to walk down the aisle.

On the other side of them sits Ryker Flynn, his gaze glued to Avery Archer-Flynn who is closer to the action, snapping pictures. She's a former CIA analyst turned photographer and Easton asked her to shoot the wedding. Ryker and Avery recently came back from a dangerous adventure down in Columbia and my head is still spinning from their complete 180-degree flip from hate to love to marriage.

But, there's no denying how good they look together. And, from what I know, all the men at P.S. had been haunted by troubled pasts and demons. Until these amazing women came into their lives and helped them pick up their broken pieces.

And, here I sit, by myself. No boyfriend. No date. Not even the possibility of a special someone.

That's kind of how it's been the past 30 years. I was never the girl who always had a boyfriend. I didn't go to my prom in high school or date fraternity guys in college and I never really fit into any of the cliques or social circles. I've always been more of a loner and prefer my laptop to a relationship.

Lately, though, I can't help but wonder what it might be like to meet that special someone. Problem is, I'm never interested in anyone for very long. A date here or there, maybe a hook-up, but then I lose interest and would rather be nose-deep online.

Is something wrong with me? I wonder. Have I been wasting my best years and one day I'm going to wake up, be 50 years old and completely alone?

God, that's depressing, but at this rate, it's exactly where I'm headed.

It's hard for me to open up, though. I hate being vulnerable. I've always been tough and a tomboy. I grew up with two older brothers, both former military, and they taught me how to be strong, independent and swear like a sailor. I'm not some weak, wilting flower who needs a man in her life or she has no purpose, no identity. Like my Mom before she died. I know who I am and I know what I want.

Unfortunately, I just can't seem to find it.

Honestly, until I saw it firsthand for myself at Platinum Security, I questioned if real, all-consuming love actually existed or if it was just something Hollywood and romance novels sold to desperate hearts. As nice as those movies and books may be, they don't keep you warm on a cold December night. And, even here in Southern California, the temperature drops in winter and I need to pull out my flannel sheets because there is no male body in my bed to keep me warm.

Other than my brothers who I don't see very often because they don't live near me, I've never had a good male role model to look up to. My Dad, the infamous Robert Vaughn, is a thief, a liar and an inmate serving 10-15 at the California State Prison in Lancaster.

Yep, good 'ol Daddy had quite the career as a successful thief until the law finally caught up with him. He's served five years of his sentence and I've never visited him. He emails me every blue moon, but I don't write him back. I have nothing to say to the man who broke my Mom's heart and left his family.

The ceremony is short and sweet. Before I know it, the priest pronounces Jax and Easton husband and wife. And, Jax drops his dark head and kisses Easton like she's the very oxygen he needs to breathe. When a lock of his hair falls forward, she pushes it back with a slim hand and they share a smile.

We all burst into applause and whistles as they turn and face us, holding hands.

"May I present to you-- Mr. and Mrs. Jaxon Wilder!" the priest announces.

I can't help but smile. I'm happy for them and wish them a lifetime of love. I know they both have had rough roads to love and deserve every good thing life has to offer. As they walk down the small aisle and pass us, Griff tosses Jax a salute. "Way to go, Jaxston!"

Only Griff, I think, and laugh. Jaxston is the name given to them by the media and Jax hates the attention and spotlight that they're thrust into at times. But, when you marry America's Sweetheart, it comes with the territory. That's why Easton made sure the wedding was small and quiet. If helicopters and paparazzi showed up, she claimed Jax would leave her at the altar.

But, we all know that is not true. From the look in his dark eyes, the man is head over heels in love with the raven-haired beauty.

I feel kind of bad, though, because I know Jax really wanted his younger brother to be here, but there's no sign of him. Not that I know what he looks like since he never comes around. Hell, Easton hasn't even met her new brother-in-law yet.

I don't know much about Sebastian Wilder other than he sounds like a wild card and a loner. A lost soul. Probably a lot like Jax before he met Easton.

Men like that...

I shake my head. I know them too well. My Dad was always involved with the wrong people and it didn't take him long to turn to a life of crime. He's extremely intelligent and likes to challenge himself. It's a shame he didn't put his talents to better use like my brothers and the men at P.S.

But, no, my Dad became a renowned thief. The feather in his cap and, ironically his downfall, was the job where he managed to steal $20 million in diamonds from a Saudi Arabian prince who's worth an estimated $14.3 billion.

Sure, that was a drop in the bucket for the prince, but to the average person, twenty million in diamonds is life-changing. But, I don't think my Dad did it for the money. Like I said, he always appreciated a good challenge.

The funny part is, they may have gotten my Dad, but they never found the diamonds.

And, as much as my Dad and I have always had a tempestuous relationship, I can't help but admire him just a little. But, I would never admit it. He's clever beyond comparison and charming beyond measure. I think I inherited his cleverness, and I've taken that cunning, quick-wit and savviness and turned it into the most amazing hacking skills you can imagine.

Dane and Rafe, my brothers, inherited his charm. No doubt about it. They're both extremely tall, athletic and possess a magnetism that can dazzle even the most cold-hearted women. Trust me. I've seen it.

I am the complete opposite. Zero charm, a little rough around the edges and I'm pretty damn sure that no man is stopping in his tracks to admire my boring brown hair and plain Jane looks. I mean, don't get me wrong. I do well with what I have, but when I look at Easton, Lexi and Avery, they all have some striking feature or two that sets them apart from everyone else.

Easton's green eyes sparkle like emeralds; Lexi's copper hair resembles the stunning autumn foliage; and Avery looks like a Victoria's Secret model with her angelic looks, bedhead blonde hair and cornflower blue eyes.

And, here I am. Harlow Vaughn, normally hunched over a computer, brown hair in a ponytail, dull blue-gray eyes probably behind a pair of glasses and not a stitch of makeup. I'd blame it on the fact that I grew up with two brothers, but Lexi also has a brother and she isn't nearly the tomboy that I am.

I just don't care about makeup, perfume and dressing up. I'm comfortable in my sweatpants, t-shirt and slippers. A little too comfortable and that's why I decided to finally pry myself out of my dark apartment and force myself to go into an office to work.

I'm 30 now, but the last five years or so, I'm kind of embarrassed to say, have been me and my beloved computers in the spare bedroom in my apartment. Totally absorbed in work. I have a lot of connections and people know to contact ShadowWalker, my handle, when they need a job done.

I don't want to be like my Dad, but, damn, how can I ignore the similarities? I spend all day on the Dark Web, involved in shady undertakings for clients who I never physically meet. We just exchange information online and I start digging through all my illegal back channels. After I find out what they need, and I always do, they wire me payment.

It's been a profitable, but lonely existence.

When Griff referred me to Jax, I wasn't sure at first. Working in an office and for someone else made me think I'd lose some of the freedom I have. But, it also forces me out of my apartment and comfort zone.

Jax assured me that I could work as a freelance contractor for them and that I didn't have to come into the office every day from 9-5 like a worker bee. So, I accepted his offer almost two months ago and so far it's been pretty perfect.

It's forcing me to meet people, getting me out of my dingy apartment and I'm really starting to make genuine relationships with the guys and their significant others. It's also making me feel a little more legit because I have an office now, as silly as that sounds.

The work is still shady as shit which I don't mind, but something about going into Platinum Security and sitting down at my desk with my mug of coffee makes me feel...more credible. And, appreciated. Jax, Griff and Ryker always make sure to let me know I'm doing a good job and that they wouldn't be able to function without my hacker skills.

And, it's nice to feel needed and appreciated.

After Jax and Easton finish their walk down the aisle, we all stand up and get ready to head over to Easton's mansion up in the Hollywood Hills where there's going to be a reception. I look forward to the endless flow of her favorite and very expensive French champagne Taittinger's Blanc de Blancs. *It's going to be quite the celebration,* I think. Especially since Ryker and Avery eloped recently and we haven't had the chance to celebrate yet.

Yes, I'm looking forward to drinking some bubbly and mingling with my friends for the next couple of hours. Then, probably heading back to the office for a little late night work.

I have no idea that my life is about to change dramatically and the dark whirlwind known as Sebastian Wilder is about to tear into my life like a tornado.

Read the full story: Dark Secrets

ALSO BY KELLY MYERS

Daddy Knows Best Series:

My Secret Daddy | Yes Daddy | Forbidden Daddy | Billionaire Daddy | Daddy's Best Friend | Pregnant with the Wrong Man | Dirty Little Secret | Holiday Daddy | Daddy's Game

Platinum Security Series:
.
Dark Kisses | Dark Riches | Dark Sins | Dark Secrets

Forbidden Love Series:

The Guy Next Door | Arrogant Jerk | Misunderstood | My Best Friend's Ex | Office Mischief | Fool Me Twice

Dangerous Love Series:

Tainted Goods | Brutal Love | Deadly Devotion | Twisted Truths

Big Daddies of Los Angeles Series:

Daddy's Rules | Daddy's Temptation | Daddy's Fake Fiancée | Daddy's Million Dollar Proposal

Searching for Love Series:

Frenemies with Benefits | Breaking All The Rules | Fake Heartbreak | Against All Odds

Standalone Books:

Ruthless | My Possessive Ranchers

INVITATION TO JOIN KELLY'S NEWSLETTER

Kelly Myers writes steamy contemporary romance. Her stories have characters that make their partners feel seen, heard, and understood.

Once you've read her book, you won't forget it and you won't stop chasing that feeling again till you grab her next book.

So, she's inviting you here to subscribe to her newsletter and stay updated with latest information on upcoming releases or special price promotions.

Sign up to her Newsletter -> https://landing.mailerlite.com/webforms/landing/m8t0h0

If you want to get in touch with her, drop her an email at:
kellymyers@kellymyerspublishing.com

Made in the USA
Middletown, DE
05 July 2025

10131810R00149